The Mutilated Bacchus

The Mutilated Bacchus

by
André Arnyvelde

translated, annotated and introduced by
Brian Stableford

A Black Coat Press Book

Visit our website at www.blackcoatpress.com

ISBN 978-1-61227-433-1. First Printing. September 2015. Published by Black Coat Press, an imprint of Hollywood Comics.com, LLC, P.O. Box 17270, Encino, CA 91416.

TABLE OF CONTENTS

Introduction 7
THE MUTILATED BACCHUS.................................... 15
MAN WANTED or, THE STRANGE TOURNAMENT
OF LOVE... 291

Introduction

This is the second of two volumes containing translations of all four of the original novels that "André Arnyvelde" (André Lévy, 1881-1942) published during his lifetime. Although each of the four is complete in itself, the four narratives form a coherent sequence tracking a single theme, and they gain considerable interest from being read as a set, in the order of their composition. The first volume, entitled *The Ark*,[1] contained the first two novels, *Le Roi de Galade, conte bleu* (1910), translated as "The King of Galade; a Fantastic Story" and *L'Arche* (1920), translated as "The Ark." The present volume contains the third novel in the sequence, *Le Bacchus mutilé* (1922), translated as "The Mutilated Bacchus," and the fourth, *On demande un homme... ou L'Étrange tournoi d'amour* (1924), translated as "Man Wanted; or, The Strange Tournament of Love."

A general introduction to the author's life and an introductory commentary on the first two novels in the series is contained in the first volume of the present set, and there is no need to repeat all of it here. Indeed, given that readers will be able to comprehend and appreciate the novels in the present volume far more fully if they have read the previous two in the sequence, I strongly recommend that they start there; if they have, the next few paragraphs will be redundant, but for the sake of those who have not, I shall use them to fill in a little of what they have missed before adding a few comments specifically introductory to the present text.

To summarize briefly, Arnyvelde's novels constitute a series of fantastic *contes philosophiques* exploring and developing the notion of the possibility and necessity of human

---

[1] Black Coat Press, ISBN 978-1-61227-432-4.

beings acquiring the psychological means of a transcendent Joy. The author had been convinced early in his adult life that the solution to the anguished aspect of the human predicament did not reside in conventional euchronian social reform but in a kind of eupsychian self-transformation that would enable individuals to find Joy in life rather than the misery and angst that currently afflicted the vast majority.

Arnyvelde had also convinced himself during the first decade of the 20th century that the path to that transcendent joy was wide open to his contemporaries, whereas it has been closed off for most of human history, by virtue of the recent extension of the human senses by optical instruments such as the telescope and the microscope, new media such a cinematography, and by recent advances of scientific theory in cosmology, biology and anomic theory. The new ways of seeing the world provided by this extension, coupled with new ways of experiencing it by virtue of new means of locomotion, had already wrought a considerable transformation, he thought, which only stood in need of psychological completion by the development of a new and better comprehension of the world and its possibilities. Unfortunately, the evolution of that new comprehension was hampered by the inertia of old ways of thinking and action, which were preventing people from moving beyond the essentially paltry and ultimately unrewarding "joys" with which they were familiar, to attain the superior Joy of which he dreamed.

The first of his novels *Le Roi de Galade*, developed these ideas in the context of a fabular narrative about Galade, a small enclave of territory lost in what is nowadays the northeastern corner of Italy, whose existence is unsuspected by the rest of Europe because access is denied by uncrossable mountains. At one point in Galadian history, however, three inhabitants of the valley succeeded in tunneling through the mountains, thus enabling the exploration of the world beyond. Jealously kept by a small elite for hundreds of years, the secret of that tunnel allowed the kings of Galade to pick and choose which innovations from the world at large would improve their own society, admitting Christianity but refusing gun-powder, before deciding in the 14th century that no further importation was necessary or desirable, and walling up the tunnel

The story is told in the novel of a king who is led by cir-cumstances to make a vow to forsake his favorite pastime—sex with the ladies of the court—for a year, and is driven by the subsequent ennui to rediscover the tunnel and set forth to explore the world of the nascent 20th century: an exploration which is exceedingly educational, but somewhat overwhelm-ing. The experience enables him to formulate a primitive ver-sion of the Arnyveldian theory of Joy, but also to understand some of the difficulties that might stand in the way of a politi-cal program that might make his own people happier than they already are.

L'Arche, written between 1914 and 1919, while the au-thor was on active service during the Great War, and intended to provide him with a psychological Ark to bear him through the figurative Deluge to an Ararat offering a new mission as well as mere survival, offers a much more elaborate account of the theory of Joy and the rewards that its acquisition ought to provide, in the form of a vision of a superhuman individual who introduces himself as an *arcandre*—a Greek-derived term probably intended to provide a more accurate translation of the Nietzschean *übermensch* than the conventional French *surhomme*. The arcandre informs the narrator that he is on the way to becoming an arcandre himself, but that there is still a lot of work to be done to complete his own self-transformation, and then to inspire and enable others to do likewise.

The story told in *Le Bacchus mutilé* begins with an at-tempt to flesh out the program hinted at in the conclusion to *Le Roi de Galade* and lyrically extrapolated in the latter pages of *L'Arche*. The general psychological legacy left by the Great War, however, was not at all conducive to continued optimism regarding the possibility of building a new and better world on the ruins of the old, and French literature of the next few years bears eloquent testimony to the disillusion felt by a great many people as they saw the old evil habits and ways returning in full force, further degraded by the effects of the war. *Le Bacchus mutilé* does not escape the effects of that general disillusionment, which might well have been further augmented, in the author's own case, by severe personal difficulties. It was not at all rare for the surviving combatants involved in the war, even if they had not been permanently damaged physically, to find that the situation to which they returned was not as they had left it or hoped to find it, and problems of readaptation were the rule rather than the exception.

At any rate, the very fervor of the hopes reflected in Arnyvelde's existential thesis, which seem to have helped sustain him psychologically through the war itself, made them vulnerable to an exceedingly steep fall if and when it became difficult to sustain them, and *Le Bacchus mutilé*, having detailed their ascent, also details their catastrophic and seemingly irredeemable fall. It might be as well for the reader to bear in mind, while following the harrowing details of that fall, that once the book had been published—probably a year or so after Arnyvelde had finished writing it—it was not long before the author started on the next work in the series, which is cast as a sequel to it, although it bears very little resemblance to its predecessor in tone or narrative strategy.

The central motif of *Le Bacchus mutilé*, to which the title refers, is the image of the god Bacchus preserved in a statue by Michelangelo dating from about 1497. The same statue had been previously invoked in *Le Roi de Galade* as one of three works of art offering the reader some idea of what the protagonist of that novel looks like physically. That novel and the autobiographical sections of *L'Arche* make it clear that the author had seen the statue in question when he visited Florence as a tourist in the early years of the century, so his memory of it when he wrote *Le Bacchus mutilé* must have been a trifle vague. That presumably helps to explain why the present text gets its location wrong—it is not in the Uffizi but the Bargello—but leaves unclear a curious enigma regarding the title of the novel and its symbolism.[2]

Michelangelo's statue depicts a youthful and somewhat androgynous individual in a slightly intoxicated pose. A little faun standing behind the god is eating grapes taken from his dangling left hand, which is also holding a tiger-skin. The principal figure would not normally be cited, as it is in *Le Roi de Galade*, as an archetype of male beauty, and its credentials in that regard were not improved by the fact that someone removed the statue's penis with a chisel prior to 1530. The cup in the raised right hand was also broken off at the same time, but was subsequently restored, unlike the penis. The statue that Arnyvelde saw was, therefore, already a "mutilated Bacchus," and mutilated in a very specific fashion. The problem that arises with regard to the symbolism of the novel is that the text gives no indication that the author was aware of that fact; it is never mentioned. The text does not say whether the copy of the statue made for the protagonist's house has a penis, nor does it make any mention of the faun or the tiger-skin, which seem to have slipped the author's memory.

Presumably, as it is not mentioned in the text, the safest assumption is that the mutilation of the original statue has no relevance to it, and that the novel's title refers purely and simply to the eventual literal mutilation of the copy and its symbolism of the mutilation of the protagonist. If one reads the novel with the additional information in mind, however, it might be thought to alter the perceived symbolism somewhat, and that the alteration in question, whether it is conscious or unconscious, is not devoid of significance.

---

[2] There is a "Bacchus" in the Uffizi, but it is a painting by Caravaggio and bears no resemblance to the statue cited in *Le Roi de Galade, Le Bacchus Mutilé* and *On demande un homme…*, which is evidently the Michelangelo, albeit minus the faun and other minor details. It might, however, have been hearing a reference to "the Uffizi Bacchus" that caused the author to misremember its location.

It is worth noting, in this context, that there is something else that receives absolutely no mention in the text of *Le Bacchus mutilé*, although one would be hard pressed to argue its irrelevance, and that is the Great War. Although the biography of the protagonist runs from a fin-de-siècle childhood through a crucial psychological awakening in 1907 to his return to his home village with messianic pretentions in the 1920s it makes no mention of what he was doing between 1914 and 1918, or whether he was aware of anything else happening in those years.

That second omission is definitely a puzzle, but although there is no way to be sure, there is one plausible explanation that springs readily to mind, which is that there is no mention of the Great War in Denis' biography because that biography was penned prior to 1914, and constituted one of the "hundred incomplete manuscripts" that Arnyvelde mentions in *L'Arche* having left behind when he went off to war. If that is the case, the stark contrast between the two halves of the story would become much more understandable, only the second part being written in the period of disillusionment caused by the war. If so, then the novel presently called *Le Bacchus mutilé* must have originally had a different title, and must have been planned as a follow-up to *Le Roi de Galade* before—quite understandably—being set aside in favor of the Ark intended for the author's psychological flotation during the terrors of the lethal Deluge.

If that is the case, then the Great War probably is present in the text, symbolically if not literally. The author could not insert references to the 1914-18 conflict into the pre-war text without reconstructing it in its entirety, so references to a literal war that had already been tacitly ruled irrelevant would not have been appropriate in the continuation, but it is arguable that the firework display during which the protagonist crashes stands in for the war, and the exceedingly awkward prosthetics that he has to wear once he is allowed to return home might well stand in symbolically for crippling baggage of a different sort, which the protagonist's *alter ego*, the author, brought back from the war. If so, it would help enormously to decode the whole of the second part of the book, and to assist the reader gain a far better understanding of the extremism of its deeply mordant—and, indeed, truly morbid—disenchantment.

It would be inappropriate to comment further in advance on exactly what the second half of the story contains, but I will add an intermediary note that might help to account for the vast difference in tone, narrative method and content between *Le Bacchus mutilé* and its sequel, *On demande un homme...*, which takes up the author's perennial theme yet again, but in a very different context and seemingly in a more positive mood.

The fourth novel in the series is perhaps more of a coda than a conclusion, and it reverts to the fanciful and whimsical manner of *Le Roi de Galade*, deliberately basing its plot on a familiar *conte bleu* motif, that of a competition between suitors to determine who will win the hand of a particularly desirable bride. The motif is perhaps best known nowadays in the version that provided the plot for Puccini's opera *Turandot*, based on Carlo Gozzi's similarly titled play of 1726 and Friedrich Schiller's *Turanzot* (1801), although the opera in question was unfinished at Puccini's death and was not completed for production until 1926, two years after the appearance of *On demande un homme...* Arnyvelde probably took the motif directly from Gozzi's source, the *Thousand-and-One Nights*, although the text also refers to variants in Greek mythology. The most interesting feature of the novel, however, is the extra twist that Arnyvelde adds to the story by dividing the heroine for whom various suitors are obliged to compete into five, and teasingly leaving it uncertain for some while as to exactly how that division is to be construed. At any rate, the "tournament" of the contrasting contemporary suitors offers the modern storyteller an excellent opportunity to compare and contrast the various practical and philosophical routes to the solution of the human predicament in a lively and witty manner, with Joy still the ultimate prize.

It is undoubtedly significant that *On demande un homme...*, the most flippant, and perhaps the least heartfelt of the four novels in the sequence, was the author's last original novel. He did produce three novelizations of film scripts in 1934-35, although they were calculatedly trivial hackwork, and he continued to write prolifically in the furtherance of his journalistic career, but *On demande un homme...* can nevertheless be regarded as a kind of farewell wave to the obsession that had gripped him at the age of twenty, but had released its shackles by the time he was forty—a release foreshadowed, and perhaps predicted, in the long lecture that the runaway king of Galade receives from his tutor following their reunion. In that speech the tutor observes that Ideas make good servants but terrible masters—a notion ruefully repeated in one of the autobiographical sections of *L'Arche* and ironically echoed in *On demande un homme...* The two novels in the present volume might therefore be regarded be regarded as a bittersweet chronicle of the manner in which André Arnyvelde escaped by modest modification his once-cherished enslavement by the idea of Joy.

The following translation of *Le Bacchus mutilé* was made from a copy of the 1922 Albin Michel edition. The translation of *On demande un homme...* was made from a copy of the 1924 Ernest Flammarion edition.

Brian Stableford

THE MUTILATED BACCHUS

PART ONE

1

The Joke had begun in the middle of June the previous year. Sénecé is supplied with drinking water by a spring in Telluire wood, three kilometers away. The pipes of that supply pass through a meadow on the Aury estate. One morning, a housewife went, as usual, to fill her bucket at the fountain in the Place Jacques. She turned the tap and looked up at the sky while the water flowed, to see whether the weather was fine and that the weathercock on the steeple had not been stolen during the night. The noise of the liquid flowing brought her attention back to the bucket.

Hello! What's that stream? She leans over, sniffs, becomes alarmed. There's no doubt about it...

It's wine!

At the other fountains, at the same time, other housewives are amazed by the same miracle. In the streets of Sénecé, people talk, shrug their shoulders... these women!... let's go see...

They see. Everyone runs to fetch bottles, pitchers, tubs. And Sénecé, all morning, is refreshed by long draughts, and celebrates at the marvelous fountains the extravagant Messiah who had, for a few hours, deflected the Telluire spring and replaced the water with wine.

Damn! How many hectoliters is that?

And the cinema in color…on the wall of the church!

The wall had just been freshly roughcast. One evening, young Leluc, going to the Café Gillon for a bottle of rum for his father, was going past the church. Suddenly, there is a flash, and there, on the wall, is a marvelous landscape, which begins to dance! Violet mountains, palm trees replete with golden clusters of dates, camels like those the child has seen in the pictures on the wall at school—but as large and majestic as they must be in reality…

Is that the Magi one can see? Good…it's changing!

A new landscape appears, slightly bumpy because of the swellings of the old wall: a pink and vermilion city beside a sea bluer than the stained-glass windows in the church in sunlight…

The child runs, he shouts, a crowd gathers…

The light is coming from a window at the top of the Aury house: a long and magnificent triangular beam, in which multicolored vaporous spirals flow; the beam of a magic lantern aimed from that high window. But with what magnifying glass, and what projector?

Italian lakes surrounded by mountains; forests in the heart of Africa; landscapes of India and China; extraordinary machines plowing, harvesting, the hundred-limbed bodies of which obey the finger of a child sitting on the seat in front of a control-panel; submarines seen in the ocean; helicopter aircraft; enormous telescopes brandished toward the sky like arms reaching out for the stars—and, indeed, catching them, since one then sees the landscapes of the moon, Mars and Jupiter…

When the beam went out, there was desolation. They could have stayed there all night! The curé made quite a fuss the next day.

Then there were the new bicycles and the American plows left at night—by whom?—at thresholds; the sheets, the garments, the schoolbooks, the tobacco, placed by night on window-sills. The cows led—by whom?—to the stables of poor farmers, always at night, and found at the stake in the morning, with a little note hanging from the horns: *On behalf of Denis Aury.*

Why the jokes? And why the benefits? Political ambition, proposed Ferroux, the schoolteacher. "It's to redeem the father's avarice a little," suggested virtuous folk. The curé insinuated that that Denis wanted to be pardoned for having let his father die without closing his eyes. All sorts of hypotheses, but nothing precise or solid at which to direct the incessantly reignited curiosity.

And above all, why did the Aury son remain invisible?

Frignot, the steward of the Maison Aury, harassed by questions, only succeeded in thickening the enigma, affirming that he had never seen Denis either—or, more precisely, had not seen him since the day when the young man had run away from his father's house—the house of the bitter, taciturn notary Jean-Nicolas Aury. Denis had been seventeen when he disappeared. He had not given any sign of life for years, or almost none.

The only person who had pampered him when he was small, the Aurys' old cook Julia, had received the occasional postcard from her darling, coming from all the corners of France, and then abroad. On one of them, Denis had written that if his presence became absolutely necessary, they were to notify a certain Leviel, a painter, whose address in Paris he gave: a little street in Montparnasse.

Now, Jean-Nicolas died and, although Leviel had been notified, Denis did not appear. Sénecé had judged the bad son severely. To be sure, such a father, a funereal miser...but a father is a father, after all, and death is death, and Denis ought to have been there. Denis was informed via the intermediary of Leviel of Montparnasse that he had inherited the château, known as the Maison Aury, the estate and the miser's considerable savings, comprising a handsome capital.

After three months of silence and disordered conjectures, a letter from Denis had reached Frignot, the anxious guardian of the house and the lands. Traveling for an indefinite time, Denis would take personal possession of his wealth when he chose to do so. In the meantime, Frignot would receive orders in writing.

Shortly after that first manifestation, construction of a factory had begun at Courtoisans, which is the next village to Sénecé. In the following week, the refurbishment of the Maison Aury commenced. It appeared, straight away, that the new owner wanted to modernize the building entirely; it was very old, and the notary, widowed early, had effectively let it rot. New widows were pierced in the soot-colored façade; the stone, scoured, offered a cheerful white flesh to the daylight; partition walls were demolished. The father's studio, always gray, crammed with filing-cabinets, a drawing room that no one ever entered and guest-rooms unused while Jean-Nicolas was alive were expanded into a vast hall with luminous galleries. From the cellars to a flowery terrace fitted under the roof, an entire electrical network was aggregated, destined to reduce the heavy burdens of service and reduce the work of heating and lighting to the flicking of switches.

When the work was in full swing the famous Leviel appeared, introduced to Fringot by a letter from Denis. The artist slept at an inn while waiting for the château to become habitable, and spent all day at the Maison Aury. He painted frescoes in the hall, the galleries and the antechambers. A small building with walls that were all panes of glass was erected in the park some distance from the house. Was it a greenhouse? There was already one of those. A further letter instructed the steward to consider Monsieur Draguin, soon to arrive, as the master of that building, which would be a laboratory.

When Draguin arrived at Sénecé, Frignot discovered that the new guest and Leviel were old friends and great friends of his master. He attempted, feebly, at every opportunity, to obtain some information. By turns mocking, evasive and, it sometimes seemed, embarrassed, the scientist and the painter avoided precise responses.

Denis' personality remained, for Frignot, nebulous. And it became even worse at the beginning of the year in which the prodigies and the tricks began in Sénecé. The best joke, the miracle was the most irritating for Frignot; Denis' letters, deposited without stamps in the box at the gate, multiplied until they were daily. They showed that the proprietor was up to date with the smallest details, exactly as if he were present, and the presence was very vigilant and clear-sighted. The steward lay in wait, spied on the domestics and the workmen, but could not discover anything, and was unable to explain how his master was so well-informed. Resolutely, he once mounted guard on the letter-box all night; the result of his vigil was simply that there were no letters the following morning.

What, in such circumstances, were the people of Sénecé to think?

Now, the mystery was to be concluded that morning in July, in two hours...an hour and a half...an hour. Only one hour to wait. Still an hour to wait! Frignot communicated the great news to Sénecé yesterday. It is at noon that Denis Aury will arrive and take effective possession of his domain, and will become for the Séneçois a visible man...finally!

The church clock chimes quarter past eleven. Work has been stopped for a long time. All of Sénecé is loitering in the vicinity of the Mason Aury.

At half past, the nearby blare of a klaxon freezes the crowd. Is it him? They recognize the car of the director of the Courtoisans factory. Monsieur Géard gets out of the auto in front of the gate, replies to greetings, and goes into the park; he is seen going into the laboratory, and coming out again a few moments later with Monsieur Draguin. Both of them go into the château, arm in arm.

At eleven thirty-five, Monsieur Leviel is seen arriving from Telluire wood. He has been working in the open air, as he has done since finishing the frescoes at the château. He walks at his tranquil pace, carrying his easel and paint-box, as usual. As he comes through the crowd he jokes, pretending to be astonished: "What's all this? Are we expecting the President of the Republic?"

"Is he definitely going to come?" asks Jeanselme, the farrier.

"The President?"

"We wouldn't go so far out of our way for the President. M'sieu Denis, of course!"

"I'm expecting him, as you are," says Leviel. When he reaches the gate he says, in his solid and joyful voice: "You're very intrigued, eh? I'll tell you something. What you've seen so far is nothing compared with what you'll see when Denis Aury gets here."

He opens the gate and goes toward the house at the same placid pace. Those who have heard him watch him, shaking their heads with a vague joy contained by the bewilderment into which overly complicated perspectives have cast them. His words are repeated, with immediate commentary, colored with extravagant suppositions.

Finally, the fever of the crowd explodes in a: "Good God, will midday never come!" cried by the shop-assistant at the Bailhard grocery.

The waiting weighs upon the Sénéçois like a stormy sky, tightening stomachs and making legs itch. The blast of a horn relieves the enormous irritation.

"Here comes the Maire!"

It's Monsieur Cahoche's auto.

"The bigwigs have all the luck!" comments a young cyclist from the factory, who has found a pretext to come and dawdle at Sénécé. "That one will see him, this Denis, don't worry," he grumbles. "Perhaps he'll even get invited to lunch."

The Maire's car advances with difficulty. The chauffeur sounds his horn repeatedly. Monsieur Cahoche, behind the glass, responds to the salutations. He is trying to be amiable, but his attitude suggests anxiety.

Ordinarily, Monsieur Cahoche is always laughing; he listens to you with little wrinkles of god humor under his eyes and a sugary "Yes, of course, we'll see to that, you'll see that we can reach an understanding" on his lips, with his head slightly tilted, his neat salt-and-pepper beard extended toward his interlocutor like a little pouffe offered in a drawing room. One always has a vague impression, when he speaks, of being in his drawing room. Monsieur Cahoche, a former solicitor in Paris, had bought the Château d'Harcors, a fine Renaissance edifice, Sénécé's other château, built on a hill facing the Maison Aury, and separated from it by Telluire wood and several hectares of fields. They live lavishly at Harcors; Monsieur Cahoche gives frequent receptions, maintaining relations with political man and important people in the magistracy and business.

The auto is obliged to slow down even more. Monsieur Cahoche becomes impatient. It is quite understandable that he too should be nervous, and more than the others, having borne responsibility for administration and order in the hallucinated village for a year. Monsieur Cahoche lowers a glass and shouts to the chauffeur: "That's all right—I'll get out here." And to the Sénéçois: "It's not worth risking an accident. What a crowd!"

He gets out, paternally moves aside a brat planted in front of him, reaches the gate, goes into the château, and goes up toward the hall.

Anyone going into the new Maison Aury is accompanied, from the ground floor to the hall on the first floor, by an uninterrupted fresco spiraling upwards with the white stone staircase. It is a singular work. "It develops the theme of the Joy of Welcome," Leviel said one day to Frignot, who was contemplating the painter at work with a kind of desolate bewilderment. A very legitimate bewilderment!

At first the gaze only seizes a multicolored tangle of rhombi, cubes, rectangles, spheres, spindles and cylinders enveloped, contorted and tormented by currents, flakes, eddies and spirals…and yet, as the eye adapts, beyond the frightful initial commotion, a veritable prodigy emerges. From that chaos, that crowd of lines and masses, forms and images are detached, seemingly born, stretching, quivering, condensing and expanding… As soon as it is discerned, each image, each form, immediately enriched by a host of possible evocations, is not only itself but a hundred others.

Such a painting, if it demands on the part of the artist a profound science of color, an infallible administration of volumes and their relationship, also demands a luxuriant inspiration. The rigorous mathematical laws that are the foundation of such an art, paralyze mediocre painters. They garrote them, confining them to dry and baroque representations, inaccessible to the majority of spectators, incapable of grasping it via the only interpreter that is offered when habit is shocked and intelligence nonplussed: enchantment.

Leviel's fresco can obtain that truly magical victory. It opens with the image of a man who is advancing through a décor equivalent to that of the château's own entrance, the trees of the park neatest to the façade, the three steps of the perron, the large glazed door, solely ornamented by eight bronze strips framing its two battens, the threshold of the vestibule and the first steps of the staircase. Around the man presses, densely, a sabbat of phantasmal forms, confused, as if incorporated into one another. The painter attempts to materialize therein the nebular escort that everyone trails perpetually behind him: the fatigues, the troubled thoughts, the bitterness, the hauntings. Here, dark patches, streaks of color, sometimes violent, sometimes sordid, muddy or glaucous puddles are permitted to indicate faces that are sniggering, moaning or biting; there, bold, bright, bright lines launch forth, ending in flattered, flaccid, disgusting masses of shadow, seeming figurations of aborted dreams. Beyond the man and his larval conglomerate, the gaze is immediately appeased. The funereal faces flow away, fading and diluted, into an expanse of soft colors and limpid lines; spirals, tufts and effluvia become gradually more precise, as fruits and flowers, in sparkling waves and undulations, some evoking arborescent fluids, some capering of sylphs. Here and there, the painter's thought is inscribed in a more objective design: a laughing juvenile face, a child dancing in the sunlight.

"The Joy of Welcome," Leviel has said...whoever follows that fresco, as he goes upwards, gradually feels the lustral certainty of that theme.

At present, Monsieur Cahoche is scarcely paying any attention to the fresco. He climbs the stairway, the sentiment of his dignity putting a brake on the impatience of his legs. He reaches the landing, breathes, mechanically passes his hand under his beard, tugs his gloves over his wrists, reaches the hall and goes in.

He pays no more heed to the splendid strangeness of the décor that surrounds him. He is not dazzled by the light, which is the sovereign magnificence of that décor—a July light, entering in a river through the bay overlooking the park, a light pouring torrentially from the glazed cupola that covers the hall, a light as heavy as all of space. He will admire some other time the gleaming friezes running between the divans and the shelves laden with books, and Leviel's vast frescos illustrating the room's four panels.

He does not spare a glance for the dazzling statue standing at the entrance to the gallery that opens facing the entrance to the hall. It is a perfect replica of the Bacchus of the Uffizi, in which it seems that Michelangelo has expanded the corporeal Joy of being. Monsieur Cahoche perceives Frignot, salutes Géard, Leviel and Draguin, who seem surprised to see him come in, goes toward the steward—but does not have far to go, because Frignot comes to meet him, embarrassed, scarcely leaving him time to say: "Bonjour, Frignot, bonjour, my friend...," before immediately demanding: "Has Monsieur le Maire received a personal letter from Monsieur Denis?"

"No," says Cahoche, "why? In truth, I came of my own accord. I thought..." He goes *grrhum!* as if something were stuck in his throat, passes his hat from hand to hand, opens his frock-coat with a gesture he tries to make casual and takes out his watch. "Twenty-five minutes, eh!"

"Monsieur le Maire," says Fringot, "this is very embarrassing to say...especially when it's someone like you...Monsieur Denis specified to me in his last letter..."

Fringot twists his moustache, biting the hairs that descend from his upper lip. "In brief, that he wanted to be alone with his friends and his lady."

"He has a lady?"

"Apparently, Monsieur le Maire. We're expecting her at any moment."

"Good, good...my word, that's true...why not? But my presence is perfectly explicable. Denis Aury is coming to take possession of his estate. It's perfectly logical that, as the primary magistrate of Sénecé, I should come to greet him..."

"Undoubtedly, Monsieur le Maire."

"With the result that if one weighs the pros and cons, Denis Aury will not find my presence more inopportune than he would think my absence impolite."

"There are pros and cons, as you say, Monsieur le Maire. It's very embarrassing..."

"Not for a man of the world, my friend."

Cahoche takes off his lorgnon, wipes it, replaces on his nose, scans the hall with a serene and cordial gaze. "What I mean," Frignot continues, "is that, given the authoritarian temperament that one might suppose Monsieur Denis to have, it might perhaps be better to do as he has taken care to specify. And then...given that a person like Monsieur le Maire, as clear-sighted and considerable in all respects...."

The Maire's gaze, blinking as it scans the frescoes, returns to the steward and stares at him with haughty astonishment.

"Monsieur le Maire," continues Frignot, softly, "would only have to set aside the curiosity that grips him, like everyone else here, and come back tomorrow or the day after, if Monsieur Denis does not visit him in the meantime..."

"Well…," says Cahoche. "But my friend, where did you get the idea that I was curious? Is it not my role as an administrator…and…But, in fact, why the devil didn't I think that it was to me that the visit was due?"

"There, Monsieur le Maire, that would be the curiosity. It's enough to turn the strongest heads upside down."

"Indeed, my friend, and it's high time that this bizarre adventure came to an end. For a year, my word…"

At that moment, emerging from the gallery, three young women appear, their arms laden with flowers that they have obviously just picked in the park. Their hair is ruffled by the branches, droplets of dew are glistening on their half-bare arms. They go to a large table, cover it with the sheaves, which they scatter with fresh litter, and then simply drop the rest on to the carpet, at the foot of an armchair. All three are dressed in white cotton smocks, indented over the breast and lightly tightened at the waist by a slender belt embroidered with brightly colored arabesques. The same embroidery runs along the edges of the short sleeves. Each of them is wearing a necklace that dances over the throat. One is jade, another amber, the third coral. The three women are beautiful; the color of their flesh and their gestures have the soft plenitude that is a kind of concrete sign of easy and spacious wellbeing.

"Are they…?" queries Cahote, looking at Frignot in surprise.

"Domestics, Monsieur le Maire, nothing more. The lady's chambermaids. I understand Monsieur le Maire's thought. They're not the usual sort. Monsieur le Maire will be astonished if I tell you their names. They're named after their necklaces: Jade, Ambre and Corail. So it appears! Monsieur Denis' letter said so, and they told me the same thing. Oh, to be sure, it's necessary to prepare to see things!

Having disposed the flowers, Jade, Ambre and Corail have left. Cahoche taps his foot, strokes his beard, and murmurs, with a slight laugh: "I presume that it won't be boring here…" He takes out his watch again. "Oye! Quarter to… I'll go…"

He puts on his hat, sketches a step toward the door and remains in place, immobilized by the deafening blast of an auto horn, an unusual song cutting through the air, in which a musician would have recognized the inaugural notes of the choral sequence of the ninth symphony.

"It's Lène!" cries Leviel to Frignot. "The gate, old chap, quickly!"

Frignot runs off. Leviel, Draguin and Géard follow him. Cahoche is left alone, somewhat disconcerted. The three strange maidservants reappear, traverse the hall, and head for the staircase in their turn. Cahoche follows them, overtakes them, says: "Pardon...," and rejoins Leviel, Draguin and Géard in the vestibule. "Excuse me Messieurs, I wouldn't like to disturb..."

They move aside to let him through. Now he is on the perron. He is half way along the drive when the gate opens wide, pulled by Fringot.

In front of the gate there is a tidal wave of curiosity-seekers, jostling one another in their unbridled desire to see. There are people in the trees and children perched on the crest of the wall. Cahoche is annoyed. Caught between the auto that is about to come in and the crowd that will see him leave, he does not really know what he is doing there. He ought to be on the perron with the guests of the Maison Aury, or in his own château, waiting in a dignified fashion for Denis' visit. At any rate he has to adopt an attitude, at least strike a pose.

Oh well...he has come to fulfill his administrative role, to make sure that everything is in order... His mission complete, he goes serenely back toward his auto...

For the moment, Monsieur le Maire is wasting his effort, because no one is paying any heed to him. The ocular attention of the crowd is caught, like iron filings by a magnet, drawn to the monumental auto that is there, and by the woman sitting in that auto: a young blonde woman in a green dress, her upper body outside a large mantle of brown wool that has fallen in heavy folds behind her waist.

The car has turned, passed the threshold, rolls majestically into the drive. Cahiche steps back and, gravely, with a gesture magnified by pompous elegance, bows to the lady, whom he can see through the large windows, and who smiles politely at his salutation.

Now that he can take advantage of the frantic attention of the crowd he leaves, simultaneously prompt and solemn, and goes back to his auto. But there is still a matter of saving appearances! He stands there, hat in hand, his gaze dilated behind the lorgnon, while the car reaches the foot of the perron, and the door opens, liberating the great green flame that has just dazzled his eyes and electrified the fibers of his being...

No, impossible! His mayoral consciousness grips him again. Sapristi! It's isn't over! It has hardly begun. There is time to revise...

Let's go... His temples are throbbing rudely. The gate. Ten paces. The car.

Gaspard has not budged from his seat. He is there, tranquil and cool. He isn't a Séneçois, a peasant—he's seen many others! Although the auto that just went past... That auto must be at least a hundred horse-power...

"To the château, Gaspard."

Drawing away. The silent, smooth departure of Cahoche's forty horse-power, until that moment the finest car in the region. The road. The banks, the boundary-markers, the trees the only spectators. Monsieur le Maire can let himself go. Well! No, it certainly won't be boring at Denis Aury's. Ambre, Jade, Corail...and that one... There's a man to whom that green flame belongs, a man who can hold her in his arms, place his lips on that bare shoulder that was visible...on that neck...on that hair...that hair...Oh Lord!

"I beg your pardon. Your beauty startled us to the point that we haven't thought of introducing ourselves. This is Louis Géard, and Pierre Draguin. I'm Bernard Leviel."

"I know," Lène replies. "Denis has told me who the three of you are."

"And this is Frignot," Leviel adds.

Frignot has unconsciously struck a military pose. He has been a sergeant. He senses the same prickling in his limbs, and the same mist over his eyes that overtook him the first time he had to return a general's salute.

Lène sees the three pale young women on the first step of the perron. "Bonjour, Ambre, bonjour Jade, bonjour Corail."

The three men line up. Lène advances and climbs, escorted by the women. And now they are all in the hall.

"What light!" says Lène.

Her nostrils tremble. She parades her gaze over everything in the room. Her visage is tinted pink by a pleasure both delicious and solemn. She goes straight to the flowery armchair. She sits down and says: "Denis will be here in a few minutes."

They have forgotten the time.

Lène is dressed in a green sheath of jersey and silk, pleated at the waist by a trip of fawn leather. Two slender ribbons of the same fawn color attach the dress to the bare shoulders. Only an artist could have composed the color of that dress. The bright and fluid green is the very flame of copper in fusion. The russet silk stockings have an ardent and heavy sheen like the wing-cases of scarabs. The shoes, fawn mules, secured at the ankles by across-piece, only enclose the end of the foot and the heel, leaving the arch, gilded by the stocking, exposed.

Lène is not merely beautiful. Something utterly unusual animates and exalts that beauty, circulating in the weft of her flesh. A kind of immaterial sap, a presence of wellbeing, which one senses in the young women who serve her, is revealed in Lène, much more richly, and more assured. She has drunk from the very spring of wellbeing.

Leviel is involuntarily put in mind of an expertly trained and well-nourished horse, whose coat is shining...

Lène is shining with Joy. The veins of that young body are carrying, mingled with the blood, the effluvia of that state of Joy. A strange, suave emotion takes hold of Leviel. Of the order of a fervor. Joy! Yes, that is really what it is! And besides which, what else could have recreated that hair, rendering it sublime? Neither nature nor the light, alone, could have achieved the golden vapor that seems to be incessantly renewed, to be the visible breath of the radiant presence that is palpitating and respiring in the limbs and the fibers... Crowning the graces of the body, the hair is also its fluid hymn. It accompanies and concludes every movement with silvery waves. A curl that snakes over the ear prolongs the nacreous freshness of a laugh; a lock that shines on the forehead completes the rosy gleam that springs from the nail of a lifted finger.

A rumor in the park draws Fringot toward the bay. There are still masons at the Mason Aury finishing the garage, and electricians putting the finishing touches to the innumerable circuits that run through the château and the laboratory. Footsteps are heard running through the edifice, in the upstairs rooms, in the antechambers.

Suddenly, the large gallery that opens behind the Bacchus lights up with a blaze. Draguin, Géard and Leviel start. The wait that they have had for their mysterious friend, and the atmosphere, seemingly saturated with nervous energy, of the entire village, the electricity of which has become more intense as the moment approaches, have combined to render noises, silence and things troublesome and irritating...

But suddenly, as soon as they are illuminated, the lights in gallery are extinguished. Three men appear behind the Bacchus, entering the hall. They are wearing blue overalls, two of them carrying bags of tools. All three are robust fellows, young and bearded, with eyes that have a slightly mocking gleam. A fourth workman follows them, this one older, who says: "Excuse me, Messieurs, Ladies," and heads for a commutator in the antechamber.

Frignot goes toward them, upset.

"What you doing here?"

"A last adjustment to the lights, M'sieu Frignot," says one of the three workmen, with a vague hint of irony in his voice. He goes to the table, nor far from Lène, and checks a contact-point. Lamps light up, and then go out.

Furious, the steward marches up to the older man, who is in the antechamber. "Are you mad, Goivin? You've left it until the last minute? It would be a fine thing if Monsieur Denis were to find you here when he arrives. Take your men away, quickly!" He takes out his watch. "Two minutes to noon! Great gods, get out of here!" Then he returns to the hall. "I beg your pardon, Madame," he says to Lène. "I don't understand at all. Goivin's an old supplier of the château, established in the village for years. Everyone's lost their common sense today..."

Draguin has gone to the bay, and leans out, as if listening. "We ought to be able to hear something," he says. "Noon is about to chime. Is he arriving by auto...or by airplane...?"

Lène smiles.

"How do you expect him to arrive, Madame?" Draguin asks her.

"He'll certainly be here at noon," Lène replies, simply.

Meanwhile, the workmen move slowly toward the hall. One of them, adjusting the strap of his bag, murmurs: "Perhaps he's already in the château, Monsieur Denis..."

"What is he saying, that man?" grumbles Frignot, following the excessively slow movements of the men with a visible exasperation.

"...And perhaps he's waiting for noon to make himself visible," concluded the workman.

"That's stupid!" Frignot explodes, his fury muffled by anguish. "How would I not have discovered him? He's not going! Monsieur Géard, you command them better than I do..."

"Sending us away, Monsieur Géard," says the workman nearest to the engineer, politely, "might perhaps prevent Monsieur Denis from being here at noon..."

"How's that?" said Géard.

"What if Denis Aury were one of us?"

"Oh, that's a good one!" Fringot guffaws. "Monsieur Denis a workman! He's not you, Julien Nouant! I've known you since the days when you played truant instead of going to school."

The first stroke of midday chimes on the church of Sénecé. A confused tumult rises up on the road. Géard, Draguin and Leviel look at one another apprehensively. Ambre, Jade and Corail have their eyes fixed on Lène. She is leaning back in her armchair looking at the workmen with an impatience full of amusement.

One of the three men calmly takes off the false beard that made him resemble his two companions. A frank pleasure dilates their faces; they tug their beards to demonstrate that they are real.

"Of course!" says Leviel. He burst out laughing, and Draguin and Géard join in, all three laughing broadly, with a glad timbre.

It is Denis Aury. Above his blue overall, his face is clear and youthful, gilded by joyful humor. But that clarity, that youth, that delight, is more of the fresh gleam of certain colored granites than the luxuriant sheen of a beautiful plant or that of a healthy and vigorous animal. The glittering glaze of stone is allied to an impression of extreme mineral hardness. In that living substance, hardness become firmness. The clear, youthful bedrock of that face is intelligence and will. A flutter of the eyelids, a crease in the lips, a suddenly serious attention, are sufficient to bring the sculptor of the rude substrate: the habit of thought. A rare spectacle, a face testifying to meditation, not hollowed out or rendered severe, but entirely radiant with it!

Géard, Draguin and Levil have seized Denis' hand

"Monsieur...," says Frignol. He is crimson. He does not know whether he ought to laugh too, or yield to a muffled anger that is rising to his throat, at having been fooled for such a long time. Well! For a year you've been rubbing shoulders...

The contentment of seeing Denis come into his inheritance ends up overwhelming the anger, which turns to: "But that damned Goivin was in on it! And them!"

He points at the two workmen.

"These two know," said Denis. "Because of our build and our beards, all three of us were often mistaken for one another, which dispersed suspicions. That helps me a great deal to come and go. And now, Frignot, you can let Sénecé know that I've arrived."

It was easily conceivable that like Frignot, the people of Sénecé who had known Denis as an adolescent, had not rediscovered him in Père Goivin's sturdy workman. The young man who had run away from the Maison Aury at seventeen was of medium height, timid and shy. The image that people had been able to retain of him was ill-adapted to that of the tall fellow who had called himself Amédée, who was seen working at the château and, on Sundays, idling in the cafés or along the roads, not sensibly different in his behavior from his companions of a similar age doing similar work.

On first reflection, the disproportion of stature exhibited by the two Denis—the one who was remembered and the one who reappeared—might have suggested to romantic minds the idea of a substitution and the usurpation of an inheritance. There was room for many adventures in such a long disappearance...almost twenty years! But it really was the same Denis. A hundred small evocations of childhood would have convinced Frignot promptly and calmed excited imaginations. In any case, it had been a long time since old Julia, in spite of her octogenarian eyesight, and in spite of the false beard and the name of Amédée, had penetrated the identity of her little Denis, and Goivin's strange workmen had confessed to her. Only the tender old rogue had kept her discovery preciously to herself.

It was the same Denis. And yet, there really had been a substitution; expressly, a reaction. The imprecise, hesitant, frail child had transformed himself into that strong and radiant man.

2

I

To save himself the few hundred francs of expense that he might have spent in sending his son to college, Jean-Nicolas Aury had once succeeded in unearthing an extraordinary tutor. Wandering though an inexorable deluge of misfortunes, assisting the assaults of that ill fortune by his laziness and his hobby-horses, Benoît Rufle, after his early days as a teacher in an establishment run by spinsters, had fallen into one of those indefinable states whose stigmata are painted more eloquently than all the precisions that might be attempted.

One day, to earn a crust and a few francs, he had been cleaning the glasses in a little bar where he hung out from time to time, by turns as a client and an odd-job man; that day, after having finished the liter of cheap wine granted to him by the bistro he had picked up a newspaper left on the counter and was looking at the small ads, a habitual and disillusioned gesture. Although, on several occasions, he had tempted fortune, his attire had always completed in front of the potential employer the catastrophic effect produced by the evident symptoms of an incurable idleness and a singularly ductile morality. In that moment of peace, in the warm bar, Benoît Rufle felt disposed once more to cast the net of his flaccid whims into the mysterious ocean of employment...

"Damn it!" he suddenly exclaimed. "That's a bit rich!"

A smoky indignation stirred within him a vague and decrepit sentiment of corporate solidarity, the old self-respect of a former teacher, on reading the advertisement placed by Monsieur Aury of Sénecé. That ministerial officer was asking for a tutor for a twelve year old boy and offering a monthly salary hardly sufficient to pay for candles, cigarettes and a weekly aperitif.

"Must be scornful of education!" sniggered Benoît Rufle. He calculated, however, that in spite of the country lawyer's stinginess, the function necessarily assured food and a bed.

He asked for something with which to write. What was he risking? And on the lined paper furnished by the bar, he drafted a letter to Monsieur Aury. He listed his qualifications, and mentioned that family misfortunes had reduced him temporarily to a precariousness of resources unworthy of his value, but which nevertheless incited him to accept the proposed "emoluments." Unable to give a personal address because he had no fixed abode, he gave that of the bar, informing the proprietor, and harboring no illusions, went to post the letter.

The miracle was accomplished, destiny having put in path of the man who had come down in the world the most accomplished of accomplished misers. The response arrived, which invited Benoît Rufle to present himself at the Château de Sénecé. It was so inconceivable, so utterly unexpected, that the poor fellow, after having read it, was seized by vertigo, and was obliged to sit down, dropping the letter and beginning to gibber.

"Let's have a look at it," said the bistro owner.

At the top of the sheet was printed: CHÂTEAU DE SÉNECÉ, *Étude de Maître Aury, notaire.*

"Damn!" said the bistro owner, rudely but cordially, to Benoît Ruffle. "Just what you wanted. Here, drink a little calvados; it'll put you right."

Benoît drank the calvados, wiped his eyes, reread the letter and recovered his spirits.

He needed to think. "I'll be back," he said, and went out to take a little walk. The event caused the lugubrious salad of his past to dance between his temples, fulgurantly. "If you miss this chance, my lad, it's all over..."

He saw himself respiring honest country air, strolling alongside florid hedges, behind which white apple-blossom was fluttering. He placed his hand on the shoulder of a little boy who was listening to him with large candid eyes. But what did he know that he could teach the child? Bah! The rules of grammar, the dates of reigns and treaties, and a confused geography were resuscitated in foggy battalions in his memory. Oh Lord! The country! Real trees...a child...a room...a bed...daily bread...

"That's it!" he said, in a resolute voice to the proprietor of the bar, when he went back. "Would you like to help me become a member of society again, like everyone else?"

And immediately, his great desire became a plea, so moist with emotion, that it seemed as if he would have burst into tears of anyone pressed him. It was necessary that someone help him, lend him a few clothes, in order that he could present himself decently, and money for the journey. He was irresistible, so wretched and so bewildered by hope, that the bar's owner softened.

"One can't let an educated man to whom destiny is holding out a branch to fall back into the utmost depths," the café-owner said to his wife. "There are things to which one doesn't have the right to remain indifferent." And he gave Benoît Rufle want he needed.

Immediately after the civilities, the gentleman began: "Monsieur, we will fall into accord or not immediately—no middle ground. I, my son, the cook, my steward, my gardener—in brief, everyone here—practices the vegetarian regime. An excellent regime, Monsieur, which has given its proofs. The good country air, for its part, nourishes and keeps the blood rich and abundant. Our air is as good as any alcohol, wine and meat."

The notary paused momentarily, and tapped the table with his bony fingers, which made a sound like hailstones on the sheet metal.

"My procedures are irreducible. If they suit you, I'd like nothing better than to confide my son Denis to you. Otherwise, I'll have the regret of not continuing this conversation. I count on not handing over the monthly salary fixed by my advertisement, but of keeping control of it in order to capitalize it. The salary will be your property, it goes without saying, augmented by the interest, on the day we part. In what hands could it be better placed than a notary's? You ask the reason for that procedure? I have no embarrassment in telling you. If you require, in those conditions, some pocket money for your tobacco and the slight fantasies with which it might please you to ornament our way of life…wine, sugar—what do I know?—candles, if you read in bed…for I can only furnish you, for my part, with one candle per fortnight…in brief, your superfluities, your little coquetries..." He smiled severely. "That pocket money, which will be yours, absolutely yours, I will give you, in hard cash, sound and of full weight, as payment for labors such as copying deeds, engrossments, registrations, expeditions, which you will do outside the hours of your lessons and which, I won't hide from you, will allow me to economize on my clerical expenses. That's it, Monsieur. Take it or leave it."

He sat back in his armchair, cracked his knuckles, passed his hand into the flaps of his waistcoat and swung his legs.

Benoît did not flinch. He knew full well that he had only one immediate choice: to eat here or to fall back into Hell. He could always "see how it went." He could get himself out of it. He put on a pretence of hesitation, looked at the ceiling and then his fingernails, sighed slowly, and replied: "Those are very harsh conditions, but, you see, I'm so tired of life in Paris and its agitations, that the pleasure and relief of being in the country will help me do without many things."

"My conditions are precise, Monsieur, and permit no reservations."

"Then I accept them without reservations, Monsieur. At the very least, we'll try them, such as you have been kind enough to state them to me. Would you care to introduce me to your son?"

Jean-Nicolas pushed back his armchair and stood up. Benoît Rufle was able to see a small, thin man with a ruddy face furrowed with violet capillaries, agitated by brief nervous tics. The pale eyes, striped with yellow, had a piercing and glacial gaze.

The notary opened the door to his office, shouted: "Denis!" and returned to his armchair.

The door of a nearby room grated. A child appeared, clad in a blue mariner's blouse and blue cotton trousers. He had a somnolent expression, and his feet dragged slightly over the parquet. Without saluting the visitor, he advanced toward the table.

"This is Monsieur Rufle," said the father, "who is taking responsibility for your education."

Denis turned to the man and looked at him; his eyes expressed no sentiment.

That silence and that immobile gaze disconcerted Benoît. During his journey he had formed the image of going to the child, taking him by the hands, embracing him, and sealing with that first gesture an alliance that he wanted to be affectionate and fraternal with all his resuscitated heart, since the hope of a new life...

"Bonjour, my dear Denis," he said. "I don't frighten you, do I?"

"Well, answer!" said Jean-Nicolas, brusquely.

"Bonjour, Monsieur," Denis replied. He went to Benoît and held out his hand. Benoît kept the small hand in his. "I hope that we shall be friends," he said.

"Take your master to his room," said the notary. "Go on, get acquainted. I have work to do."

He opened his files.

"Come, Monsieur," said Denis.

As soon as the landing was passed, the stairway, neat and solid enough from the ground floor to the notary's office, became lugubrious and worm-eaten. The dark red walls were shedding their plaster in large flakes, some steps oscillated underfoot and other creaked like mice.

Benoît's room was at the very top, under the roof, illuminated by a skylight. It contained a narrow iron bed, a small nightstand, a wicker chair and a white wood table. The flowery wallpaper, perhaps once pink or blue, offered brown and russet patches on a gray-green background, black blisters and dangling strips, spotted with mildew, the eccentric works of time and humidity. Benoît's bedroom was half of a grain-loft; on the other side of the loft was the bedroom of the cook, Julia.

The teacher looked at the rotten paper, the poor bed and the bare table but immediately sniffed blissfully.

"It smells good," he said. "It smells of nature."

"It's the apples and pears, Monsieur, and the hay in the loft."

"I'm very content to have them for neighbors. Let's go see them…"

He waxed ecstatic over the fruits, set out in an orderly fashion on the floor, sniffed them voluptuously, laughed at the onions hanging from the beams, and sank his hand amorously into great heaps of foliage drying against the wall.

Opposite, at the far end of the loft, was a chaotic heap of broken furniture, punctured frames, old cushions leaking feathers, books and a pell-mell of indiscernible objects coated in ageless dust. Between that confusion and the wall there was a kind of niche, simultaneously dark and quiet, a seemingly velvety refuge in the sordid mess. Benoît went to it, followed by Denis, whose eyes blinked and, for the first time, took on an expression—of anxiety.

In the shadow of the niche, Benoît perceived a long soft cushion on the floor, hollow out and rucked up, as if by the frequent presence of a body. An illustrated book lay beside it. The depths of the niche were populated by a miscellany of objects: pictures, stones, leafy branches. There was also a bowl full of water.

"What's…"

"It's my corner," said Denis. His head taut, his tongue slightly stretched and gripped between the lips, his eyes suspicious, he followed Benoît's exploratory gaze.

"And your belongings!" said Benoît. "That's to amuse you? What can you do with all that? Those stones...that bowl..."

"The pebbles...," said Denis. He looked at his feet, the wall, stared at a picture-frame, studied a spider-web in the corner of a joist. He avoided Benoît's gaze.

"You don't want to tell me? You can tell me when you want, if it annoys you. We don't know one another well enough yet..."

Denis then looked Benoît full in the face: his aged face scarred with wrinkles, his eyes red-rimmed by a perpetual epiphora, which gave the impression at that moment of a spark of tenderness.

"Those pebbles, M'sieu...perhaps there's one that is the prince of the Earth."

"Oh? Well...what an odd idea," said Benoît, softly. "And the little bowl?"

"That's the water that...that I took from the pond, M'sieu. Perhaps it's the fairy Ondine...and that branch there...the fairy of the Cherries."

"What makes you think that, my dear Denis?" asked Benoît.

Denis tilted his head, put his hands in his pockets, took them out again, twiddled the thumbs briefly, and then, in a muffled, timid voice, full of a great question that visibly came from his innermost depths, he said: "Tell me, Monsieur, have you seen the fairies?"

"The fairies? But..." He suspended his reply. It was necessary to be very prudent with a child about whom he had to learn everything before teaching him the few poor things that he knew. "Why do you ask me that, Denis?"

"No reason, M'sieu," said Denis, whose face became deadpan again.

II

He had scarcely learned to read when his mother died. He was seven years old. The ability to spell out letters, to pronounce the words they formed, to grope his way to the meaning of the word, was the whole of his science when he became an orphan. In any case, poor Madame Aury, had she lived, would scarcely been able to take her son's education any further on her own. She was a good woman, a shrewd administrator of the budget fixed for her by her parsimonious spouse, clever at making clothing and linen last. The daughter of a small vine-grower in Burgundy, Jean-Nicolas had married her with a meager dowry when he had been a clerk with a notary in Beaune. She had followed her husband's ascension without ever having the leisure or the means to refine her mind.

Jean-Nicolas, having become senior clerk, had been skillful enough in accumulating the funds that had permitted him to buy Maître Bessonet's little studio in Sénecé. The latter had left him a placid and mediocre business. The crafty Jean-Nicolas had soon appeared to his peasant clientele to be an excellent adviser, even though his stiffness barred any route to sympathy. A favorable opportunity had facilitated his acquisition at a very low price of the old Château de Sénecé. He had transferred his studio there. Avarice took hold of him after a few successful operations; the increased value of lands that he had brought on his own account, the adjudication of the woods and farms of which he was, via intermediaries, the beneficiary.

Acquitting himself as rapidly as he could toward his lenders, and then gorging his strong-box on a fortune that was his sovereign property, constituting an innumerable seraglio of mauve leaves of the Banque de France, gold louis and invulnerable bonds, became his goal, his obsession, his all-consuming sacerdocy.

Several times, when he bought the château, and afterwards, before his increasing clientele, Madame Aury insisted that he permit her to ameliorate their everyday existence, augmenting her domestic resources and even acquiring a few distractions. He laid out complex bills, which whirled before the worthy-woman's soon bewildered eyes, invoking the re-payment—long since accomplished—of his creditors.

"Later," he said. "When we have money and no longer owe anything to anyone. Then you'll see..." And with that, he demanded further economies.

Madame Aury died of a fluxion of the chest, and the fallacious promise obsessed her until her dying breath.

"Your famous 'later,' my love, 'you'll see...,' it's now necessary to call 'too late...,'" she said, with infinite plaintiveness.

With his mother dead, Denis was absolutely alone with Julia. Jean-Nicolas had achieved a settlement with his conscience by deciding, irrevocably, that he would get Denis a tutor when he was twelve or thirteen, and then teach him his profession, in order to leave the studio to him. Until twelve or thirteen, provide that he did not drown, fall off the roof or, above all, occasion any expense beyond the tiny budget that Julia controlled, Denis would have nothing to do but play in the park, help the gardener in the vegetable-garden, feed the chickens and rabbits in the yard, accompany Frignot hunting, and otherwise amuse himself as he liked. Let nothing be heard of him! Let no one come to annoy the notary with stories of torn garments, worn-out shoes, toothaches or earaches...that was Julia's business.

The hours and the days surrounded the child with a co-coon of ennui. No companion of his own age. The notary would not have consented to his son going out to play with the village children, nor for them to play in the grounds of the château. From behind the gate, however, or sitting astride the wall, Denis saw the games of those children. Did he want to join in with them? In a few words, as curt as commands, Père Aury had informed him that he belonged to a particular caste, and that the son of a notary must not debase himself with peasant children. Denis experienced a vague pride in not jumping down on the far side of the wall or going through the gate, which also prevented him from talking to other children at a distance.

In addition to that pride inspired by his father, he had an immense and mysterious reason for not interesting himself in the Séneçois. All of them—children women and men—appeared to him to be made of the same human dough, invariable, devoid of surprise, always dressed in much the same fashion, with gestures almost always the same. Denis had constructed a world of fairies and enchanters governing a humanity from somewhere beyond anything that could been seen in Sénecé: a humanity dressed in prestigious costumes, in which were mingled, pell-mell the brocade robes of Merovingian princes, the velvet garments of marquises and the golden uniforms of Napoléon's maréchals.

It was a living library; they were the images of a host of romances, bibles, history books and accounts of voyages, passionately contemplated, learned and animated; the few lines accompanying each image laboriously spelled out and their meaning expanded with scant effort in a brain and a soul normally avid for life, on which reality frowned everywhere.

Although all children who can believe in fairies construct an enchanted world and sense its presence, Denis' imaginative life and credulity was distinguished by an intensity all the more vivid because no one corrected it. Without guidance, having learned nothing that separated for him the past from the present, the real and the phantasmagorical, how could he not have entangled them intimately?

He was incessantly prepared for miracles. It only required the slightest hazard, no matter how unlikely, which a favorable circumstance might produce at any moment, for General Marceau to emerge from the wall, for that holy branch to be transformed into Saint Michael, or that hazelnut-bush into a grand vizier. There was, somewhere, beyond Sénecé, a mountain from which the crusaders could see Jerusalem; there were men clad in sculpted armor, and horses caparisoned in velvet; somewhere there was a rock to which A...n...d...r...o...m...e...d...a was enchained, a forest in which the hawthorn changed into a fairy struck Riquet-à-la-Houppe and made him as handsome as the day...

Thus he grew up, requesting the stones in the garden, branches, the wind and dragonflies to recover their true form and take him into the sumptuous and exciting world of books. Thus, when Beonît Rufle arrived at the château, Denis was living, apparently bleak and gauche, while bearing in the secrecy of his heart a perpetual expectation.

"The world is wicked, my dear Denis. If there are fairies, one never sees them. At any rate, I've never encountered one myself. The truth is that we all only know what we can know...in accordance with our character, or habits... There are certainly books, but one can't trust them blindly. They contradict one another. One will prove to you, as hard as iron, that the Good Lord made light, the earth and the people on it in six days; another will prove to you, as clear as daylight, that the earth emerged from the sun. And you won't be any further forward!

"Since I'm here to give you instruction, listen, my dear Denis. It's better to act in life as if there were no fairies. One decides to do something. One wants to do it, solidly, firmly, as a man, what! And one doesn't expect anything from anyone. Me...let's not talk about me...I haven't believed in fairies, and I haven't had will-power. There's nothing worse. You need a great deal of will-power. Well, the best thing is to have a métier in hand—but what I call a true métier: mason, carpenter, locksmith, mechanic, for example. Yes...you pull a face, because your father has told you that you're a petty bourgeois. Go on! One never knows what might happen. You think you'll be a notary. Well...if it's in order to be like your father...if I were in your place, I'd prefer to earn my living daubing plaster or making keys...

"You're free. When you're not happy somewhere, you pick up your trowel or your hammer, and you can say: '*Au revoir*, Messieurs, Mesdames, everyone, I'm leaving.' You can go anywhere, as you please. Oh, I'm not at all sure that you'll find what you've seen in your books anywhere. The crusades, King Arthur...Sindbad the sailor and the bronze horse that can fly...don't shake your head. The world... Wherever you go, it will be like Sénecé. Larger, naturally...you're going to say that, in consequence, it's not worth the trouble of going...that it's not worth the trouble of giving yourself so much trouble in order to be free, strong and independent...

"Oh, in truth, if you could understand... There's no more happiness anywhere than in lying on the grass out there, near the beech-trees, and watching the insects running through the grass. There's nothing in life worth as much as that joy...

"You'll go, eventually, and you won't know what happiness is. And me, in the meantime, I'll scribble deeds and lists to buy candles, in order to read the books in the library from which I'll extract as best I can the lessons that I give you, since your papa doesn't want to hear talk of buying scholarly books...

"Come on, I'll tell you about the gathering on the Field of the Cloth of Gold...don't bite your pencil..."

Far from having split the cocoon of ennui, the arrival of Benoît Rufle in Denis' existence had made the child's days more colorless and heavy. Benoît had chased the fairies and Prince Charmings away. He had put in their place a hostile, somber world devoid of the unexpected, a kind of Sénecé extended all over the world, with the leitmotiv, the tiresome repetition of the necessity of a métier, in order to be able to move freely in the world.

Denis had passed the age of thirteen when, one day, he heard from his room a loud burst of laughter coming from his father's office. Laughter was not often heard in the Maison Aury, especially not laughter like that, resounding with health and good humor. The child wanted to have his share in such a singular event. He went into the office from time to time, and the notary gave him documents to file, to occupy him and habituate him to it. Denis picked up one of the files he had, slipped quietly into his father's room, and started tidying up, silently.

The elder Aury paid no attention to his son. Sitting opposite him was a man who was fairly young, robust and elegant. He was a Parisian painter, whom an inheritance had just made the owner of a small plot of land in Sénecé, and who was making arrangements with the notary for the sale of the land. He listened sagely to the notary's advice, and then, as soon as he opened his mouth, his questions or his replies had a light tone that rendered everything he said accommodating and agreeable. When the affair was settled, he rubbed his hands and then scratched his head.

"Perhaps I'm making a mistake. The area is pleasant. Your château has character. View of the road...the interior... Damn it, Monsieur Aury, your home isn't cheerful. Oh, if it were mine...with a park like yours! One ought to be able to hunt deer there."

He considered Père Aubry, drawn into himself, in his armchair, listening with polite indifference, and contented himself with blinking his eyes, or shaking his chin with little remarks: "Tee hee... yes...!" The painter, because that type of narrow rural bourgeois amused him, and doubtless also because he only knew how to go forward at speed, carried on talking, and warmed up, lending himself to his tirade. He talked about the pleasure of living, the voyages that had inspired him, cited an exotic land through which he had traveled the previous year, described its customs, its spectacles...

He was suddenly interrupted by the noise of dropped files.

The notary started. "Pay attention, Denis! What's got into you?"

The child picked up the scattered papers. He would have been very embarrassed to say that the visitor's words had resuscitated confusedly within him the great mysterious emotions that he had once experienced in fairy tales, and had cast a flash of light into the bleak verities of Benoît Rufle, an intoxicating suspicions of other marvelous truths...

The memory of that afternoon was to obsess him. He planned fantastic adventures: to run away, to enlist as a cabin boy, to have himself stolen by gypsies. After long and turbulent meditations, one evening, he climbed over the château wall and went to knock on the door of the locksmith Goivin. Candidly, he confided to the amazed man his desire to learn a métier, without anyone being aware of it., in order to be free...free to go one day to see how the world was made, before taking up his father's métier for life.

Goivin asked to think about it. Madame Goivin, having been consulted, concluded: "We're risking the gentleman getting angry...but we'll gain the amity and gratitude of the son. All things considered, Goivin, and in spite of the inconvenience, it's a good investment for the future..."

Denis commenced his secret apprenticeship. He went to Goivin's house almost every evening. The neighbors, seeing light filtering through the workshop's shutters late into the night, were astonished and there was talk. To the rumors that were brought to his attention, Goivin simply replied: "Yes, work's going well. Orders from the town. I'm not discontented."

One evening, when Denis, dressed in one of Goivin's overalls, was struggling at the work-bench, someone knocked on the door.

"Hey, Sénecé-la-Prudence!" cried a loud, joyful voice. "Will you open up to Vendôme-la-Branche-d'Or?"

Goivin ran to open the door, and came back with a tall fellow carrying a satchel and a stout cane.

"Welcome, Branche-d'Or," said Goivin. "Everything going well? Make yourself at home."

"You're still working at this hour, Prudence?" Business must be very good in these parts."

"No better than anywhere else, friend. It's a young lad to whom I'm teaching the trade in my spare time. Sit down and I'll go get us something to drink..."

"You want to be a locksmith, then?" the man said to Denis. "It's a good trade. You're lucky to have fallen in with

Père La Prudence. He has his renown. I've heard talk of him in Lyon, from which I've come, and Bordeaux, and Orléans. There are comrades who remember him, from the time when he made his tour of France. It wasn't yesterday—but a good workman leaves traces..."

Goivin came back with glasses and a bottle.

"I was telling your lad that people still remember you, La Prudence, in the shops you passed through once At Lyon, for instance, my last, at Berlaud's..."

"Berlaud...Berlaud...oh, Berlaud! Lyonnais-la-Clef-des-Coeurs! I should think so!"

The two men were caught up in a tide of stories, names and memories. Denis did no more work that evening, and listened until a late hour to tales of the journeys of Vendôme-la-Branche-d'Or and the incidents of Goivin's tour of France.

III

The passage of the Vendômois and the explanations avidly demanded of Goivin thereafter resolved for Denis the great problem that was haunting him. Capable of being an aspirant, and then a companion, he would go to the city. Goivin would be his godfather, and he had already chosen his name: Sénecé-l'Espérance. He would be received into the Association. Once received, he was saved. He would only have to travel the world, from town to town, working for the bosses who were indicated to him.

He had no fear. Obliged by the notary to familiarize himself, during the day, with deeds and contracts, he was exasperated by it. It was much more amusing to fashion a key cut from the blank, or a dovetail, far more noble to cause an accurate and smooth form to emerge from a piece of iron than to transcribe the articles of a union or a legacy concerning people who are nothing to you. Soon, adieu stacks of paper; he would be free! When he had worked solidly all day, he would employ his leisure hours in looking, discovering and learning.

The puerile hope of fairies and prodigies was perhaps not entirely extinct within him; at any rate, it had left him with a thirst to get closer, passionately, to he knew not what innumerable surprises, of which the world beyond Sénecé must be full. Bold, the file! Bold, the screw-cutter! His hands held his liberty, the liberty to confront life, to take his place among men. In order to begin, he only had the concern of becoming an aspirant. That was the certainty of never lacking work. He knew that he would always find fraternal aid among the gavots.[3]

Goivin was a Master-Companion and gavot. He told the apprentice fine stories. Certainly, in the twentieth century, the Companions no longer made the tour of France with a bunch of ribbons in the hat and a buttonhole in the coat. Journeys by rail had replaced the joyful journeys on foot, but the fundamentals, the rituals and the principles of the Association remained intact. There was always, in every city and every town, a "Mother" in whose home a Companion was assured shelter and nourishment until he was placed, and a "Roller" who would find the pilgrim a place.

The rivalries of corporations and sects were greatly attenuated. Oh, the great battles of the Association! He, Goivin, in his capacity as a gavot, was an "Indian," a "Child of Solomon," a "Companion of Duty and Liberty." Denis would encounter in the Association, Dutifuls and Dogs, Children of Maître Jacques or Children of Soubise, Companions of the Holy Duty of God. Once, gavots and dutifuls had killed one

---

[3] *Gavot* is an argot term referring to a veteran member—normally one with forty years' experience—of one of the ancient artisans' guilds, which were still active in France at the end of the 19th century, although in the process of being replaced by trade unions of a modern kind. The term has no English equivalent, English artisanal guilds being differently organized, but I have translated most of the other jargon terms the Denis learns from Goivin into their literal English equivalents.

another. A Dog encountering an Indian on his route would feel obliged to insult him immediately and then fight, and there were some who went as far as murder.

One had as rigorous and as sacred an idea of the ritual to which one was affiliated as Catholics had of their church. The French did not detest the English more after Saint Helena than the Gavots detested the Dutifuls and the Children of Soubise the Children of Solomon. That savagery was in the past, thank God! Denis would be able to fraternize. One man was as good as another and all true workers belonged to the same family...

However, it was necessary to consider the good side of the rivalries. People had acquired a much more elevated concept of professional value then than nowadays. At present, the least of unionized workmen had the right to consider himself the equal of any other worker, knowledge and talent passing into the background. Corporate pride, if not taken to excess, was a great stimulus to competition. Not that Goivin despised the trades unions—on the contrary. "You'll see for yourself, Denis..."

In general, the trades unions did not like the Associations, partly because to say "companion" was to say "good workman." And there were inevitably poor workmen, good-for-nothings, the jealous and the denigrators, in the unions, open as they were to anyone...

It was also because of the bigoted articles of piety that still encumbered the rituals of companionship. In opposing that, the unions were not wrong. In any case, as was evident, there were companions in the reddest unions. Everything was coming together. The articles of piety were the framework of the old principles of Companionship, and those principles still served for the reception of aspirants. They too had their good side. They represented a discipline, severe rules, which bound the companions together side by side, friends and brothers for life.

It was necessary, to be received, to pass through the proofs. Some were harsh and baroque. "You'll doubtless take a beating...be made to drink vinegar, perhaps worse...eat dirt...a heap of practical jokes...they're symbols. The slaps one gets over quickly, and you'll understand the seriousness behind the practical jokes: ideas of honor, courage and fidelity. If they go about it a trifle vigorously, that's to get the ideas more firmly into your head, and so that they'll remain there until your dying day..."

And then, the pride in fine work! Goivin told the child epic stories, among them the combat in Montpellier in 1800 or thereabouts. The Companion Carpenters of Duty had played for the town against the Companions of the Duty of Liberty. In those days towns were staked between rites of the same corporation. Each society made a masterpiece, and a jury decided the prize. The winning society had the town for a hundred years—which is to say that if the dutiful carpenters won, no gavot carpenter would be able to find work in Montpellier for a hundred years. Oh, people went at it hard in those days! The unions, however, for all their faults, had established more egalitarian mores, and everyone, from the moment that he could use his hands, had the right to earn a living anywhere.

"So, the gavots and the dutifuls had made their masterpieces—a pulpit—in order to be masters in Montpellier. The prize was given to the dutifuls. They went through the town chanting victory. But scarcely had the prize been awarded than a gavot went to his corporation's masterpiece, smashed it with his foot, and before the wreckage of the pulpit shouted to the judges: 'Let the dutifuls do the same. We'll reconstruct ours, in no time.'

"The gavots' masterpiece was made of eight thousand pieces of wood, so well-conceived and well-realized that each of the pieces adapted to its neighbors by the perfection of its dimensions, its mortices and tenons, alone. The judges, marveling, reversed their decision and gave the prize to the gavots. Exultant, they spread out through the town. They ran into the dutifuls, full of triumph. They told them about the judges' reversal and mocked them.

"Then, my little Denis, they hurled themselves upon one another. The blood ran for three days. There were gavots and dutifuls arrested and convicted of murder. Savages, I tell you! But even so, eh, Denis? Eight thousand pieces of wood! So well-shaped that one could scatter them to all the devils and then reassemble and reconstruct the masterpiece. What artists!"

For Papa.

Benoît Rufle, going to open the letter-box at the gate one day, found a letter from Denis. Very anxiously, he handed it to the notary. Denis announced that he would already be a long way from Sénecé when his father opened the letter, that he had left of his own free will, that no one should worry about his safety and that he would soon send news. He promised his father always to be honest and not to owe anything except to his work. A solid handshake for Monsieur Rufle and a big kiss for Julia.

What work was Denis talking about? Why had he run away? A child who had a life ready made before him, the inheritance of a prosperous studio...

Julia's lamentations brought some clarity to the completely disorientated notary. Of course! The little one had no comrades, never any distraction! Monsieur Aury judged and treated everyone around him as he did himself. As if the affection of a poor old cook and the stacks for paper in the study were sufficient for a growing boy! It was hardly surprising that he had got a heap of things into his head that no one suspected. To whom would he have confided them?

"There are many children who would have liked to be in Denis' place!" replied the notary, and added: "One isn't on earth to amuse oneself."

The vague remorse, the amazement and the anger generated by that disappearance lasted all the way from the morning to mid-afternoon. When that time had passed, Jean-Nicolas, as if corseted by cold rage, retreated into himself a little further, ordered Julia never to mention Denis to him again, and decided not to make any fuss and wait. Hunger and the realities of life would soon oblige the young adventurer to return to the nest...

I

A chaos of sentiments in Denis, a pell-mell of disappointments, puerile delights, bewilderments, a sabbat of horribly complex problems, hopes simultaneously vacillating and stubborn of resolving those problems, and of finding the key to the joy that, in spite of everything, he sensed quivering within him...

What Joy? Doubtless that of youth, doubtless that of new liberty. Strange liberty! From daybreak to nightfall the young man belongs to a factory whistle, to a raucous ululation that comes to take possession of him in his bedroom, makes him gallop to a big black gate with broad scars of rust, wide open to the torrent of a host of workers, of which he is one, takes him to a narrow workshop into which daylight, having introduces itself painfully through the dirty puddles and packets of spider-webs that cover the windows. That is where he works, accomplishing a stage before commencing the tour of France: monotonous and tedious labor amid an incessant din of turbines, valves and pistons.

What can he think about in that racket, amid the exchanges of coarse jokes, whistles and the jeremiads of his companions? Liberty can only come to him when the ululation cries "Enough! Until Tomorrow!" He is scarcely in any state to celebrate its arrival. He is racked by fatigue, stinking of an air charged with vapors, oil and acids, numb, his head buzzing. It requires courage for him to climb up to his room, clean himself up a little, go to have a morsel in a little eatery near his lodging-house and run away from his leprous street to make a tour of the broad and luminous quarters of Paris. He needs to overcome not only his lassitude and reduction to animality but also to resist the invitations of his comrades at the exit from the factory, or get past their sarcasms and their hostility.

"Snob!"

"Monsieur is a loner…!"

"Monsieur prefers more distinguished company..."

Oh, they do not spare him their gibes. Even if he does what the others do, speaks their language, drinks like them and joins in with their heavy banter, he remains "the bourgeois." All the more so because he one day let slip: "My cook..."

Was it to find what he has found that he fled Sénecé? The foremen, the old workers, are brutal. How far away they are from the paternal gaze of Goivin! And those among the old who belong to the Association are the worst, imbued with archaic traditions that oblige the aspirant to ritual formulae of respect, to a servile docility toward the "ancients." The workers of his own age only think, outside the factory, about girls, sports, café-concerts and card games.

When, out of what he earns, he has paid for his room, his brief meals and his laundry, he scarcely has any money left for pleasures. But for what pleasures is he thirsty? All of them…those that the people must have whom he sees, on certain evenings, in the Champs-Élysées: the men in suits, the women covered in furs and diamonds, borne away in automobiles with florid interiors, as vast and illuminated as drawing rooms…the pleasures that one finds in the lands of sun or snow advertised by the multicolored posters on the railways stations…but it is not with his poor costume that one can savor any of the luxuries he covets. Outside of his present garments, he only has his blue overalls, stained with filthy grease. For what can he hope?

A neighbor at the work-bench, to begin with, has taken charge of removing all his illusions. There is an argot term that characterizes very precisely the kind of man that Mazou is, a tall, lanky fellow of twenty-five, not a bad worker, who boasts of being an anarchist; that term is "loudmouth."[4] Nothing ever emerges from his mouth without a snigger behind it, in which one senses the entire social machine ready to come in stage. An observation by the foreman, an implement getting blunt, a dropped piece of work, no less than the last session of the Chambre, the derailment of a train in China or an earthquake in Colorado, are the rigorous consequences, the inevitable reactions of the disorderly functioning of a poisoned Society, gangrenous to its foundations, on the verge of collapse and putrefaction.

"Don't hope for anything," he told Denis, one day when the latter permitted himself to dream aloud. "Outside of the bordello, the card table and an occasional drunken binge, all other joys are closed to you. They're for the rich. So long as the world is the way it is, there'll be everything for them on one side, and nothing on the other for us. Fortunately, the great dance is in preparation. Oh, a nice sweep of the broom! Wait until Capital comes tumbling down! You'll see, the managers, the messieurs all in gold and the lovely ladies all in pearls—away to the boiler, people! Everyone to his turn!"

He intoned, with a kind of furious delight, to the charming tune of *Temps des cerises*, a song of revolutionary victory and universal love in an egalitarian world: "When the time of anarchy in here..."[5]

---

[4] *Râleur*, which I have translated as "loudmouth," that probably being the nearest equivalent in English slang, also implies that the noisily opinionated individual in question is peevish, ill-tempered and quarrelsome.

[5] The song *Le Temps des cerises*, the tune of which was composed in 1868 by Antoine Renard (1825-1872) in 1868 to fit words previously penned by Jean-Baptiste Clément, became closely associated with the Paris Commune of 1871, in which Renard was intimately involved. Its many subsequent interpreters included the ardent feminist Odette Dulac, whose version, dating from the turn of the century, Arnyvelde probably heard while he too was occasionally performing in Montmar-

Denis shook his head. "It might be a long time yet before the world changes hands. Me, I'd rather profit from my youth. There's a host of things I want. By putting in the necessary energy, I don't see why I should get them. People have been seen who started from humble beginnings. With their intelligence, their determination..."

"Valets, traitors! At a given moment, they'll have made use of their intelligence for some crapulousness. They'll have stepped over the body of a comrade, or made themselves lackeys of the bosses..."

Denis seemed dubious.

"I tell you," Mazou went on, with implacable assurance, "when one's on this side of life, it's forever. No hope of getting out, if one doesn't want to betray one's brothers in slavery and suffering. Will you too accept to profit from what is simply the result of the crimes and egotism of the rich, and the misery of the plebs, from the torturers of the Inquisition to the prison-camps of bourgeois and capitalist labor?"

At that moment, Denis thought about his father, the bitter gentleman out there, heaping up and locking away his useless stacks of gold coins and wads of banknotes...

He had not replied to Mazou. He had bowed his head.

For a time, the persiflage of the anarchist had troubled him fully. Then there was moment of clarification of two equally harsh and somber destinies: return to Sénecé, prepare himself to be a notary, inherit from his father one day, and from that day on, enjoy in a cowardly fashion a wealth he had not earned; or continue on the road that he had opened to himself, be a worker, earn his daily bread by bestial labor, gradually climb the rungs of a terribly short ladder, become a foreman, an overseer...and then what?

He has heard it said often enough, since early childhood, that one is not in the world to amuse oneself. However, his

---

tre cabarets. By 1922 Dulac had become a writer of some note, and was probably acquainted with Henriette Sauret.

young blood, by its ardent flow, his muscles and his nerves, are protesting violently against that dusty precept...

At the very least, he has to dispense that fire in his blood, that impatience in his nerves in the joys that are permitted to him.

He tries. Thanks! Thanks for interminable sessions around dusty little marble tables in dismal taverns, warming himself, employing his strength, his reflection, his impetuosity in triumphing with a pair of aces or four queens. Sports tempted him; immediately, he dreamed of being one of those champions about whom everyone talks, and the mere mention of whose name fills his comrades with feverish veneration. His first attempts tempered his vast ambition. And anyway, was that what he imagined when he leapt over the wall of the park, his heat hammering, and running to Goivin's house to forge his liberty, the armor and the blade of great adventures through the incalculable world: one day to be a "record holder," at rugby or cycle racing?

There are goals more noble, more spacious... He does not know what they are...they pass before him in sparkling nebulosities, with the vague forms of Venetian palaces, transatlantic liners advancing majestically over adamantine seas, tiger-hunting with maharajahs in the jungle...

But Mazou's bitter tirades, still loud in his ears, intervene. Is it true, then, that to be a leader, a powerful individual, a vanquisher of life, to sail freely over the seas, to live in palaces, to hunt with maharajahs, is to wade in the blood of murdered plebeians?

But there is amour...the most beautiful of joys, and which is not accursed! Denis is eighteen; he is neither deformed nor gauche. He has heard and knows of romances in which burning intoxications, in the arms of blonde mistresses, are the most precious happiness of all, which open the heavens to humans...

Amour...

Immediately, the same day when he underwent, with several boys of his own age, the proofs of the Association, jokes burst forth about his still being a virgin. Oh, the thunder of laughter, the fusillade of gibes, when Denis had been made to admit it! No one would go to bed that night until the lad was deflowered! And he was dragged off to the brothel. The girl...he no longer remembers her at all...was summoned who, in seven or eight minutes, initiated him. He went back to his comrades, rather proud of himself, something like a real commencement of a man, someone, in sum, who now had the right to play his part in conversations where there was talk of women.

Amour...he would have liked to encounter the Golden-Haired Beauty, or the Clever Princess...which is to say, a creature that corresponded to them, in reality. It was stronger than him, stronger than the anathemas of all the Mazous; it was not his fault if, as soon as he dreamed, his dream bounded toward the major splendors...

Amour...the girls he meets, the mistresses of his comrades, the female factory workers and those of the neighborhood, are merely poor little women bundled up by the devil, and utterly deprived of everything he would like to find, for want of other magnificence: a soul, a particular sensibility, with which to share his great confused thirsts. Those gamines are all perpetually envious of one another, perpetually denigrating one another: if Germaine Thuilard has nice boots it's not very clever...she debauches herself every Thursday with an old commercial salesman...it's not very difficult to have a red leather handbag like Marie Lebasquet's...

Denis has written to Sénecé several times. But what can he write, in the cruel struggle in which he is stifling? He has just sent a few words to Julia. He is well...he is working... What point is there in saying any more? And how would he explain it—the fog over the world and over himself, in which he is circling like a horse in a treadmill? It seems that everything is combining to aggravate his stagnation, thicken the uncertainty that surrounds him. The smallest incidents...

One evening, as he was finishing his dinner, he distractedly picked up a few pages of a book that the child of the eatery's proprietor was amusing himself pulling apart and scattering. They were illustrations from a legend: a woodcutter striking the trunk of an oak with his ax, effortfully; a king passing by, out deer-hunting, escorted by lords.

Why am I not that king, instead of a poor woodcutter? lamented the poor forest-dweller. Immediately, he became the king. The sun began to shine on the hunt, becoming so ardent that the cortege had to halt, interrupting the ride in quest of shelter. And each of them complained, and the king-woodcutter, humiliated, wished that he was the star powerful enough to trouble his royal pleasure.

Scarcely has he formed his wish than he is the sun. He is radiant, bursting with pride, contemplating the wretched earth and its human anthills. Suddenly, a cloud passes by, which masks everything. *I wish I was that cloud!* thinks the stupefied sun. He is the cloud. He advances magnificently through the air. But an obstacle stops him, tears him apart, disperses him in vagabond wisps. He wants to be that obstacle, which vanquishes the vanquisher of the sun. Now he changes into an immense tree, with foliage so high that he can transpierce the clouds. He dominates the forest. He reigns over the other trees, the animals and the ground. He spreads out all his branches voluptuously.

A terrible shock suddenly shakes his base. He is being attacked, wounded, disemboweled. Oh to be the reckless individual who is assailing his majesty...And, having become that person...he finds himself once again the woodcutter that he was to begin with...

That naïve apologue completed Denis' confusion. It illustrated his devouring anguish. It was the veritable symbol of that anguish and the pitiless verdict passed upon it. What good were all his ambitions his labors, his dreams? Nothing served to lead to anything. The rich, the fortunate, were also circling eternally, finding themselves, at the conclusion of their joys, like the woodcutter at the foot of his oak. It was just that the circle in which they turned was larger and more brilliant than the one permitted to Denis. Let him return to Sénecé then.

There, at least he would be sheltered from those vain temptations, those ironic mirages of grandeur and joy, with which the atmosphere of the city whipped his eighteen years...

But what a defeat that return would be! The shame, when he thought of it, brought a cold sweat to his brow.

Thus he was, for hours, lost, adrift, full of distress, and the spring of life in his arteries was like the gold in an alluvial deposit that no boat has yet approached.

II

One morning, there was a great discussion in the workshop, Brochin, the fitter, who liked to comment on the events that he had read about in his newspaper on the way to work, started talking about a lecture to be given that same evening by a prince—"A real one, a sort of king, the Prince of Monaco,[6] in fact"—at the University in the Faubourg Saint-Antoine.

"That's good!" exclaimed Brochin. "This evening, a prince. The other week they had Père Clemenceau. They're advertising Flammarion, the astronomer. And recitations by the artistes from the Comédie-Française. And singers from the Opéra. The best thing is that one can talk to the lecturers and the artistes. They come to mingle with the audience after the lecture, neither more nor less than comrades. You ought to approve of that, Mazou. It's your ideas."

"Me?" said Mazou. "I spit on it. It's humbug, sucker-bait, bird-traps. An invention of capitalists to amuse the people

---

[6] Albert I (1848-1922) of Monaco had a long and distinguished career as an oceanographer, and did several lecture tours popularizing the science. He lectured at the Université populaire du Faubourg Saint-Antoine (U.P.) in 1907; if that date is accurate within the internal chronology of the text—and there are other confirmations of it—then Denis' return to Sénecé, "nearly twenty years" after running away must take place in the mid-1920s probably shortly after the novel's publication date.

and turn them away from the great upheaval. While the Monacos are filling their eyes and ears, they aren't thinking about going to smash the strong-boxes. These lectures are a waste of time, a diversion, that's all."

"All the same, to learn things about which one had no idea is a good thing; it aids progress," said an old hand. "A fellow becomes capable, by educating himself, of rising above his station; you shouldn't say that it's humbug."

"A slave he's born, a slave he'll stay, your fellow," said Mazou. "What's the point of knowing about things he'll never be able to enjoy? To make himself more miserable..."

"See himself more miserable, he'd be more disposed to revolution, in a sense," observed Brochin.

"Seen like that, yes," said Mazou. "But it's a trick. All the nonsense that they tell him out there, it can only trouble him, and delay the moment when he'll jump on Capital with both feet. And then, what do you expect me to say to you?" He set down his implement violently. "I have nothing but scorn for people on high who want to disturb themselves to talk to the people. With what have they acquired the education or the talents that they want to hand out as alms to the worthy gawkers who widen their eyes at the auto that has brought them? And their auto, eh? It's from the sweat and the misery of the people, thanks to the disgusting state of things that gives to some all that education and talent permit, and to the others alcohol, the factory and brutalization... That's my opinion. You're fixed."

There was a silence; shoulders were shrugged. The files grated more forcefully. Brochin whistled *Viens, poupoule, viens...*[7]

A young man suddenly began to laugh. "You know, Brochin, there are some who say that your U. P. is a fine dance-party. Me, that's the way I've heard talk of it. And that

---

[7] A song by the celebrated cabaret performer Félix Mayol, which became very popular shortly after the turn of the century.

there are society women who go to lectures expressly to meet strapping fellows from the suburbs, who make a change from their monocled messieurs."

"There are always people to drool over anything good that anyone tries to do," replied Brochin disdainfully. "Perhaps you'll be lucky enough to bag a duchesse, ape though you are."

"At times...," sniggered the workman

"Lads," said Brochin, suddenly, "I've got an idea—which is that Mazou takes advantage of the fact that one can talk to lecturers as friends, even when it's the Prince of Monaco, to go and tell the prince to his face what he's just explained to us. It would be funny—we could laugh for five minutes...and perhaps it would make tomorrow's papers..."

"What good would it do me?" said Mazou. "I'd be arrested at the exit. Evenings like that are full of cops. You can well imagine that princes get a police escort!"

"It would make you a martyr, an apostle of your ideas," said Brochin, cheerfully. "But you're just like all the rest. In talk, yes, here in a little corner of the workshop, it's forward ho—break everything, overturn everything! But when the moment comes, you swallow your tongue and stick your hands in your pockets"

"You think so?" said Mazou. "I don't need to be pushed so hard. I'll talk to the prince. I'll give him a lecture too. We'll see. Yes, I'll go. If only to show you...who's going to come with me?"

"Keep talking," said Brochin. "I'm not worried. You'll stay quietly in your place. You're even capable of applauding!"

"Come with me!" said Mazou. "You can't excite people and then duck out!"

"I have the family to dinner this evening," Brochin said, by way of excuse.

"All right. And the others?" He turned to Denis. "You, my lad...it'll be character-building."

"Then again," Brochin said to Denis, "it'll teach you about fish. Go on, then. If Mazou doesn't do anything, you'll profit from it anyway. The prince is a man who fishes up extraordinary things, it seems. He's an oceano..." He picked up his newspaper, folded up in front of him and stained with grease. "An oce...anographer. Trafficking in the deeps, in short...."

The bewildered silence of a packed crowd, heaped up, sweating with attention as much as the heat. A man on a little stage, sitting in front of a white wood table, bare and dirty. To the right of the lecturer, a screen on which photographs and drawings of marine animals file past. The prince relates the mores, and the monstrous battles of species leagues below the surface, fish brought up from twelve thousand meters of water, which burst on arriving in the air, those which rotate like luminous wheels, those that live motionless, like enormous diamonds...

A fantastic and real world come here to be added to the known world, to throw thousands of hallucinatory, unsuspected forms into the midst of the forms familiar to humans, to fill and enrich the imagination with lines, glows, actions different from anything that had been ventured in decorative works and heraldic adventures, surpassing the diabolical and magical creations due to legends and the grimoires of the Kabbala...

Denis breathed out. The wonderstruck curiosity that held the entire room in thrall became in him a burning emotion.

When the prince had finished, the audience stood up and applauded tumultuously, and no one left. The prince came down from the little stage, and started heading toward the exit. He passed through compact groups of workers saying to him; "Thank you, Monsieur le Prince..." He shook extended hands.

Denis had the audacity that he had seen in others. He took the prince's hand, and the other squeezed his fingers.

"Good, good," murmured Mazou, beside him, very red-faced.

Denis had completely forgotten the challenge issued to Mazou that morning. The latter, with a hint of embarrassment, said to Denis: "No, I won't go as far as shaking his hand. As for my speech...I'll save that for another occasion. No need to play the fool. For the moment, I'm nabbed. One can't say that those things aren't amazing...are you coming, lad?"

During the return journey he became furious and sarcastic.

"Oh, they know that! Oh, the strings! Naturally, one is caught by them. They go to search for startling stories ten thousand meters under the water. Of course! One goes for it...as one went for Peau-d'Ane and Bluebeard at four years old. I tell you that they're capitalist machinations. One lets oneself get intoxicated by them. It's alcohol, worse than the other..."

"You can't deny that there are photographs," said Denis. "Photos aren't invention. What we saw really exists..."

"Are you any further forward?" Mazou mocked.

"Of course," said Denis, timidly but gravely. "If I often saw things like that...."

He did not finish. What he might have said could not be expressed. His own words came back to his ears as if they were foreign. It corresponded to something extremely troubled, which pinched his breast and caused a fog to roll behind his brow...at a completely new thought that had crossed his mind so rapidly and softly that he could not see it. It merely left him a vague contentment, and that trouble in his breast.

Mazou continued his tirades. From time to time Denis said "Oh, yes...," for the sake of politeness. He was scarcely listening. He paid attention to the streets they took, for the evening when he came back.

III

There were not only the lectures in which the most subtle aristocrats of the mind came to throw to their plebeian audiences the wealth and the singularities of a universe colored by their genius, or to develop the most complex metaphysical and social propositions. In the corridor that led to the public hall, a glazed door opened into another lecture room. There, a few young men—poets, sociologists, scientists—accomplished, in their apostolic fashion, the mission of educating their working class brothers, avid for all intellectual light, more intimately.

It was there that Denis met Pierre Draguin.

Draguin was a teacher in a primary school. He was passionately interested in chemistry; in his leisure time he still found time to read enormously, and savored no joy more elevated and voluptuous than that of meditation. His disparate knowledge was perhaps only superficial. In fact, he was able to talk about anything, and could as easily draw a cross-section of a motor as explain the movement of the Orion nebula toward Aldebaran and recount the history of a painting in the Louvre, discussing its composition and establishing its esthetic lineage. He had studied occultism and was seeking, with the aid of mechanics and chemistry, to transpose into the experimental domain of physics the mysterious arcana obscurely developed in the doctrines of the Yogis or the books of Jacob Boehme, Claude de Saint-Martin and Éliphas Lévi. The habitude he had of talking to children rendered him particularly patient and intelligible, albeit a trifle pedagogical.

Draguin was twenty-four years old, sported a short black beard, and his eyes, very large and bulging, had a calm sharpness and a restful confidence that was impressive, penetrating the interlocutor and causing any contradiction to hesitate.

Denis arrived at Draguin exactly as a breathless, blind streaming, drowning man who has had the luck to reach the shore by thrashing about wildly, arrives at a clump of grass on the bank.

Thus was Denis floundering in a torrential and chaotic discovery of the World. The frightful diversity of the seeds hurled forth by the illustrious orators of the U.P. grew in that anxious soul into an extravagant florescence, in which nothing corresponded to the inconsistent instruction of poor Benoît Rufle or the troubled conceptions that the child had been able to form for himself by groping. Through a disorderly tangle of ideas and notions, entirely new and rudimentary, his anxiety, devouring in the times when he was bogged down in a cogitation without issue, metamorphosed into a tumultuous hunger for hard facts, reference points that could provide him with havens, or which formed for him the axes of the world that was delivered to him piecemeal, the innumerable variety of which dazzled and unbalanced him.

That imperative and poignant hunger, as furious as the one that clawed his entrails, that hunger for a lucid vision of the monstrously complex ensemble of things, took on in Denis an entire character, directed the rude debate in which his entire being was taking part. And the ardent investigation was all the more coercive because Denis sensed himself as somehow naked on the threshold of an immense caravanserai of Possibilities.

Very rapidly, from the sessions that had followed the Oceanographer's lecture. He had understood that he was entirely ignorant of a reality that he had only judged funereally limited and gross because of that very ignorance. Before that new reality, he had no guide. If there was anything in Denis that could react or influence his actions, it was—a legacy of his childhood—his propensity for folding back into himself, his ascendancy, the deep determination to know, the irremediable necessity to see clearly, that gripped him on his entrance to the U.P.: a stubborn necessity doubtless continuing that which was, in his father, voracity for gold, here transferred to the spiritual sphere, and aiming, in Denis for the possession of his own consciousness.

Among the young workers who followed his conversations, Draguin immediately picked Denis out. The latter asked bizarre questions, precipitate and murky, which made the other listeners, most of whom were docile and slow-witted, smile. But Draguin had recognized therein, doubtless for having experienced it himself, the stormy trouble of intellectual geneses among autodidacts, the anarchic seething of ideas, which, at the slightest excitation of one by another, caused them all to rise up at the same time and jostle one another in order to pass into the life of words.

On some evenings, after the course, Denis and Draguin went part of the way home together. An exciting stroke of luck for Denis! He felt an attachment toward the teacher compounded out of distress, wonder and fervor. The serene assurance with which Draguin talked about everything filled him with a strange wellbeing. Oh, that one had certainly reached the haven toward which Denis was desperately steering! If his gestures had been expressed as his soul designed them, he would long since have thrown himself at Draguin's knees and cried out to him: "Direct me! Be the shepherd of the intoxicated host, be the brewer of the furnace that is my brain!" But modesty, timidity and a vague fear of ridicule, and that anarchy of consciousness, stopped Denis—and perhaps, also an imprecise pride, made of the hope of attaining for himself the key that, in a miraculous fulguration, would illuminate and order the chaos.

One evening, Draguin said to Denis: "Would you like to spend Sunday at my house? You'll encounter good friends, who'll be pleased to meet you. And above all, no formality. Come as you are. We too earn our living, and you won't be the only one to have calluses on his hands."

Draguin lived with his mother in a very modest apartment in Boulogne-sur-Seine, not far from the school at which he was a teacher. His room was sparse in furniture but three of the walls were covered in books. On the fourth there were a few photographs: the Parthenon; Leonardo's John the Baptist; an Adoration of the Magi by Gentile de Fabriano; Holbein's Christina of Demark,[8] and three portraits: Leonardo, Beethoven and Nietzsche. When Denis arrived, one of Draguin's friends was already in the room.

---

[8] The original text has "Christine de Norfolk," apparently confusing two of Holbein's most famous portraits, one of Christina of Denmark and one of the third Duke of Norfolk.

"Oh, there you are! I was talking about you to Géard. I'll introduce you: Denis Aury, Géard, engineer at Normiot-Lestrie, the airplane manufacturer. For the moment, Géard is an aviator and mechanic rather than an engineer. He's working on a apparatus that he'll try out one morning soon. We'll try to witness its first flight."

Blushing, Denis shook a solid hand, which gripped his own firmly, and felt the hand studded with calluses. A wave of pride passed suddenly—and fearfully—over the embarrassment he had felt on the way, in spite of Draguin's cordial words, in thinking of himself, with his costume and mannerisms of a petty factory worker, among men worthy of being called "my friends" by his master...

"Bonjour!" said a new arrival. "Ah, there's comrade Aury. Delighted to meet you."

"Leviel, painter, and temporarily a designer for a furniture manufacturer. One day, furniture manufacturers will throw themselves at his feet and fight one another to realize his audacious and logical inventions..."

"For the time being," said Leviel, "when I dare to design for my boss an armchair that deviates slightly from Henri II or Louis XV, he asks me if I intend to continue my métier at Charenton..."

"We were only waiting for you," said Draguin. "We're now complete. Let's go for a walk."

They traversed Boulogne and the Pont de Saint-Cloud, went into the park and reached the wood of Ville d'Avray.

Draguin, Géard and Leviel chatted about a thousand things: the decorative gropings of an "art nouveau" with which snobbery was infatuated and was beginning to manifest itself in architecture and furniture; they denounced its eccentricities but agreed, nevertheless, that the principles inspiring it were preparing an era of ingenious and genuinely new forms, which would finally sweep away the sempiternal influences of the old styles, and in which décor would respond to the new activities of a humankind that the great modern dynamisms had rendered more nervous and mobile.

"However, will we ever create as a whole a beauty to surpass that of the Greeks and the Renaissance?" said Draguin. He talked about a young American dancer, Erica Florian, who, to the rhythms of Gluck and Beethoven, resuscitated in her movements and attitudes the eternal grace of the Victory of Samothrace and Della Robbia's angels.

Leviel opposed to him the prodigious works undertaken in the Place Saint-Michel for the construction of the Métropolitain:[9] the slow sinking of immense metal caissons in the river and the ground of the square, the mysterious splendor of the work that was being done inside those caissons. In the darkness of the giant cylinders, one could hear machines roaring; butterflies of fire, incandescent caterpillars rising from the dark rumble and going, with a straight and swift flight, to stick to the concave walls. They were the bolts and rivets, spring from profound forges, manipulated by invisible workers...veritable Nibelungs of that great subterranean labor, which was opening to humans the liberty of circulating underground, as the submarine was delivering the underseas to them, and the airplane the lists of the air..."

"You make use yourself of the word Nibelungs to depict the workers," said Draguin. "You're thus affirming the eternity of the great symbols and that of authentic beauty, whether it's a matter of Erica's resurrections or the tetralogy. The music written by Wagner for the drama that plays on the fabulous worlds of the Eddas accords perfectly with certain vicissitudes of today's world. Look, in addition to those workmen in the Place Saint-Michel, I can easily imagine. For instance, the theme of Fafner and Fasolt imaging the orders launched to the banks of two continents by a Rockefeller, or, if you like, the song of Siegfried discovering the Valkyrie expressing the moment when a Curie attains radium, after having traversed the flames of her meditations, her calculations and her experiments..."

---

[9] The climax of the long-drawn-out excavations to construct the Metro tunnel under the Seine was reached in May 1907.

"That's turning the proposition around," said Leviel, "for I meant, precisely, that the modern forms and new activities of humankind are worthy of inspiring musicians, dancers, poets, philosophers, works and deeds as vast and magnificent as those inspired in the past. It is, therefore, not Siegfried's song that ought to come to my lips on thinking of Curie discovering radium but a song that would express that great moment and was inspired by it. Let's understand one another. I'm not sustaining at all, as certain, that the caissons of the Metro would be a subject for a painting move moving than Mantegna's Saint Sebastian or Rembrandt's Bathsheba. Nor should our makers of operas and symphonies choose as themes a fast automobile or the flight of a Wilbur Wright! I'm imagining something else entirely..."

He drew breath, lifted up his felt that and loosened his collar.

"I shan't go to see your dancer, Draguin! She symbolizes the perpetual adoration and the perpetual recommencement of a beauty that aggravates and stifles me, which puts a spell on us all and whose place is no longer anywhere but in museums. I love that beauty, but on the condition that it limits itself to its historical role, and doesn't persist in governing not only our arts but also our sentiments and our passions...yes, our passions! It's a vast process that I'm sketching here! That beauty persists, in parallel with our old dogmas, beliefs, moralities and the passions of the times when the sun was thought to be a fixed star and the earth for the center of the universe. Into the Museums, your Erica Florian, with the cathedrals, the synagogues, the mosques and all the pieces of canvas and marble that offer us representations of landscapes, interiors, men, women and all the old aspects of the visible world! Into the Museums, the novels and dramas of love, and their heroines, Iseult, Brunhilde, Cleopatra, Beatrice, Juliet, Mélisande..."

"Damn!" said Géard. "And what are you offering us in their stead?"

"Simply that which the Demiurge offered at the moment of Genesis," Leviel replied. "Since we're the contemporaries of an absolutely new world, I want a beauty, arts and amours in conformity with modern humanity, as it is in reality beneath the obsolete appearance that we continue to see in it: two legs, two arms, a torso, two eyes..."

"Damn!" Géard interjected.

"The true humanity, such as we ought to see it now, is a marvelous apparatus of universal perception and receptivity, which the telescope permits to reach out to the stars, the microscope and electrolysis allow to participate in atomic iliads, and which the newspaper enables, every morning, in an instant, to pass through all the vicissitudes of a day of the planet, awakening therein a hundred souls and a hundred hearts, triggering connections therein...with a Bullock Workman reaching one of the highest peaks in the Himalaya,[10] a Shackleton advancing toward the Pole,[11] an Edison bringing his latest invention to perfection, with the girl who drowns herself in despair in a pond in the Pyrenees, and one who commits infanticide in a village in the depths of China...the true human beings, whose senses are enriched by all the instruments recording and determining the electricities, magnetisms and other energies that surround and constitute them; whose arms are augmented by all the titanic machines for piercing mountains, deflecting riv-

---

[10] Fanny Bullock Workman (1859-1925) and her husband William Hunter Workman set several altitude records while climbing in the Himalaya in 1899, without the aid of any modern equipment, and subsequently lectured all over Europe recounting their exploits. They mounted a major expedition to Kashmir in 1906, when Fanny, without her husband, set another new altitude record on Pinnacle Peak—probably the feat to which Draguin is referring.

[11] Although Ernest Shackleton first went to Antarctica as third officer on Robert Falcon Scott's 1901-04 expedition, from which he was sent home early on health grounds, it was not until the 1907-09 expedition that his name came to the fore as one of the setters of a new distance-record, so this reference seems to confirm the dating of this period in Denis' life.

ers, constructing houses, etcetera; whose legs are augmented by the wings of the airplane and multiplied by automobiles, locomotives, metros, telegraphs and telephones...the true human beings, who are the beings whose instincts, desires and faculties, served by that innumerable organism, have what is needed to extend toward orgies, ambitions, endeavors, amours and joys a little more subtle and specious than those to which the humans of the times of Nebuchadnezzar, Tristan or even Lorenzo de Medici aspired!"

"Which ones?" demanded Draguin, gravely.

"Taking for the point of departure any human organism, those of which we artists are sketching the lines, those of which you philosophers are proclaiming the metaphysics. For my part, I'm working on it..."

He put his hat back on. They kept silent or a moment.

"In the meantime," said Draguin, "our thirst for beauty, if it wants satisfaction, is obliged to drink from the past and its accomplished esthetics. While awaiting the Dante who will be inspired by I don't know what unsuspectable kind of future Beatrice, allow me to be moved by the Divine Comedy..."

"Certainly, as by a work in a Museum," said Leviel. "That being admitted, I'll gladly go with you one of these evenings to see your Della Robbia angel dance."

They laughed cordially. Draguin whistled a passage from the Pastorale, to which he had seen the American dance. Shortly afterwards, he began, in a loud voice, after a malicious glance from Leviel, to declaim the tirade of the Queen of Sheba from the *Tentation*.[12]

---

[12] The reference is to the speech made by the Queen of Sheba in the version of Gustave Flaubert's *Tentation de Saint Antoine* that he completed in 1856 but did not publish at the time; it was eventually published as *La première Tentation de Saint Antoine* in 1908, suggesting a slightly later date for this scene than the previous references, but some time has elapsed since the Prince of Monaco's lecture, so the two implied dates are

When he had finished, all three of them launched into an excited discussion, declaiming pages from the book in question, streaming with gods and mages clad in phrases that rang and blazed in Denis' ears and eyes.

The latter has insufficient intellect and heart to receive, grasp and absorb his comrades' words, controversies and ardent duels. He listens, respires, adores; he is happy, he is intoxicated; he is unfamiliar with the majority of the things about which his friends are talking, but it does not matter. He is in the state that Jason must have been in, alone in the Garden of Colchis. The Golden Fleece is there. He can go forward. He knows that it is shining; he can see it shining, through the fog of those passionate declamations...

Here are prodigious dispensers of strange treasures, and treasures giving to whomever handles them that great balsamic laughter, that exaltation, those spacious gestures and those beautiful grave gazes.

From time to time they pass other Sunday strollers. Scraps of conversation are picked up mechanically. The price of a straw hat...an alpaca waistcoat to go to the office...there's a chalet that way, were the beer is cooler... People are sprawling on the grass, playing cards, poring over unfolded newspapers...

Denis is astonished that the passage of those four young men, of whom he is one, does not make those players and walkers start, that the radiance of Leviel, Draguin and Géard does not crash through the straw hats, the alpaca waistcoats and the card games, bowling all those paltry things away in a deluge of fire...

"Make arrangements, then," said Draguin to Denis, "To run and join us one evening when you get out of the factory. We'll join the queue at the Opéra and climb up to the forty-sou seats to hear the *Rheingold*. You'll dine like us on a little bread and a piece of chocolate, while waiting for the time to

---

not inconsistent, and the previous two indications could easily date from a scene set in 1908.

go in. And Leviel, in spite of his theories, will come with us. You'll see his eyes, when the orchestra finishes the over-ture..."

IV

Birth, tribulations, duels of two inextricably associated beings: a Denis for whom the intimacy of Draguin and his friends is like the visage of the great unformulated certainty; and a Denis imprisoned every day by the factory, enslaved by massive and invariable actions, searching confusedly to take refuge in the enchanted memory of the diversions of the other Denis...

A few evenings after the day at Ville-d'Avray, he has re-ceived the musical baptism. He has abandoned himself meekly to the great tide of sounds, which, which his friends listened, rendered their faces so meditative and so luminous that one might have thought that they were bathing in an invisible world, receiving and savoring behind heir closed eyelids some unknown ecstasy...

More than the stage, its magical sets, the complex drama and the music, it is the attitude of his companions that has impressed him, as if melted and molded in a sacred emotion; and it is also the ambience, the grave voluptuousness of the audience filling the cheap seats...

That audience, testifying to the same fervent enjoyment, he rediscovered one Sunday afternoon, when his friends took him to the Concert Colonne; he discovered it again on the evening when he went, with Draguin and Leviel, to see Erica Florian dance.

An artistic initiation has been sketched in parallel. On Sunday mornings, Denis meets Leviel again at the Musée du Louvre. Draguin often joins the expedition. It seems to Denis that he is in an immense cathedral, of which the Rubens, the Titians and the Veroneses are the stained-glass windows, win-dows that draw from themselves the light that they spread in suave fires and adorable figures. Leviel and Draguin are the tender officiants. They know all the mysteries of the marvelous images and the responses to the problems they awaken in Denis, and which mingle with the terrains of his thought under the plow.

When they leave the museum they go along the quais, and over the Pont du Carrousel to the Rue Bonaparte, where they go to have lunch in a little restaurant near the École des Beaux-Arts. Chez Establion is frequented by the pupils of the school, and young men of letters: a rowdy and passionate assembly, which makes the little restaurant a kind of market-place of ideas.

Denis listens, observes, is enthused and rebels, following at point blank range the oratory conflagrations, and never ceasing, stunned and delighted, to admire the fact that the sole desire to convince one another of the purity of an abstraction, or the excellence of an esthetic, can provoke such heated agitations. All of that youth seems to consider as worthy of interest only that which springs from the life of the mind. The subjects perpetually discussed at the factory never enter into their comments or their arguments. Food, wages, clothing, social injustice, the coercions of material life...all those questions, out there of exclusive importance, seem here, compared with the problems of art, science and metaphysics, hardly to exist, almost invisible, like flies around the columns of a palace.

Often, at Denis' table, a friend of Leviel and Draguin comes to sit, André Ravot, a young composer who gives piano lessons and teaches scales to children to earn a living. On some evenings he invites his friends to come and have tea with him. As soon as Ravot is sitting at his piano, the Spirit of Music possesses and bewitches him, enclosing the listeners in an inviolable spell, from which everything that is not Music is banished. While playing, the young man sings, imitating the instruments, supplying on his own the orchestra, the characters, the drama and the soul of the drama.

There, gradually, in a sacredly fraternal atmosphere, Denis familiarizes himself with the gods of the Olympus of sounds. He is able to hum himself the dances of Prince Igor,

the spring song from *Die Walküre*. He can whistle triumphantly the song of the Forge when, at the end of a long meditation,
he clarifies some great idea. Suave musical presences accompany his internal deliberations. A candid effusion causes him
to whistle the song of the Bird to the sparrows in the streets,
with the confused hope that one of them might fly to him, to
take him away, through the rackets of the omnibuses and car-
riages, and the insipid flux of pedestrians, toward he knows
not what magical creature or transcendental verity, the key to
the universe, the arcanum of all the problems in the world...

On the evenings that Denis does not spend at the U.P. or
meeting his friends, he shuts himself in his room to read.
Draguin lends him books. He discovers, by turns, Plato,
Izoulet, Carlyle, Emerson, *La Bible de l'Humanité*, *La Vie de
Jésus*, Edgar Poe's *Eureka*, *Jean Christophe*...[13] After each of
his readings he stirs and reconstructs the world, religion and
the laws that guide humans, shares the dreams of a Luc
Froment,[14] wants, like Christ, to have himself crucified for the
great suffering of humankind, desirous of being a hero worthy
of the songs of a future Carlyle, loves, suffers, has all the fe-
vers of genus with Jean Christophe, and watches in the crumbs
of the bread that he eats for the Force that, according to Poe,
causes the atoms to integrate Unity.

---

[13] *La Bible de l'Humanité*, is by Jules Michelet (1864; tr. as
The Bible of Humanity); *La Vie de Jésus* (1863: tr. as *The Life
of Jesus*) is by Ernest Renan; both attempt to provide skeptical
corrections to the Catholic faith. The first three volumes of
Romain Rolland's *Jean Christophe* were published in 1904
(the sequence eventually ran to ten). Jean Izoulet (1854-1929)
was appointed to the chair of social philosophy at the Collège
de France in 1897, but his most notable book, *La Cité
moderne, métaphysique de a sociologie* [The Modern City:
The Metaphysics of Sociology] (1895) fell out of fashion quite
rapidly, and is now virtually forgotten; it might, however,
have been one of the sources of the ideas expressed by Leviel.
[14] The hero of Émile Zola's *Travail* (1901; tr. as *Labour*).

It is the bright and dark magma of thoughts, systems, dreams, images, music and works that he carries within him, takes with him to the factory, and which rends him sensible, in direct proportion to his acquisitions and his dazzlement, to the coarseness of his companions in labor. By a strange inversion, however, that sensibility soon takes the form of remorse.

He experiences a kind of shame, in that atmosphere of ignorance, mocking and hateful myopia, of invisibly having the prerogative of so many sumptuous notions: the shame of being the only one there, he thinks, who can perceive and possess such a numerous and magnificent universe, because of the unjust privilege that is its basis, that of his birth; of his childhood secure from base concerns and a miserable ambience— the initial privilege that permitted him to dream in a park, to prepare himself, in the company of fairies, to receive one day, more easily than the others, the gift, the revelation of the graces that make life sublime.

That remorse, scarcely born, is immediately, and as if naturally, prolonged into an immense pity. A need, soon a duty, are designed of their own accord, which grip and enfever the child: to say to all of those who will never have any effluvium or aroma of the higher joys, to give them and spread over them the new treasures with which he is replete, and the infinity to which he has the keys. If they knew, like him, what the veritable enjoyments are, and their inexhaustible profusion, if they knew the major beauty, that poured out in torrents by the masterpieces of art, great books, true music, nature and the world, enlightened by the exaltation of the soul, it is toward that beauty and those enjoyments that they would devote their labor and their strength.

But how would those somber men even conceive of that exaltation, blind and deaf slaves as they are, locked in their stunted ideas, bound by the fatality of their caste, by the fatality of the social system, iniquitous in its essence? And that iniquity itself…oh, no less wretched and stupid is the blindness of the rich, the cause of monstrous disequilibrium, the eternal disharmony! If the rich too turned their will toward happiness, their power and their passion toward the only worthwhile wealth, the unlimited intoxication of knowledge, the ever more vast and more profound intelligence of the universe...they would abdicate the murderous egotism and the frenzy of gold whose only motors and only goals are the bitter possession and implacably limited enjoyment of material goods and monetary sensualities.

A vision of the salvation of the world by the universal comprehension of true joy sets Denis ablaze, all the more dazzling because it is a simple, primary, naïve synthesis that, in its fiery course through the child's imagination, rejects the logic of facts and all contradictory realities as a locomotive rejects its cinders...

He searches for the word of salvation that the rich have never heard or read, and which the plebeians cannot understand, the word that Leviel, in his tirades against the false foundations on which modern humans have sketched the mind, has expressed the spirit. It is not possible that the man who holds simultaneously in his consciousness the vision and the distress of the distress, the certainty and intoxication of the true joy, should not cry out, should not pour out his certainty of the great happiness offered, available to all.

Denis will find the key, the open sesame of Eden, the word that will be resplendent before humans, between them and their happiness, like the arch of light raised for the gods by Donner between heaven and earth.

However, he does not know the real nature of his exaltation, and that it is, in the final analysis, merely a magnified reflection of the drama playing within him, and in which he alone is the theme, the theater and the actor. It is in him that the joy and misery exist, in the image of which he makes and remakes the world.

Denis, similar all day to any of his companions in the workshop, his hands black with oil and filings like theirs, a serf earning his living, but so rich in interior images, does not think of complaining about his chains. Get away! Him, who can while manipulating the cutter, stroll in thought in Valhalla, evoke Leonardo, Rubens and Holbein, while his neighbor, Brochin has nothing in his poor depths but the latest café-concert tune or the incidents of some paltry feuilleton...!

Not thinking of admitting that he is suffering, the enlightened Denis has transposed the unacknowledged suffering of the imprisoned Denis to those who are the concrete expression of that suffering. And it is the prisoner that he laments subconsciously, in the rude men among whom he lives, and, beyond them, in all those who swarm throughout the factory, and the neighboring factories, and throughout the dark quarter. And it is by virtue of a generalization common to children and dreamers, which facilitates the humanitarian tendencies of the moment, that it is, again, the unconscious lamentation for himself that he extends to all the wretched individuals of the great wretched human race.

4

I

Someone taps at the door of the dressing-room.

"Who is it?" asks Lène Garain, who is finishing having her hair done.

"It's the theater electrician, Mademoiselle."

"Come in. What is it?"

A man of about thirty has opened the door and is standing on the threshold.

"This ring is yours, Mademoiselle."

"Why yes..."

Lène turns toward her hairdresser and rummages in a wooden bowl where there are a few items of jewelry. "Give it to me...thank you very much...where did you find it? I left it in here..."

"Outside your door, on the floor. I brushed it with my foot, it rolled..."

"Bizarre. I was sure I'd put it in here...as sure as one can be about such things...the main thing is that it isn't lost. Thank you, my friend; you're very kind. You'll do me the pleasure..."

She opens a small bag, rustles banknotes.

"It's no trouble…"

"Go on, don't make a fuss. Take this, as a comrade..."

"No…all the more so as I don't deserve anything at all. It was me who came into your dressing-room and took the ring from that bowl."

"What are you saying?"

"I had to talk to you, and sought a means of entering into communication...."

"Oh! Right…you're not banal..." Lène became serious, a trifle haughty. "We'll talk about it again, my dear. I don't have time this evening. I'm expected. *Au revoir*...."

Habituated as she is to the little adventures that the desire of men concocts around her twenty-two years, she thinks the electrician's behavior excessive. Should she inform the director? It isn't very prudent to have an employee like that in the theater.

But the man has not gone.

"It's not ugly, your diamond," he says. "A little small. It would give me pleasure to offer you one three times the size, which I saw in Boucheron's window..."

Lène has always avoided adventures. She does not want to compromise either the material security or the cordial affection represented by her friend, nor the brilliant destiny that her young renown is fashioning for her with one success after another. One does not know—or, rather, one knows only too well—where a reckless action light lead. That said, one can always smile at the unexpected and allow oneself to be brushed by an amusement that passes like a perfumed breath of wind. There are, after all, many men who understand these things, and go no further than is appropriate. The important thing is to know in time to close the door in the face of a Possible who intrudes too far into the sagely-established order of wellbeing and career.

"If you offered me Boucheron's diamond as you've offered me my ring," she says, "I'd be arrested the next day for receiv...you're too kind. Then again, Boucheron's is better guarded than this dressing-room. No, decidedly...will you permit me to finish getting dressed?"

"I'm not stopping you."

"How can I make you understand that I'll be obliged to call someone if you don't leave?"

"How can I make you understand that Boucheron's diamond will be brought to you by an employee of his, if not by Boucheron himself...?"

Lène, who is standing up, on guard against some possible brutality, sits down again, calmly pulls her skirt down over her ankles, and pats her bare arm.

"Pardon me, Monsieur, but with whom am I dealing? Are you an amorous billionaire disguised as an electrician or an electrician slightly touched by delusions of grandeur?"

"I don't have delusions of grandeur, but, properly speaking, the possession of grandeur. I really am an electrician. I work for a small employer in the quarter, from whom the theater has borrowed me for a few days, and I'm also amorous, if that narrow word can signify the very grave sentiment that impels me toward you. As for my resources, without exactly making me a billionaire, they are, in addition to my wages as an electrician, a factory with six hundred workers working at full capacity, a château surrounded by game-rich forests, and cultivated fields extending over a thousand hectares."

"Why aren't you in your château, your factory, your forests and your hectares?"

"I was waiting for the moment, when I saw you, to return there."

"Very curious. And you quit all that to be an electrician?"

"An electrician, yes…and many other things."

Lène's hair is done. She puts on her necklaces.

"One question. Why have you employed this very peculiar fashion of introducing yourself? The ring…the theft…Arsène Lupin. If you wanted to make my acquaintance, there were thirty-six other means for a man with a thousand hectares and six hundred workers. My address is in the *Tout-Paris*, Monsieur."

"I wasn't thinking about you two hours ago. My apologies, but I knew nothing about you except your name, read mechanically on the posters. If you had not come this evening to this twentieth-class theater to lend your collaboration to a benefit, we would never have met. I saw you on the stage just now, distractedly, from my corner at the control panel. I confess that my attention was initially directed at the play, but suddenly, I saw you…or rather, I saw in you a certain being…beyond the actress in the process of declaiming. How can I put it...? I saw in you a being that you are, beyond the one that you believe yourself to be..."

"How complicated! And what did it look like?"

"Too complicated, in fact, to describe in a few words. Someone is expecting you, and here you are, about to leave. The being that appeared to me corresponded with a fulgurant brilliance to something for which I was searching. Lène Garain, you cannot know how great and sacred is the salvation that rises towards you from my utmost depths..."

"But who are you?"

"It was necessary that I go to you immediately. That which is in you, to which I am bringing my salvation, to which I shall make myself known, cares no more than I do about petty worldly gesticulations. The thirty-six means of civility that you would have preferred would have encumbered the straight route that links us together. Having recognized you, I decided to immobilize your destiny for an instant, at that very moment, in confrontation with mine. That is done. The story of the ring is irrelevant. I used what I found to hand. Facts only have the importance that one gives to them. It is up to the player of the game to give them their dimensions. Mountains that close the horizon and bar the way to the goal for the weak and timorous are crumbs that are lost in the dust of the road traveled, once the goal is attained."

Turning the gold medallion on one of her necklaces, Lène enjoys making the light of the electric bulb fixed above her hairdresser's head dance on the walls. She leaves a moment of silence after the man has finished. Then, continuing to rotate the disk, she asks: "Do you remain dressed like that, as a workman, at five o'clock in the afternoon?"

"Usually, yes. Why?"

"If you had a costume like everyone else, your landowner's costume, or another—in sum, one that would not cause my concierge or my chambermaid to chatter, I'd invite you to take a cup of tea with me at home."

"No. It's you, for the first occasion, who will come to my home. I live in a frightful furnished room in a house in a wretched street in the Italiens quarter. Have not fear, except of leaving that room with a queen's crown and mantle."

"Only that?" says Lène, bursting into laughter.

"I'll expect you, tomorrow and the day after, at five o'clock. This is my address..."

He takes a little notepad from his pocket and a stub of pencil, writes, tears off the sheet and places it on the dressing-table. "There. Denis Aury, Hôtel de Mont-Blanc, 17 Rue Bourgon."

II

"Bonjour! Well, I've come. Go to your window—you'll see a veritable revolution in the street. People are on the door-steps. Your bellboy was so bewildered when I asked for your number that he called me *Monsieur*, stammering. However, I dressed as simply as I could... By the way, your diamond ar-rived this morning."

"Good. Do you like it?"

"I refused it. It was magnificent. You must be slightly mad. To give away stones like that and live here... Anyway, there are such funny things in life..."

"Why did you refuse the diamond?"

"Because I want to understand first. Where can one sit down? It's a miracle that I didn't tear my dress on your stair-case. Look at the plaster from the wall on my elbow... Thank you... And where will you sit?"

"On my bed. It's not important. I'm glad to see you."

"I'm thirsty. After such a journey! Give me some tea. Where are the advertised crown and mantle? Can one see them?"

"Not immediately. As for the tea, I'm very sorry. I don't have anything here that permits me to make it. I bought this bottle of port yesterday. Will you accept a drop?"

"What's this goblet? But..."

"It's yours. Shall I pour?"

"But it's solid gold..."

"A bagatelle. Shall I pour?"

"And you? You're going to drink out of that crude glass?"

"It's the hostel's glass. An honest glass from a wine merchant next door to a factory, who has a clientele of workers."

"Is that your factory?"

"Oh no...mine is much larger. It isn't in Paris."

"What do you make there?"

"Radium."

"That can be made, then?"

"It's very interesting. One has certain stones brought from Madagascar, Colorado and Portugal; one reduces them to powder, and after certain manipulations, one obtains a final pinch of powder that is radium."

"But..."

"It currently sells at between eight hundred thousand francs and a million per gram."

"I've read that in the newspapers. And it sells well?"

"Almost as well as rice powder. A little more port?"

"Can you imagine...I've had a bizarre thought since yesterday evening...it seems to me that I've seen you before, somewhere?"

"I believe I told you, the evening before last, quite sincerely, that I'd never seen you before. And you wouldn't have paid any attention to me. I can scarcely imagine..."

"You've traveled a little?"

"A lot..."

"It was two years ago. I was in Monte Carlo with my friend. We noticed a gambler. He wagered stacks of bills. He put his watch on the table. At a certain time, whether the stack had grown or only a few remained—enough, however, to continue testing his luck—he got up and left. That's extremely rare. Occasionally, when one is winning, one finds the energy to leave...but most of the time, one stays. He was marvelous...automatic. That's why we noticed him. Well, I think that you bear a striking resemblance to that gambler."

"When was this, did you say?"

"February, two years ago."

"It really was me. I was amusing myself with my will-power."

"I was sure that it was you! But you didn't notice me?"

"No, Mademoiselle, I don't remember."

"It appears, however, that I was very pretty."

"I don't doubt it."

A silence.

"It's explicable," Denis goes on. "It's because I was still searching. I hadn't found my joy. Since then, I've found it. And I saw you the day before yesterday for the first time because you had its face."

"What is it, your joy?"

"The simplest and most inaccessible thing, a matter of squaring the circle for the majority of people, but in reality, a kind of Columbus' egg. Not a certain kind of joy, as everyone arranges more or less to have one...some by collecting postage stamps, others by buying a cottage in the country with their savings...but a joy that is a permanent state, which becomes part of being, like the circulation of the blood or respiration."

"In other words you're happy. You've found happiness..."

"There's something immobile in the word happiness, as there is in the word bliss, if you like, which doesn't express the active faculty, the kind of continual birth of states of voluptuousness, exaltation, emotion that everything one looks at and everything one does provokes."

"One must get a little tired after a day of such states..." She laughed. "All the same, your famous joy lacked something..."

"What?"

"Me...since you came to look for me."

"That's not quite accurate. I saw you, and I stopped you."

"For a quarter of an hour."

"Today, yes. And it doesn't matter if, at the end of that quarter of an hour, we say *au revoir* or *adieu*, and you go back to your theater or your habitual life. I'm now with you for as long as you feel bewildered, Lène, with all your soul and all your instinct, and incessantly more bewildered, attracted to me...or, rather, to what I bring you."

"My God! Is it now that you're going to bring out the crown and the mantle?"

"Not immediately. Oh, don't laugh. If you knew..." Denis has blushed momentarily. "I beg your pardon," he says—and his face becomes calm again, almost solemn, brightening suddenly as if a surge of light had risen from his heart.

"Those are big words," says Lène. "You have phrases too!"

"Listen, Lène. I'm a kind of impulsive adolescent, of which there are no longer very many nowadays. Those of today like sport, dancing, and the more serious turn to business, politics, the exact science...."

"My friend is at the Bourse," says Lène, approvingly. "And to distract himself, he does research in linguistics with one of his friends, a professor at the Sorbonne."

"When I was eighteen," says Denis, "there was a kind of social effervescence in the air, which I breathed in, like many other young people...and I thought I had discovered that it would be sufficient to lift a little finger in a certain fashion to make the earth turn in the other direction..."

"I know. When I was ten or eleven, Maman, who was an accompanist, sometimes took me to soirées at the Université populaire, where she played the piano. I heard a great many tirades about your turning the earth the other way. God, how boring it was! Fortunately, there were the singers."

Denis goes to a little shelf unit containing a few books and small objects. He picks up one of the objects.

"Do you believe in talismans?"

"What's that wretched little mirror?"

"It's a great talisman."

"Oh! Let me see."

She takes the crude item, contained in sheet metal, turns it over, and looks at Denis, disappointed and mocking.

"It is, in fact, nothing but a four-sou mirror," said Denis. "One would never suspect that an object so banal could serve to make a man…almost as a woman's womb serves to make a child…"

"What do you mean?"

"In the days when I was obsessed with the future happiness of my fellows, I was a humble worker, a lathe-operator in a factory, and I was preparing for my tour of France. My dreams gripped me seriously. I was positively dazzled by the idea that there was enough beauty in the world, and that people had arrived at possessing enough science, and means of realization, for the earth to have attained an absolutely new state—so new and so rich that, in order to savor it, everyone would have to let go of the old beliefs, and all the old sensualities for which they slaved, got excited, and killed one another…"

"Ha ha! What would have been left?"

"That new life…a kind of perpetual celebration on an earth of grace…"

"Never ill, never dying! No more passionate dramas, no more milliner's bills to pay?"

"Very nearly."

"Ah, our childish dreams!" She raises her arms, laughing.

"It's because I hadn't changed in that respect, in becoming a man," says Denis. "Except that I submitted my chimera to experiment. I still think that such a life is possible, but the possibility that I dreamed of as universal, I've understood that it can only be individual."

"Too heavy for me, that…and the little mirror?"

"I'm getting to that. In the midst of the enormous hotchpotch of ideas in which my eighteen years were struggling, I was struck by a singular advertising campaign launched in the newspapers by an American company. It called itself something like the Laboratory or University of Psychic Sciences, and announced that in order to obtain the secret of happiness and success, to know one's strengths and the means of utilizing them, one only had to send twenty francs to an indicated address.

"That coincided so bizarrely with my preoccupations that, laughing in advance at my credulity, I saved up twenty francs and sent them. I received four little books nicely bound in green with gilded decorations. There was question therein of respiratory methods, magnetism, procedures for concentrating the will, and Jesus Christ... Don't smile, Lène...

"At hazard, I began to practice some of those instructions. I got headaches, rapid heartbeats, and also a few amazements. In a negligent fashion, I mentioned my books to a very dear friend—negligently, because I had not confided to anyone my state of mind and my great dreams... Pride, dazzling the friends I loved, and also the rest of the world, if I discovered a truth that I was searching for; prudence, in case I failed pitifully. 'These American methods,' the friend said to me, 'are too materialistic. They have the fault of only occupying themselves with certain physical possibilities, albeit very curious, without taking account of what lies behind them, which is even more curious.' With that, he lent me a few books in his turn...I'm not boring you too much?"

"Not too much," says Lène. "Except that I'd really like to get to the little four-sou mirror. And then there's the mantle and the crown, which I don't often see..."

"They're coming," says Denis. "They're on the way."

"Hmm! What if they arrive too late, and I've gone?"

"There's no danger of that. So, that friend lent me certain books. I find myself abruptly thrown into a frightful literature, a thicket of charades, tales of werewolves...in brief, into what is known vulgarly as Occultism. I flounder in stories of theosophy, spiritism, correspondences between the stars and our viscera...the sun in the region of the stomach and the moon that is on our forehead, etcetera. I pass through I don't know how many crises, sometimes mystical, trying to take seriously the presence within us and around us of planetary spirits, sometimes simply feverish, trying to manipulate certain mysterious forces hidden by my cabalistic authors under compact symbols impossible to fracture if one doesn't have the sacred key…what they call the great Arcanum. At the end of such labors, what perseverance! I think I've arrived at discerning the immense secret, the omnipotent word that, if my reading can be believed, will open up, to whomever pronounces it with the required plenitude, the kingdoms of the earth, the heavens and the intermediary regions…"

"Is that all? And the word…?

"The simplest of all, Lène, the most debased on all words: love."

Lène pulls a face, as if to say: *That's your great secret? The meanest of romances…* She looks at Denis. It seems to her that she can see such a radiance in his face that she remains a trifle nonplussed.

"The famous secret that was the so-called supreme truth, behind the mysteries of religions, nature and life…"

"Get to the point!" says Lène.

"That truth combined marvelously with the ideal that I had attained, on my own, well before having stuck my nose into that strange literature. To love…what? Not the earth, say the religions, nor life, because they're wretched and wicked… Now, that's not true! The earth is overflowing with treasures to conquer life offers innumerable objectives of joy. Was it, then, to love in the sense of novels, and Massenet's operas? That love, in taking up all the space, in enclosing in one single being all the possibilities of love, veils the multitude of other objects of adoration. Veritable love ought to be the perpetual effusion of all the forces that are within an individual…love of the senses, love of the heart, love of the muscles, love of the mind, love of breathing, love of walking, love of being! That's what I had understood. That conception was so splendid that I wondered then whether, beyond my naïve childish enthusiasms, the world permitted it."

"And this is where the disenchantments begin," says Lène.

"This is where the enchantments begin. There, where I was living, the worker I was saw nothing but rancor, maledictions, absurd superstitions, ferocious egotisms...such was the world."

"And that's the truth."

"Every hour of that reality gave the lie, in the most stinging and brutal fashion, to any idea of love."

"And that's true everywhere. If you don't think that the theater, behind the petty politeness of the façade..."

"Right. Hard work, attempting to love! Now this..." He picks up the mirror. "One of the practices of the little American books consisted of staring in a certain fashion at one's own image in a mirror, and commanding in oneself some virtue, or some energy, appropriate to determined victories. It's a very singular fact that persistence in a will thus projected and well-directed, acts on and can model the individual physically as well as mentally. I caused to emerge from this little four-sou mirror my very real possession of the world, Lène, and my radiant certainty...for it's the will to love that I planted between the eyes of my image. And that will, gradually inclined me to reject what there was in every object and every person in the rude quotidian reality everything that was sad, ugly or base, leading me as if instinctively to that which, in every person and every object, was pleasant and precious...

"Thus, I gradually discovered that in every object and every person, there was always some attractive point. Thus, for me, the world was incessantly enriched with objects of love, emotion and pleasure. And gradually, in that prodigal world, multiplying its delights in that fashion, my body began to love, as I might put it, by means of every one of its cells. And the innumerable celebration of my eyes, my lungs—of all my being, in sum—triggered the physical miracle. My blood flowed more richly, the delight of walking made my legs more robust, my chest expanded... Look, Lène."

He takes a photograph from the shelf. "This is me when I was a mere factory-worker. Look at me now, inhabited by the joy of being."

Lène is no longer laughing. She looks at the man standing before her, smiling, from whom a youthful majesty emanates.

"Five years ago," Denis resumes, "I was working as the foreman of a crew on a railway line, which a French company was electrifying in a region of South America. There's no need to take you through the phases of my material life. I had succeeded well enough in earning my living comfortably, by climbing a few rungs of the professional ladder. A good enough worker, I had taken care to find jobs that would enable me to travel the world. As for my fortunate mental dispositions, they were inherent in all the circumstances of my vagabond life... One evening, in the posada near the works, where I was stating, I was handed a letter that had followed me all the way from Montparnasse, from an address that I had given to my natal château."

He laughs. "I've forgotten to tell you that I was born rich. My father was an important country notary, and I was brought up like a property-owner, my dear... One morning, I ran away to become a locksmith. I'll tell you about that another day. The letter that caught up with me in the depths of the Americas told me that I had become a millionaire. My father had died suddenly.

"My first impulse was that I would refuse the inheritance. That money, for reasons that dated from the first awakening of my conscience, appeared to me to be abominable...money sucked out of social circulation by a vampire, utilized in the most absurd, most criminal onanism..."

"Oh, my God!" says Lène.

"I'm talking about avarice. I can still see that immense night, at the end of the earth—that night in which, alone, under the glimmer of tropical stars, I wandered with my destiny on the edge of my conscience. Certainly I would refuse that money. Pride agitated me, suddenly, so that it seemed that my limbs were creaking like the masts of a ship caught by a tornado. What use might I make of the money that had come to me? What might it bring me? I felt that I was rich already, in myself and by my own efforts, rich before and without that money. I felt in the truth of my muscles, my blood and my brain that I was rich with the fortune of the joy of being.

"And in that same moment, the pride—that of the interior work realized by my own powers of love and will—suddenly resuscitated within me the fever of my twenty years, the great vision attained by the excited child, the idea of a joy more vast and marvelous than the one with which I had just trembled...the plenary joy once dreamed of, the joy promised to modern humans, to the new humans, the joy that ought to emerge from the powers of love and will, with the material powers of which humans dispose, in order to enjoy the earth.

"If I kept the money, I was a king. And what a kingdom was offered to me!"

"In brief," says Lène. "You didn't refuse the inheritance."

He laughs. "Refused, the money would have been dispersed in a few works of administrative pity, and the dribs and drabs would have softened the final days of a few invalids in the hospices... I set aside the shame that I felt before that gold in the naïve times in which I discovered the world. The duty that appeared to me that night was quite clear. I would attempt to create the new humanity. I would keep the money."

"Of course..."

"But before beginning to live in accordance with the plenary verity that would be permitted to me, I resolved to get to know my own being better, and the world whose living matter I intended to sculpt. I resolved to continue the experiment that had led me to the idea of joy, to extend it to the extent of reality, and to confront that joy, its surety and its strength, with the most redoubtable fragment of that reality...I mean with wealth."

"Enter stage left fine suppers, luxurious women and fast cars!"

"Have you ever seen ants at work? Sometimes, one of them holds in its mandibles a wisp of straw ten times as long as itself, and advances with great difficulty, tottering, twisting, and dragging its wisp bravely. The rich drag their good fortune as the ant drags its bit of straw...and around them, there is still the entire forest, of which every tree, every bush and every particle of soil might be a fortune...but the gilded wisp is sufficient for them.

"When you saw me in Monte Carlo, I was not far from concluding my voyage through the world of the wealthy. Oh, I lived delectable hours and savored to the fullness of their merit to sumptuousness of palaces, the elegance with which the rich conduct themselves in all the little contingencies, the pleasure of having all the gestures that a crease of the trousers might attempt carried out by valets. Hunting mouflon in the Incudine is an extremely picturesque sport, and the express that carries you in a few hours from a supper in the Rue Royale to a bazaar in the Corne d'Or is not a despicable animal. I quivered, here and there, at the contact of women, often of quality, in whom the grace and glamour of attire added to the perfection of forms, and an admirable science of voluptuousness..."

"Say no more!" says Lène.

"No conceit," Denis continues. "I only want to come to this: the opportunity presented itself a hundred times over for me to be caught in the trap. Among the seductions of luxury, gambling, and even amour and its tragic delights, would one of them be strong enough to absorb into itself all my will to love, all my hunger for joy?

"I didn't get caught. Whatever the attractions were, I bore too radiantly within myself the sentiment that there was always something more to know, to want, to love, in the vast life beyond the present possession. That's the truth.

"The great misfortune is the ignorance that humans are in of the multitude of the objectives of joy, and the fact that they're magnificently equipped to attain them. The passions are only destructive if they're limited to a few paltry windfalls, always the same since the earliest ages of the world, Villon wrote verses that were able to illustrate both the power and the blindness of humans...they die of thirst beside the spring."

Suddenly, enthusiasm bursting forth, Denis straightens up. "But I, Lène, you understand, drink at that spring! And I'm not afraid, and I know."

Lène darts a mocking glance around her. "And in the meantime..."

"This room...this primitive poverty...the last experiment. The most decisive, the finest of all. I'm returning, freely, to the forms and hours of my enchained adolescence. And, knowing that I only have to make a gesture, write a check, to escape, I can now enjoy seeing whether my interior certainty is great enough, on its own, to triumph—as well!—over the basest ugliness. My joy, which surpasses the bounds of wealth, also has to defy the gehennas of the wretched. Then, materially and spiritually, I shall have the right to live and to stand tall and certain among men...like Michelangelo's Bacchus, which is in the Uffizi in Florence, lifting up the cup of life, while dancing, above his cheerful head..."

Lène tries to say something.

"Tomorrow, Léne, I shall pursue my route voluntarily, and again, alone, because the day has not yet come..."

"What day? After all that you've done..."

"The one when I shall truly take possession of my fortune, possession of my material kingdom—which will be the day when I think that I have finally taken complete possession of myself."

He looks at Lène. She does not understand.

Imperatively, he concludes: "That's it. Doubtless, I shall be this poor man for another year, and you won't see me again. For you alone, and for this hour only, I have broken my discipline of poverty. It was necessary that I stop you. It is from the depths of my instinct that the force arose that threw me toward you and called out to you. I have brought you to the décor of my childhood, in order that the living image of my attained joy should stand up there, where, with all my childish fervor, I believed in the reality of that joy..."

"I'm only a petty actress..."

"I know nothing about you, your milieu, your ties, and that's irrelevant to me. I'm looking at you. The force of joy is in you, naked and virginal, ready to break out of the thin crust of what you believe to be your destiny. I shall expand and model that living force. You will be beside me. And all the forms of joy will be before you, as numerous and renewed as the vibrations of light."

He holds out a check book to the young woman.

"In the meantime, take this. Since yesterday, there has been unlimited credit at this bank in your name. Act as if the earth were your realm. That will be the truth, which I have brought you, which I have promised you……"

The young woman's face has become grave.

"In a year," says Denis, "you will receive news of me. My labor will not be finished. I count on using a further year to learn about the country in which I want to test the power of joy. I have pleasant projects..."

But Lène, standing up, returns the check book to Denis.

"I don't want that. I won't touch that money. I would only be able to spend it on banal things, those that anyone in the world can buy. I'm not capable, alone, of making myself a queen. And what an idea! You're really going to go an entire year without seeing me again? And you could do it…what a strange individual you are!"

The sound of a siren splits the air.

"Brrr…who's being murdered out there?"

"It's the signal to stop work at the factory, a few paces from here."

"What time is it, then? Oh, God…I have to run. I'm going to torture myself with questions..."

She adjusts herself in front of a little mirror above the dressing-table.

"Until a year from now, then…… You're not afraid that I'll forget you...or that you'll forget me …and find someone else much more interesting than me? It's very cunning, what you're doing, fundamentally. Naturally, I'll think about you, and rack my brains wondering what this joy might be…your joy… Sunk, Rothschild! What a phenomenon!"

She is at the door.

"A year, truly…that's very dangerous and very long. In the meantime, I must run. Let's say: *au revoir*. I'll think about what you've told me. My poor head!"

"*Au revoir*," says Denis.

He holds on to the hand that is offered to him momentarily.

"All the same," she says, "you haven't only set my hand on fire…"

PART TWO

1

I

"Monsieur Denis won't be long. If Monsieur le Maire would like to wait..."

"Thank you, Frignot."

Cahoche, left alone, installs himself in the armchair, gazes sanctimoniously at the hall, the frescos, the marbles...and then gets up, approaches the frescos and stands squarely in front of them, like an art-lover absorbing himself in his contemplation. However, without moving his torso or his limbs, he moves his head this way and that. There, on a cornice, are a few photos, including one of Lène. He goes toward the cornice at a slow, mincing step. He holds his arms clasped behind his back. His fingers dance a little on his palms. He is only a slight distance away from the photos when Denis comes in.

Denis is wearing a white woolen sweater, leggings and boots. He has a briar pipe in his mouth, which he puts down on the table, and comes toward Cahoche with his hand wide open.

"I beg you to excuse me. I'm delighted to see you. I was delayed in Telluire wood. I was thinking, before a corner that's mine, about the different work required install an ice palace there."

"An...? You're entirely excused. I'm also very glad finally to make your acquaintance. But I don't quite understand...an ice palace in Telluire wood?"

"Yes. There's a clearing there, not very far from the road, which is perfectly suited to it. Once the ground is

98

cleared, the basin and the pipes installed, I'll transmit the cold and electricity from the factory. I'd like to hold the inauguration on a fine sunny summer's day. Skating in twenty-five degrees will be very amusing for the Séneçois."

"You're being serious?"

"It's only one detail of an ensemble of constructions about which, have no doubt, I've thought very seriously. In any case, it will be necessary for us to have an important conversation on that subject. I need, I won't only say your administrative approval, but your moral collaboration...your sympathy."

"My sympathy is naturally acquired, my dear Monsieur. As for the rest...the essential thing, as you'll understand as well as I do...is that the tranquility of Sénecé...the good mores..."

"It might be," says Denis, smiling, "exactly what you're saying there that might be complicated..."

"You're alarming me...all the more so as...your little jokes...the spring of wine...the cinema on the church..."

"Here we are, right away, at the nub of the question. Those little jokes before my appearance..."

"And that appearance itself, my dear Monsieur! That sojourn in Sénecé incognito, in those workman's overalls..."

"It interested me, before everything was finished, to work with my hands on the installation of the lighting in my château. Let's say that my incognito was something akin to...what a diving suit is for someone who wants to explore the sea-bed."

"I don't really see..."

"It's only an image. Someone who wants to build solidly, to know the resources of the soil he has chosen, needs to study the soil, the stone and the vegetation carefully."

"Undoubtedly..."

"What poor information would he receive if he shouted at the top of his voice what he has resolved to build? Everyone would boast to him about the water and the air, the minerals and the orchards. Everyone would do his best to mask the vices of the place and souls..."

"What is it, damn it, that requires so many precautions with regard to our worthy Sénéçois?"

"I'll tell you: an experiment that I plan to carry out here, and of which the ensemble of the constructions of which I've thought is only one detail, in the same way that what you've called my 'little jokes' were only a prelude."

"An experiment...for your radium?"

"Completely separate. My radium—my business, rather—will simply aid me to underwrite the expenses of the experiment, which will be considerable...properly speaking, incalculable."

"And that experiment...?"

"I could tell you that it will be social..."

"Ah!"

"But the word would be inexact. It will be...ontogenic."

"Ont...oh, damn it! What does that mean?"

"In the etymological sense, to do with genesis, creation...a type of being..."

"Curious. And what purpose will it serve?"

"The solution of a passionate problem. The establishment of a certain concrete proof that will be, for the future of humanity, something at least as important as the discovery of the locomotive by Stephenson, or bacteria by Pasteur."

"You have thoughts of that sort? My compliments—that's marvelous! You could live in leisure...but you're going to encumber yourself... It seems to me that you have the bother of your factory, and the employment of your income... You have a fine château, a wife who seems to me, from the little I've seen of her, to be adorable. You have hunting, voyages, receptions... Humanity? Ha ha! Unless you're ambitious for honors...the cross, perhaps...or an electoral mandate...."

"No. Suppose, more simply, that my pleasure in living is such that it goes beyond the pleasures that you've listed...and that its overflow forms, quite naturally, of its own accord, my experiment..."

"An odd calculation. And you've chosen Sénecé..."

"In truth, because I have my château here, my land, the primary facilities all found. What I needed was a little human collective, as rudimentary as possible. The Sénéçois will suit my purposes very well. In brief, I have the intention, much as a biologist introduces seeds into a new environment and observes their reactions and their development, to precipitate the little human colony represented by the Sénéçois into a culture broth..."

"Eh?"

"...which will be nothing less than a complete metamorphosis of the ambient conditions of life."

"Total? Which is to say...?"

"Let us suppose, at once, a state of the world such that it has the power to renew, so to speak—or, better, to recreate—human beings, their sentiments, their actions, their instincts, even...to recreate their physical organism..."

"I can well suppose... We're in the heart of fantasy. What sort of state are you talking about?"

"A state of happiness."

"Ah?"

"A happiness...in being, in living, which will be breathed through all the pores like the air, like light. It's happiness that will make the metamorphosis...ontogenic."

"Good, good—and by what miracle will a happiness so...extraordinary...?"

"Quite simple. Happiness will find its aliments in every minute, because each of them will be limitless, enriched and multiplied by love, art and science..."

"We're very far from our worthy Sénéçois!"

"Not as far as it might seem."

"Go on! And even further from ninety-nine centimes..."

"Stay with me. Notice that it will require, to attain this state of happiness, the possession of the faculty of love, the sensibility of art and a science sufficiently profound and numerous of reality, in order to discover continuous motives for pleasure, wonder and sensuality..."

"Admitting a reality that contains those motives, of course."

"Of course. Which is to say, in fact, that before any other factors, it will be the science, the consciousness of such a reality, that will determine the faculty of love, the sentiment of joy, the happiness of living... Now, before the impossibility of rendering that reality concrete to any mass of individuals trapped in the normal, which is to say, of enabling them to attain that inevitably preliminary science and consciousness, one means presents itself: to put those individuals in a position to accomplish instinctively the actions of that happiness. To put it another way, to utilize in their regard, and by paraphrase, the old advice of an illustrious sectarian: they will perform the actions of Joy, and Joy will come to them..."

"Go on—how's that?"

"Practically, by throwing them into a world where that joy is possible, and by surrounding them with objectives of action that will be the generators and the aliments of that joy. That's your culture medium."

"Pardon me, but...that's your experiment?"

"Exactly. I shall begin by liberating the Sénéçois from the majority of material coercions. My gifts of instruments, bicycles, clothing and livestock, are only a preliminary example, a feeble sketch of the liberation I envisage. On the other hand, and simultaneously, I shall fill their liberated life with the attractions and advantages that I think capable, as I told you, of recreating humans, their sentiments, their instincts, and even their physical organism."

"But damn it, with what objective?"

"I've told you. To see..."

"What?"

"The reactions, the developments..."

"And afterwards?"

"That will already be sufficiently interesting. My hobby...my petty rich man's passion...as others collect the heads of deer, or potteries of the Tang dynasty. But in order not to hide anything from you, with the hope that one day there will be, in the vast world, one village, one tiny race of humans, born of humans, whose rites and amours will be regulated, whose houses will be constructed, by that which, formerly the blind instinct of life, will have become the instinct, and then the spirit, of joy., and will bring the world the touchstone and the flesh of..."

"Of what?"

"Of the redemption of humankind."

Cahoche takes out his handkerchief, mops his brow and then his pince-nez, readjusts the latter on his nose, and slowly, as one advances into a field full of traps, says: "I can foresee difficulties. But your little experiment...we'll all be dead before you've displaced a pebble...."

"My plan, in this little corner of the world, it to go ahead rather brutally."

"Which is to say?"

"I once saw a film in the cinema. It showed the growth of a potato, from the moment when the honest tuber put out and extended its rootlets through the humus until the moment when its stem was laden with flowers and fruits. Thanks to the ingenuity of the operators, the months necessary to that succession of phases only lasted for a few seconds on the screen, because of the accelerated movement of the strip. That's what I want to do in Sénecé: accelerate reality like a film."

Cahoche smiles thinly. "Ha ha! And the *Natura non facit saltus* of our old authors?"[15]

"A fragile argument. The victories won by modern scientists over the natural order have rendered the apothegm obsolete. Abundant examples of those victories are offered in every

---

[15] The Latin axiom, meaning "nature does not make jumps" was a principle of natural philosophy in Aristotle's time, but was assertively repopularized by Gottfried Leibniz, Isaac Newton and Linnaeus, among others.

domain. For instance, in biological chemistry, the experiment of Gudernatsch..."[16]

Cahoche sketched a vague gesture.

"In 1912, he observed, having nourished young tadpoles with the thyroid, that is subjects commenced metamorphosis several weeks in advance of other tadpoles normally nourished, which served as a control."

"Very interesting, but..."

"Bohn, in 1920, cites an experiment attempted on greenfly. Even more interesting. To explain the fact that those insects are sometimes winged and sometimes wingless, temperature, humidity and the conditions of nutrition had been invoked in vain. Now, when the stem of a rose-bush bearing greenfly in placed for twelve or fourteen hours in sand washed, sterilized and saturated with a solution of magnesium sulfate, a hundred per cent of the greenfly that hatch out acquire wings..."

"Marvelous!"

"In the same way, by means of chemical substances inhibiting oxidation, Dewitz obtained wingless insects..."

"Marvelous, marvelous...but I can only listen to you. My scientific knowledge is meager. My subject is the Law. Oh, on that...but after all, can human beings, even rudimentary, even a population of country folk be compared to tadpoles or greenfly? Whatever the methods are on which you're counting...to accelerate, as you put it...you're going to run into a host of traditional sentiments and actions, in an envelope of old instincts..."

---

[16] John Frederick Gudernatsch (1881-1962). The names Bohn or the Dewitz are both moderately common among scientists of the relevant period, but I can find no evidential trace of the experiments cited; if this part of the novel was written priot to 1914, however, the date of 1920 and the experiment to which it refers would necessarily be fictitious, whereas Gundersnatch's 1912 experiment might well have been recent..

"That's as may be. I firmly believe that a great part of the force of instincts is outside of us, in the persistence of environments and forms. In sum, the only social state that we know, in spite of the centuries and all their adventures, has remained, in its mental foundations, in its essential rituals and their exterior monuments, such that the profound instincts of the species have always found themselves among familiar images, sliding in the persistence of the original rhythms, almost as easily as a bowling-ball rolls in the groove that brings it back from its target to its point of departure..."

"A curious comparison!"

"That's perhaps one of the picturesque aspects of my experiment—that of finding out what will remain the part, what will be the resistance of profound forces—let's say, if you like the 'innate'—in the face of entirely new external conditions. And inversely, what will be the part, the influence, of those conditions acting from the exterior upon the interior, the action, if you'll forgive the wordplay, of the original on the original."[17]

"In sum, if I've understood you correctly, you've formed the plan of turning this worthy little region completely upside-down...."

"I don't deny," says Denis, tranquilly, "that it might produce a few small somersaults here and there among your adminstratees. I'll even warn you that a certain number of the irreducibly old might prefer to go to end their days somewhere else, where life is more in conformity with what their ancestors have bequeathed them, since Adam..."

"A peasant doesn't let go of his land just like that. Those irreducibles will be rude adversaries for you."

---

[17] Unlike French, English cannot distinguish *original* [in the sense of eccentric] from *originel* [in the sense of primal]—although, in truth, French does not usually make the distinction either, the former spelling commonly being used in both cases, as in English.

"Bah! They'll be rolled away in the flow of my partisans. They'll complain, but they'll adapt. Then again, I don't make any claim to be able to induce metamorphosis in the old, or even the middle-aged, with a wave of a magic wand. That's of no importance. I shall work on the young, and even on the children. They will provide the impetus…and the others will follow…"

"Good. And as I say, we'll be dead and buried, you and I, before having seen the first blade of grass of your paradise grow…"

"No," says Denis. "The blade of grass will grow much more rapidly than you suspect. Look, I'll show you something rather impressive…"

He goes to his table, sits down, and pulls toward himself a rectangular box surmounted by a dozen electric bulbs, in the side of which a telephone mouthpiece opens. That apparatus is linked to another, made of a round foot supporting a stem, at the summit of which shines an ebonite disk. The disk is surrounded by an octagonal apparatus, a kind of spider-web of metallic wires.

Denis turns a screw on the outside of the rectangular box, presses a switch, and then shouts: "Pierre!"

An instant later, a silky crackling resonates in the spider-web.

"Would you please try rocket number 7?"

A further crackle. Denis pushes the apparatus away and returns to Cahoche. At that moment a slight explosion strikes the Maire's ear. Through the open bay window, he perceives a luminous dot departing from one of the lateral terraces of the château, which rises into the sky, whistling. At a great height, the dot bursts, releasing a little yellow flake, which sways in the air and elongates, without evaporating. In the atmosphere, a serene blue until now, it seems that the flake attracts the vapors suspended in the air. Around its indolent extension, fine clouds form, which grow rapidly, thickening, soon obscuring a region of the sky.

"Impossible!" said Cahoche. "Do you have the reci-pe…?"

A large droplet falls and lands on the Maire's nose as he leans out of the bay, his face turned toward the atmospheric comedy.

Suddenly, it begins to rain, hard, and Cahoche steps back hastily.

"Amazing."

The water crepitates furiously on the cupola; a lugubri-ous light fills the hall.

"What are people going to say?" exclaims the Maire. "Everyone's outside, building haystacks…"

"We'll interrupt the downpour," says Denis. "It was only a little experiment."

He returns to the apparatus and shouts "Pierre!" again.

"Yes…?" replies Draguin's voice, seemingly emerging from the box with the six bulbs, while one of the bulbs sud-denly lights up.

"That's perfect. Let's try effluvium 5."

"Understood…"

"Would you care to return to the bay, my dear Monsieur Cahoche?"

Without any machine or projectile being manifest, the clouds are violently disturbed, driven away in a circle, rotating around an invisible object, their masses shifting and distend-ing, as if they were encountering the walls of a tower of fluids. Blue sky reappears above the château.

"We can circumscribe the storm, by selecting a point at will," says Denis, "as you can see. But it's necessary to think of the haystacks. Send the rain to the devil!" he shouts into the apparatus.

And, as if the strange physicist who is receiving Denis' instructions has the power to unleash the most irresistible of gusts, like a broom chasing away dust, the clouds disperse in all directions, flying away and disintegrating into scattered wisps.

The sky having reappeared, Cahoche comes back into the hall heavily, his face crimson, deformed by a mixture of amazement, uncertainty and hilarity. He takes a deep breath, searches for words, and says: "And…you have many sorceries of that kind?"

"My friend Draguin is very ingenious. However, it's necessary that the invention be absolutely perfected, and that it succeeds every time. We're still exploring. But what you've just seen is an indication. Electricity will play an important role in my experiment. Three years from now, or four—neither you nor I will be dead, I think—the electrified fields will plow themselves. In the houses of Sénecé—I'm not talking about light or heat, which will happen of their own accord—the housework, the cooking, the laundry, the making of clothing, almost all manual labor, will be accomplished by the simple flick of a switch. There's no sorcery involved, believe me."

"Oh, that's a manner of speaking. I know perfectly well that modern science…but permit me to get straight to the point. Admitting that a day will come when everything in Sénecé can be done by pressing a button…how will the Séneçois occupy their time? It will give free rein to all their turpitudes, which labor bridles. They'll never be sober! As for mores…rendezvous in the spinneys, on the banks of the Courtoise and behind the haystacks are numerous enough already. Listen, Monsieur Aury, in my capacity as Maire of Sénecé, your experiment is really giving me a scare!"

"Quite superfluous. My plan foresees, as people become freer, offering to their leisure a multitude of goals of activity and pleasure, completely unprecedented."

"Aha! That's what I expected of you. What?"

"Trust me. Come on, Monsieur Cahoche," Denis says, suddenly bursting into laughter, "you'll see…it will be very amusing. And what if there is a brief period of disorder, a slight disruption of habits? It will settle down."

"You can't be astonished that I have, as Maire, a few reservations... Otherwise, as a man of the world and a neighbor, I'm all yours. So let's leave it at that..."

Cahoche is on his feet, and pacing back and forth.

"You've made a palace of this old studio of your father's. Shall I have the honor of being introduced to Madame Aury? We'd be very happy, Madame Cahoche and I, to have you at one of our imminent receptions. You'd meet the bishop, a president of the Court of Appeal in Paris, an administrator of the Crédit Foncier..." On seeing a crease in Denis' lips, he added: "And you know, we have a good time anyway. The president sometimes consents to recite monologues..."

"You're very kind. My wife has gone to Paris with our friend Leviel. She might be on her way back. I'll tell you exactly..."

He returns to the box with the bulbs, turns the screw in the opposite direction to the one in which he turned it a little while before, clicks the switch again and commences a new manipulation.

"Lène!"

The spider-web crackles. A bulb lights up. Lène's voice resonates, cheerfully. "Darling?"

"Where are you?"

"We've just passed through Crennes."

"Monsieur le Maire de Sénecé is with me, and would be very glad to present his homages."

"Delighted...," says the voice.

Cahoche bows mechanically. A silence.

The voice resumes: "We'll be there in a quarter of an hour or so. We're bringing Berson back with us. He's bringing you some beautiful sketches for your pylons..."

"Perfect."

Slight vibration of a click in the octagonal network. The lamp that lit up goes out.

"That's...truly...convenient," Cahoche stammers.

"We always remain in communication. The auto contains a wireless apparatus similar to this one."

"I'll gladly take the liberty of waiting for Madame Aury."

"You've heard her say that she'd be delighted..."

Denis lets a moment of silence go by, a fugitive smile gilding his cheeks. "No doubt she'll accept your kind invitation with the greatest alacrity. It appears correct to me, nevertheless, to indicate to you right away, in case you attach any importance to such things, that we aren't married."

"Oh! Ah...! Pooh!" says Cahoche, with a false lightness. He takes off his pince-nez and wipes it. "I'm not unaware that in Parisian society... For my part, I'm a freethinker, but I recognize that Madame Cahoche, in that order of propriety, retains a few petty prejudices...hmm... The somewhat particular aspect of these situations, the species of...constraint...that a person...let's say like Madame Cahoche... Madame Aury...assuredly...solely by virtue of the fact of being your companion... Nevertheless...there is in unions that the priest, or let's say even the notary, has not put the seal, a character of instability... It also happens that...that the prestiges of amour cast their sparkling veils...over the origins..."

"Lène was an actress when I met her. She's no longer anything but my...companion, as you put it."

"An actress...," repeats Cahoche, his voice somewhat troubled.

"I understand you perfectly," Denis continues. "In addition, too many divergences might be anticipated. I fear having to proceed, quite rapidly, without your collaboration."

"But..."

"In fact, I shall make my arrangements in consequence."

"Our disagreement would have a bad effect on your plans...in all fashions...not to mention that the village, surprised the see the two landowners at odds...I'm very popular...people listen to me..."

"I believe," says Denis, whose strangely clear and determined voice is accompanied by the most amiable smile, "that we have, for the moment, nothing more to say to one another."

Slightly nonplussed, Cahoche starts, and buttons up his jacket mechanically "Eh! How you go on…it's necessary to see… You know that this is the provinces…and what's worse, the country. If I weren't Maire…if we were in Paris… Although Madame Cahoche… But in the final analysis, I'm master in my own hearth. Oh, damn it all, you have a way of cutting bridges!"

Meanwhile, he moves away slowly, entertaining crafty thoughts, toward the armchair on which he deposited his hat and gloves.

"It wouldn't astonish me," he says, stopping half way, "if I'd seen…Madame Aury perform. I only caught a glimpse of her on the morning of your arrival, and two or three times since, in her auto. But it seemed to me that, one of these winters…we spend much of the winter in Paris, naturally… And you…"

"We travel a great deal," says Denis, evasively. "I have no idea where we'll be this coming winter. Perhaps here…perhaps I'll visit some of my uranium deposits in Portugal, Norway or Tonkin…"

"Madame Aury accompanies you on these…industrial excursions?"

"The industrial purpose doesn't take away any of the beauty of the countries visited."

"That's true…I meant…often, essentially technical preoccupations…unless one has, in addition, the soul of a connoisseur…like you. One only has to look at these frescos, that statue…"

"By Michelangelo."

"That's what I thought…it could only be by someone very well known…" Suddenly, Cahoche stops dead. "That whistle…isn't that the auto bringing back Madame Aury?"

"You have keen ears," says Denis "Indeed."

"And your opinion, Monsieur le Maire?"

Propped up against the back of the circular divans, drawing and water-colors are displayed, which Berson is taking from a large folder and which Lène is disposing. Denis and Leviel are commenting on the images. Cahoche is standing a few paces behind him.

"I won't permit myself..."

"Come on, Monsieur Cahoche," said Leviel, bluntly, "let's at least suppose the impression of the Séneçois when they see this machine, in iron and wood, rising up across their fields..."

"Well...if you'll permit me, I think...that they'll be utterly amazed, and slightly scandalized, when they see so much trouble taken and money spent on the ornamentation of these masts and pylons..."

The masts represented by the water-color are in smooth yellow wood, and their insulators are topaz-colored glass, evoking the form of ears of wheat. Certain projections of the pylons, which Leviel has arranged slightly to one side, are reminiscent of the delicate works of filigree in which Hindu and Moorish artisans excel; their interlacements of iron wires firming a tight trellis, curving inwards in places in serpentine fashion, in rose-like formations, nodes and arabesques, figurines in metal, glass or faience.

"A florescence on these masts," says Denis, pointing at the first drawing, "spaced eighty or a hundred paces from one another, will give the impression, in their ensemble, of giant stalks of wheat, sentinels of a sort watching over the crops developing at their base."

"Or the heralds of fabulous unknown harvests to come," says Berson.

"But we know very well what they will be," Denis replies, "and that they will come!"

"Yes, if worthy old Mother Earth can see things like you...as an artist...," says Cahoche, smiling.

"We shall help her, Monsieur le Maire," says Leviel.

"It's necessary to believe in miracles, Monsieur le Maire," says Lène, "When it's Denis who has promised them."

Cahoche does not say anything more. He wipes his lenses frequently. In drawing closer to the images, it seems to him that through his garments and all the pores of his skin he is respiring Lène, being impregnated by her fresh and sumptuous grace. The bright young woman is wearing a white dress whose sleeves, of a blond like that of old book-bindings, are embroidered with large golden flowers.

A bell rings. A lamp on the telephonic apparatus lights up. A voice says: "Monsieur Carmenton has just arrived..."

"I beg your pardon," says Denis to Cahoche. "I have some business to settle with this visitor. You must have seen it in the newspapers...the scientist who has succeeded in photographing microscopic images, of blood corpuscles and bacilli..." To Lène and Leviel he says: "Would you care, if our Maire has the time to spare, to show Monsieur Cahoche some of the curiosities of the château?"

"I'd like nothing better," says Cahoche, with vivacity. "If it's not abusing Madame's time..."

"It won't be a chore," says Lène politely. "We can make a more ample acquaintance..."

"Leave all your drawings there, Berson," says Denis. "You'll stay for dinner with us." He goes to the telephone. "Send in Monsieur Carmenton, and ask Monsieur Draguin to come and join us."

"...In sum, it will possible for you to film, as you have done for blood, the molecular movements of a certain number of absolutely immediate substances familiar to these peasants?"

"Better still," says Draguin, "will the cinematography of electrolysis be feasible? The light microscope can attain the colloidal particles. The crystal reflection of X-rays permits the conception of a microscope using those rays, which will attain atomic movements..."[18]

---

[18] In fact, the first usable images produced with an X-ray microscope did not materialize until the late 1940s, when Law-

"How long will you give me?"

"How long do you need?"

"It's impossible for me to give you a reply."

"By devoting yourself exclusively to the necessary research and it applications?"

"Exclusively? That would also be impossible for me."

"Supposing that you could do it?"

"Five years...perhaps three..."

"My dear Monsieur," says Denis. "I'll put one of my autos at your disposal to facilitate your comings and goings from your laboratory in Paris to Draguin's. I'll arrange for you to obtain a leave from the Ministry. Here's a books of checks that you only need to fill in for your purchases of materials and your honoraria. And in two years, the pellicles will be ready to turn in the magic lantern that we'll aim from that terrace..."

"That's very American! Scientific research is sometimes teasing, its processes infinitely complicated..."

Denis smiles, with a hint of irony.

"For example," says Carmenton, "all the gold in the world wouldn't have enabled Becquerel to discover the radioactivity of uranium if the photographic substances hadn't developed, by slow progress, a perfection that permitted the sensitivity of the revelatory plates..."

"That slowness of progress," says Denis, is due in large measure to the pitiful conditions in which scientists strive. I shall create for you a kind of social estate in which the scientist can dispose, by raising his little finger, with as many material needs to serve his research as a banker has to buy baubles for a dancer."

"There are many more jewelers and milliners than manufacturers of scientific apparatus."

"You'll encourage them..."

---

rence Bragg developed a practicable technique, but the possibilities of X-ray miscroscopy were first discussed in the late 1890s, soon after Röntgen had made the discovery.

"Do you want to set a limit to my expenses?"

"How, since you don't know as yet what instruments it will be necessary to have constructed?"

"That's fine."

"Would you like to visit the laboratory and judge its resources?"

"Very gladly."

The three men leave the hall. Carmenton and Draguin head for the laboratory. Denis goes to rejoin his guests. He finds them on the threshold of a large meadow behind the château, where the erection of three hangars is nearing completion. Berson is discussing with Leviel the ornaments of the mosaic set in the cement lining the hangars: images of reptations becoming soaring lines, scarlet sheets thinning down and curving gently into golden spirals.

"A figuration of the dynamism of the airplanes that these elegant stables will shelter," says Leviel.

Scarcely has the Maire seen Denis approaching than he exclaims, as soon as the latter is close enough, in an affected manner: "Astonishing! Unprecedented! It's an enchanted palace…the palace of a fairy queen!"

The group advances across the meadow. Lène puts her arm around Denis' neck. She turns eyes full of mischief toward him.

"He hasn't looked at very much, you know," she murmurs.

"Yes, at you," Denis replies, in a love voice. "He'll let us do whatever we want. It will put him in thorny situations with his administratees from time to time, but he'll sort them out. He'll arrange everything rather than lose contact with us. But be careful! He's not a bad man, and he sings madrigals gallantly enough…"

"I'd have to ask him to trim his beard," says Lène.

Denis had counted on the first crops of his electrified fields to rally the grumblers, the hesitant and the incredulous. A few months had sufficed for the installation of lines of force under his lands and the first apparatus in his farms. Crews taken from the factory in Courtoisans had toiled hard, and Denis and Draguin had supervised the work, aiding it with their good humor, and lending a hand to the labor now and again.

As soon as the first machines had begun to function on the farms, half a dozen Séneçois had allowed themselves to be won over by the new methods. It began with the smithy, and it was an outburst of anger from the farrier Jeanselme that unleashed the era of great transformations. Scarcely had the shearing of sheep and the shoeing of horses by electricity been put into practice by Denis' tenant farmers than many Séneçois had acquired the habit, cordially welcomed, of taking their animals there. The work was done so quickly and so little difficulty that there was no need, the farmers said, for any retribution. That was what pushed Jeanselme to rage and vituperation one day. He protested that the Aury farms were taking his business, ruining him and that there was nothing for him to do but break his bellows and turn in his anvil.

He was very surprised, the following day, to see Denis coming into his establishment.

"Would you like, Jeanselme, your forge to be fitted out in such a fashion that you can do everything by electricity, as on my farms? Not only will you get your business back, but the new machines that I'll put in your hands will give you a taste and facility for a lot off works with iron that you've never attempted."

"You're having me on! No disrespect, but you might as well offer to curl a bald man's hair. I don't have a sou, since your machines have taken the better part of my clientele. How could I pay for your machines?"

Jeanselme the farrier had been the first person to use and benefit from the singular system of credit organized by Monsieur Aury, which permitted him the working capital and the resources of the factory. Monsieur Aury bore the cost of construction and materials, and one had twenty years to pay it back.

"I'm quite tranquil," Denis had said to those who came to ask for details. "The profits and economies, with my methods, will be adequate for you to have reimbursed me without any difficulty in five or six years, and you'll be rich by then..."

Jeanselme's example had drawn in the baker Lauvin. When people learned that the oven was lit, the dough kneaded and the loaves baked before Lauvin had even got out of bed, and when people saw unprecedented pastries displayed in the baker's window, which his leisure had permitted him to meditate and perfect, Manevy, the miller, and Chaliex, the cobbler in the Place Jacques, made deals with Denis.

In the meantime, the excellent results of the first crop arrived to bring the lord of the manor a majority favorable to his innovations. The most suspicious were obliged to concede before a growth of wheat on his hectares so straight and dense that one never saw the stalks bend under the rudest wind, but only undulate slowly in great majestic masses, as if nonchalantly. The harvest yielded forty quintals per hectare, a figure never attained before, and the château's agronomists affirmed that it was only a step on the way to a much higher yield.

That victory of electriculture stimulated the irresolute. In spite of an obstinate denigrating minority, timorous hoarders and cultivators hostile to any alteration of the forms of activity solemnly inscribed in the ancestral contract between humans and the glebe, demands poured in for installations, current, field-machinery and domestic apparatus. Contagion, wonder, envy and the hope of marvelous profits enfevered the solici-

117

tors. Crews from the factory, temporarily assigned to basic works in Sénecé, found zealous companions in the indigenes, who seconded them as best they could with masonry, carpentry and the laying of cables and wires. Thanks to Géard's efforts, the materials arrived in abundance.

Meanwhile, the first beneficiaries of the Aury methods saw the fated difficulties and cares of hard labor effaced. Some of them had instinctively begun to fill their leisure with the diversions that had previously been the pittance of Sundays and feast days, and the only ones they knew: the idle strolls of the seventh day, the jovial meals, the games of dominoes, boule and billiards at the tavern, trips to town with the epic binges whose indispensable apotheosis was a visit to the brothel. In the interstices of the sprees, the muffled voice of morality and the original habit of labor directed the idle hands, bewildered by no longer having the employment of age-old gestures, toward a host of minor tasks. People did odd jobs around the house, tidied up, or took an interest in the new machines.

Cultivators turned their itchy fingers to experiments in grafting, in the garden and the orchard. The bulk of domestic work being accomplished with no more effort than operating a few controls, privileged wives and daughters spent long hours sewing and gossiping, and when that was exhausted, used up time extracting the ultimate gleams from bedroom windows, the crucifix, the chandeliers and the clock-face. All those efforts of neatness and cleanliness that they had scarcely snatched from time tyrannized by more urgent tasks became urgent tasks themselves.

In fact, however, for the majority of those the electric transformations had liberated, leisure activities became more numerous and more ample than games, debauchery and the petty jobs with which they sought to fill time. The overlong hours before them were like fallow fields, which they did not know exactly what they might sow therein, and what tools they had at their disposal for plowing and planting.

II

After her singular encounter with Denis, Lène had lived a baroque year. Unable to make up her mind to talk to anyone about the strange electrician from the Rue Bourgon: a singularly aggravating and voluptuous year, in which she had hugged the secret to herself as a little girl clutches her doll. What crazy stories had she not forged? Denis' words were deformed, with time, modeling themselves in all the phantasmagorias the floated through the imagination of the actress.

The mysterious joy about which Denis had spoken was gradually transmuted into a kind of fabulous power. Perhaps then man of the Boucheron diamond had discovered invisibility, like Wells' Griffin? And that unlimited credit he had offered her…what if she had accepted, if she had kept, that check-book? Sometimes she amused herself and excited herself with ideal prodigalities. What might a wealth like the one had had offered to make freely available to her represent, considered coolly?

Alice Brionne, the tragedienne, who had the support of a reigning prince, put on an intolerable display at rehearsals of her five-hundred-thousand-franc furs and her four strings of pearls… *Pooh!* thought Lène. *If I had the check-book…* She looked at the haughty Brionne, with the slightly acidic pride of having refused the means to put the show-off in the shade…

An entire year lived in duplicate, with a kind of bittersweet savoring of the most enormous possibilities, accompanying the majority of petty quotidian gestures…

Sometimes, however, she laughed at herself and thought that she would never see Denis again. She repeated the fable of the Heron to herself.[19] Miracles no longer existed. Even

---

[19] The fable of the heron was widely known in France in Jean de La Fontaine's version, but dates back at least to Roman times. The heron is surrounded by fish in the morning, which it refuses because it is not yet ready to eat. In the afternoon it rejects poorer fish in the hope that better ones will come

admitting that Denis might come back, she would soon find herself before a man like all the rest, perhaps a little more eccentric—a fine talker, certainly—but so what? It is not the case that check-books are inexhaustible, nor that a certain conception of joy, whatever it might be, could make an actress the omnipotent mistress of all the treasures of the world! "The heron, the heron, my dear..." Probably, nothing at all would happen. Nothing with remain but a ludicrous memory of the meteoric gallant...

As the date for which Denis has promised news of him drew near, a telegram arrives at the theater. At the exit from the performance, there is a splendid auto, and when Lène appears, Denis, dressed with sober distinction, who is standing next to the vehicle, comes toward the actress.

"Bonjour, Lène. Are you ready to come with me?"

Since she read the telegram she has been ready for any enchantment. As casually as possible, she replies: "Go with you? My God, where to? Until when?"

"Until the moment when you say: *Halt*. In a minute, if you wish, the auto will stop, in a week, in ten years, at the slightest sign from you, to put an end to your new life."

"Ten years! You hope, then..."

"I can't foresee any hour to come, since it's to you, free at any moment, from whom I shall seek every consent."

"Well then, let's go have the cup of tea that you were unable to offer me the last time we met..."

The auto takes them away through the Bois toward Bellevue. When they go through the gates Lène began to get anxious. "If we leave Paris, I'm lost...where are you taking me?"

"Paris isn't leaving you. This auto is yours, which will put Paris five minutes away from all your desires."

---

along, but in the evening, all the fish have gone and it has to soothe its gnawing hunger with a snail.

They arrive at a large garden, which the auto traverses, and then the threshold of a villa of fine appearance, luminous and very modern.

"A pied-à-terre," says Denis, "while waiting for my château to be completely finished."

Three ravishing maidservants are waiting for the auto in front of the villa. One of them takes the actress' coat. Another opens the doors for the couple. The third disposes the armchairs.

The tea is served.

"You're at home," Denis says, "and it's you, this time, who is offering me the tea. If you regret having invited me I'll leave immediately."

"I don't regret it yet..." Lène laughs, and searches the mirror furtively to see whether her free and easy manner is still fully visible. In reality, her blood is galloping, she is all expectation for the extraordinary event that cannot fail to materialize...something beyond the offer of the auto and that of the villa, which are of an order of munificence that a pretty and celebrated actress can always encounter.

The extraordinary is unleashed. It is not the villa flying away with its guests toward the stars, or the furniture transforming itself into living beings. Denis is not suddenly surrounded by flames...

He talks, softly. In response to his voice, a kind of wellbeing, a suavity, takes hold of Lène: an inexpressible pleasure, through it seems that objects and the atmosphere become fluid, caressant, loving...

The miracle was not to be in things or events, but interior to everything. Contrary to the fable of the Heron, Lène's most chimerical dreams were to find themselves surpassed by the most simple reality, transfigured by contact with Denis. The miracle was in Denis, was Denis himself. One might have thought that the minutes cracked before him like chestnuts at the passage of a woodland enchanter, springing forth as their spiny coats split of their own accord, and yielding their creamy pulp. A host of trivial details over which the gaze ordinarily slides were, for him, pretext for wonder or delight, which he translated so freshly and cheerfully that anyone with him immediately came to understand and share his pleasure.

Lène felt, with an incomparable delight, that in Denis' company, everything became easy, amiable and radiant. Compared with him, other people, their words and their enterprises, seemed to her to be banal and paltry, their actions and goals implacably narrow. By comparison with Denis' joy, all others were fragmentary, unstable, encumbered by bitter residues, the reek of disillusionments, of muzzled calculation.

Denis had said once and for all to Lène that the villa in Bellevue was hers, ready to receive her at any moment; that she had only to formulate a wish for things to come to her, as if flying through the air; that at the slightest gesture, the auto would be ready to race to wherever she pleased: to the mountains, the ocean or the far end of Europe.

Before all the possibilities open, Lène hesitated to wish, and waited... Doubtless, obscurely, the time would come when she felt equal to the treasures that Denis had gifted to her, when she would become conscious of the value of the fact that he had distinguished her... She was not stupidly vain. There was no shortage of more famous and more beautiful women to whom such a man should have laid claim.

The château art Sénecé was not finished, and Denis spent certain periods of time there. Lène went to meet him several times. The auto left her at the entrance to Crennes at night, and Denis, having covered the two leagues that separated Crennes from Sénecé on foot, waited for Lène in his workman's costume, and took her through the woods to a little hunting lodge, pleasantly fitted out. She left by night, and the indigenes of Crennes, like those of Sénecé, had not the slightest idea of the electrician Amédée's rendezvous with a beautiful woman from Paris.

Denis and Lène went arm in arm along the silent paths, and the actress laughed wholeheartedly at the workman's stories, the jokes that he played on the Séneçois, or was impassioned to hear him unfurl his dreams, and sketch out is means of remolding humans in accordance with the spirit of Joy.

One of those nights, they belonged to one another. When their burning torpor had dissipated, an ineffable pride enraptured the actress' mind. She thought that the gift of her body made her the equal of her precious friend, that she was delivering to him in her turn riches worthy of those he had offered her.

He said to her: "Beautiful being, for the bright impulse, toward me, of that gilded body, those lips and those ardent loins, the dear trembling and moist tenderness that is folded and restful within me, my body full of bliss and my heavy and swollen lips thanks you..."

With her head on the man's breast, she half-closed her eyes, blissful and bathed in solemn expectation. Denis did not add anything, but when dawn came, and she accompanied him a little way through the wood, toward Sénecé, he said: "The admirable voluptuousness that my body owes to you, although it is different, is neither greater nor more delightful than those of other embraces already exchanged between parts of us...."

Anxious, with a strange anxiety, made of disappointment and gratitude, she searched his dilated eyes to read within him the words that he was about to say...

"Each of the mute communications of our gaze, our emotion, our pleasure in understanding and sensing together a spectacle or a beauty, are worth as much to me as the kiss that joined us last night..."

He squeezed her warm and robust arm gently.

"This great affair," he said, with a juvenile gaiety so limpid that it eluded any impression of sarcasm, "this quasi-religious apotheosis of the gift of the body, is not in my eyes that major instant of amour, the sacrament that has given us so much literature. I believe love to be much vaster, I want the sacraments to be far more numerous and renewed. The gift of your body, darling Lène, is only one instant in the unfurling of the possessions of you that are permitted to me, the celebrations I expect from you. The gift of your body is like a proud vessel that approaches the shore, and that alone. Rich as we are, beyond that moment, there still remains so much for us to learn, to savor, to conquer of one another other, just as, when one sets foot ashore, the entire continent remains to be discovered!"

She listened, nonplussed, with a child-like soul, and sensed herself poor, her pride disconcerted. And she asked herself how, by what means, she would finally be his, what love she needed to bring him that would confer on her that certainty, that consciousness of the valuable and generous gift of herself, of which her admiration and her love experienced the passionate necessity.

The idea insinuated itself within her of giving up the theater, not uniquely because of the liberty she would obtain through Denis, but more in order that nothing foreign to him should encumber her hours. To give up...

The theater was not only her brilliant career, her beloved art, all her attachments, her social rhythm, but the tessitura of her mind, her tastes, her being. And now, what she found, and what she accomplished, and which was doubtless what Denis wanted her to find and to accomplish by her own effort...

It was her very being that she was going to surrender to him, naked. By abdicating the theater, she would be divesting herself of everything she knew, believed and cherished that was not Denis, his vision, his radiance, of which everything it struck bore the seal. She would give herself, stripped of all that there was in an on her before he appeared, and would be reborn in him, and nourish herself, breathe and drink of him, her soul inclined toward his radiance like the head of an infant toward the maternal breast.

And when she announced to him, intoxicated by her offering, glorious and trembling, that she no longer wanted to be an actress, he said: "There are, and I promise you, roles compared with which those you are abandoning will seem mere puffs of smoke..." Then he laughed. "And the famous audience of kings, before which every Brichanteau and

Brichantelle dreams of playing,[20] I shall give you, and so regal that no denizen of the theater could ever have wished for such an audience in their most avid deliria."

She understood, and knew who those kings were when her destiny was linked to that of Denis, at the finished Château de Sénecé. They were all those who composed their society, their friends, whose number was augmented every time a man or woman, and individuality, was revealed somewhere: passionate individuals, artists, inventors, explorers, scientists turned toward the florescences of life, some revealing them, others creating them, make kings of a sort, always laden with their treasures. They formed around Denis and Lène an atmosphere like a perpetual firework display of creations and enthusiasms.

And the roles that Denis had promise the actress, instead of those she had played before a hundred times in succession, with memory, learned movements and a warmth regulated by the director, were renewed with each of the subtle gift with which that entourage heaped her, for it was the work of her life that she was playing, with her happiness and her wonder; and that delicious pride, before all those who loved and admired Denis, of sensing herself, with her beauty, her ostentation, and her eyes, which shone at their stories, their works, their projects, like a living performance, suddenly depicting to each one his own richness, excited that richness to broader aims.

III

Denis had made preparations to nourish the uncertain hours opened before those privileged by his mechanical instal-

---

[20] The reference is to the ostensibly-archetypal protagonist of the novel *Brichanteau, comédien* (1896; tr. as *Brichanteau, Actor*) by Jules Clarétie, the director of the Comédie-Française (who gave Anryvelde his first premature dose of fame by accepting *La Courtisane*).

lations. He waited for the slightest opportunity that would permit him to put his plans into practice, and did not have to wait long.

One evening at the château, during the conversation at dinner, Draguin reported: "There's a good woman here who's in the process of going mad. It's partly the fault of the curé. Mère Chauvion has an only son, a mariner on a merchant ship. The child has the habit of writing as regularly as possible to the old lady. Young Paulin was supposed to be somewhere between Portugal and the Antilles when his letters suddenly stopped. Extremely anxious, Mère Chauvion went to implore help from the curé. The spiritual Aesculapius gave her a prescription consisting mainly of prayers to the Virgin and putting things in the hands of Saint Michael. A few days later, the good woman reads in her newspaper that the Atlantic has unleashed its fury in the region that interests her. Despair, further visit to the curé. Prescription essentially similar to the first, and a little lecture on the Christian acceptance of catastrophes, future reunion in the bosom of the Lord, and other bromides. Since then, the old lady believes that her son is dead. He appears to her in the décor of *images d'Épinal*, smiling in the midst of pink little angels, or writhing in the flames of Hell, jovially stoked up by fork-wielding roaster..."

"First of all," said Denis, "It's necessary to obtain some precision regarding the fate of the ship. With half a dozen telephone calls to the ministry, the various companies...perhaps there's still time. Give me the name of the vessel and a few chronological details."

Having rapidly gathered the necessary indications, and learned that there was no presumption that the vessel had been wrecked, Denis transmitted what he knew to Draguin in order that he could restore some hope to Mère Chauvion.

"It's just," said Draguin, "that relations with Heaven and Hell are damnably tenacious, once commenced. We'll need to oppose some dazzling reality to those sacred phantasmagorias..."

"In that regard," Denis retorted, "the means of proving indisputably that the young man is alive, even if he is, are much more complicated than those which consist of pointing at the Eternal Father or Lucifer..."

He reflected momentarily, and smiled at the ideas that filed through his mind. "Saint Jules Verne and Saint Wells protect me!" he said. "I'm going to attempt an adventure that those archangels of the Marvelous wouldn't deny."

The adventure was something epic and absurd. Having convinced Mère Chauvion to entrust herself to him, Denis had one of his autos take her to Marseilles, where a submarine was waiting. Leaving from Sénecé the following day, he took off in one of his three airplanes. Remaining in communication with the submarine by wireless, he explored the surface of the ocean, circling in the region where Paulin Chauvion's ship ought to have been sailing. The conjunction was made. The submarine having surfaced, a sailor went aboard the ship, summoned Paulin, and before the bewildered young man, suddenly, from one of the submarine's hatches, aided by two matelots, one holding her hand, hoisting her up into the daylight, and the other sustaining her ascent, Mère Chauvion appeared, tremulous and burlesque, in the gigantic oceanic décor, in her mantle of black satin and her little frilly violet bonnet.

At the moment of separation, singular instruments had been handed to Paulin, along with instructions.

While that tender scene was unfolding, a few thousand leagues from Sénecé, works were being carried out under Draguin's guidance in a pasture owned by Denis situated on the edge of the village, on the threshold of the countryside. A tall, broad panel of white canvas was installed in the middle of the pasture, at right-angles to the château, the terraces of which were visible from the field. A few meters from the screen, an antenna was set up, and two items of apparatus similar to those in Denis' study.

Six days after its departure, the aircraft returned. Shortly afterwards, Frignot spread the news: Mère Chauvion had

127

found her son; she would return before that evening; and to-morrow, at eight o'clock in the evening, anyone who wanted to go to the screen in the meadow to see Paulin Chauvion himself, even though he was in the middle of the ocean, and would be able to talk to him and hear him.

All day long, Mère Chauvion went back and forth in the village, incapable of explaining what had happened to her, stunned by landscapes traversed so rapidly that they seemed to be racing and changing form like the clouds...by an iron ship traveling under water like a bar of soap dropped into the Courtoise while bathing, and suddenly rising up like a bucket from a well and suddenly finding herself alongside another ship, where her son Paulin was...

On the stroke of eight, simultaneously chimed on the church and the Mairie, as Sénecé crowded the pasture, a luminous beam split the darkness, departing from the terrace of the château, and struck the screen, fixing upon it, displayed there, inundating the white surface with gold. Then its rays swirled with black spirals and images appeared.

Denis was seen in the field that served as an aerodrome behind the château. He embarked provisions and a number of instruments on to the largest of his three airplanes. Followed by a mechanic, he climbed into the airplane; a man set the propeller spinning, and the plane took off, rising rapidly.

Cinematography from the height of the airplane itself. Sénecé, then its countryside, then villages and towns, file across the screen. The oscillations of the moving plane are communicated to the recording apparatus it is carrying, with the result that the fields, rivers and entire villages, with their streets, their crowds, their houses and monuments seem to jiggle and shake, and their mass undulates like fabric over a bosom, as if the countryside, the rivers, the villages and the towns were posed on a giant palpitation, as if the earth beneath them were breathing...

The entire adventure of Denis' journey unfurls. When the reunion of Mère Chauvion and her son, amid the jovial amazement of the crow, appears, a broad, irresistible laughter, equally jovial and also tender and nervous, shakes the whole pasture. It seems that the laughter expresses what is not heard but is seen on the screen in the moving mouths and the dilated eyes of the mariners around that improbable embrace.

At that precise moment, the screen went blank. The two clocks chimed nine. A voice, young and robust, resonated in the meadow: "Bonjour, Maman. Bonjour, all my friends!"

At the same time as the voice, the projection lit up and the mariner reappeared. He was sitting on a coil of rope at the extremity of the deck. Some distance away, there was a box surmounted by light-bulbs, like the one installed in the meadow.

"Bonjour, Paulin Chauvion," said Denis. "Your Maman and your friends are here, and are going to talk to you. Come on—who wants to return this young man's bonjour?"

A murmur ran around the dark meadow. At that point, the adventure surpassed the possible. Lauvin, the baker, emerged from the crowd and said, in a tremulous voice: "Can I have a word?"

"Turn toward this apparatus and speak," said Denis.

"Hey!" cried Lauvin. "Hey, Paulin...it's me, Lauvion...Blaise. Bonjour!"

"Bonjour, my old Blaise," replied the voice.

"Hey...where are you then, my lad?"

"Miles and miles away. Not far from America,"

"Ah! And like this, you can hear me from here to where you are?" exclaimed the baker.

"Don't speak so loudly," said Denis. "He won't be able to hear you."

That paradoxical comment brings the exasperated attention of the audience to a peak. The jerky laughter of a hundred throats rattles in the night.

"Overloaded microphones render the voice unintelligible," said Denis. "It's necessary to speak as if Paulin were as close to us as his image is..."

The commentaries on that fantastic evening contributed in no small measure to augment the consideration that Denis enjoyed, adding to his reputation as a knowledgeable man and munificent fellow citizen the prestige of a man who had set off on the most astonishing and perilous escapade out of commiseration for an aged mother in distress. By the same token, irony fluttered around the church, and the next day, Raymond Alfred, the butcher, had occasion to express straightforwardly what was running confusedly through all minds.

As Monsieur Edmé Malusson, the curé, was passing in front of the butcher's shop, Raymond Alfred, idling on the threshold, stopped him and asked him if he had been in the meadow the previous evening.

"You know very well, my friend," Monsieur Malusson replied, "that Monsieur Aury and I don't know one another, since they judge out there that they're able to do without the church."

"Doesn't alter the fact," said the butcher, "that the Chauvion boy is neither with the good Lord nor the Devil, and that, with all due respect, there's the old lady, ready in recent days to go mad, who's now as well as you or me, in the knowledge of a stone cold verity that has returned her son to her..."

"I don't see what you're getting at," said the priest, ordinary a trifle bad-tempered, and suddenly red in the face. "I fulfilled my ministry in doing my best to console the poor woman...and to prepare her for what hangs over the head of all of us," he added, restraining himself somewhat.

"That's for sure, Monsieur le Curé," said Raymond Alfred, "But Monsieur Denis still has better ways of consoling than you. While one's alive, one's alive, and it's necessary to recognize, all the same, that if she'd stayed on her knees praying to the Blessed Virgin, it wouldn't have helped her to find her son."

"What do you know about it?" said the priest.

"Huh!" said Raymond Alfred, a trifle nonplused. "I know...doesn't alter the fact all this business...this and the electric wheat...and the rain that falls when you want, while, saving your respect, with the good Lord alone, it very often fell with neither head nor tail...and all the inventions that make some who were laboring father and son as many rentiers, as much as to say..."

"It doesn't make them any better!" the curé interrupted, sarcastically. "As many drunkards and fornicators. Nice! And then...what are you getting it?"

"At that all that gives you pause to reflect, Monsieur le Curé, about many things..."

"Aha!" grunted Monsieur Malusson. "Reflect, my friend. You'll be very content, at the end of all your reflections, to find the good Lord!"

They continued apace, the reflections, inexhaustibly maintained by a succession of events, as if Denis wanted to create a bewilderment, a softening of all heads.

On the very next day after the Chauvion film, the screen lights up again, and from that evening onward, the pasture does not lack a public! The projector causes the latest world news of the day to appear, sent from Havas to Denis' home by wireless. For which reason the Sénéçois are vaguely proud to find, the following morning, in the newspapers that have reached them from Paris, the story of events that they had known themselves the previous evening, before even the Parisians! For them it is as if the principal adventures of the planet, by an unprecedented privilege, make a detour in the course of their resonance around the vast world to that little meadow, in order to inform Sénécé before the rest of the earth...

Obscurely, the sentiment comes to them of being a collectivity apart, in a state of confidentiality with the universe...

Along with the information, films and images are projected: voyages all over the globe, with ports of call amid the games and labor of peoples; spectacles filmed from aircraft and submarines, others recorded with the aid of telescopes. The screen shows the sky, at first as it can be seen with the

131

naked eye, and then some of the stars seem to draw closer, growing larger, becoming giants, one revealing its rings, another its corbels of fire, another its mountains wadded with turbulent clouds. The moon confesses its pustulent topography...

Shortly thereafter, a real telescope is installed in the pasture, offering to whoever desires the terrible intimacy of the stars. And the Sénéçois go about, beginning to be penetrated and haunted, in a disorderly fashion, by the countless faces of the world. Certain revelations overflowing with amusement soon attain them more and more profoundly. Carmenton has delivered his films. Projections of images obtained by means of the microscope bring them the secret tribulations of substance.

The know that an ear of wheat, a sprig of Lucerne, an aphid, a crumb of the bread that they eat, a grain of the soil on which they tread, are the abode of monstrous multitudes, the arena of never-imagined vicissitudes. When one thinks about it, when day comes, one hardly dares eat, walk or breathe...

Assuredly, the Sénéçois would have laughed once, if anyone had told them that they did not know what an ear of wheat was, but now they discover, in the flour and in the husk of that ear, as many things to look at, detail and learn as there are in the submarine immensities or in that enormous China of which the screen in the pasture shows them the palaces, the temples, the unctuous and baroque rituals...

The muffled notion forms within them that there is everything still to know, everywhere, that the most commonplace object, every instant, every gesture, every word, is made up of invisible, mysterious and thus-far-unsuspected hosts. The sentiment of molecular life inserts a heavy, imperious, tenacious timidity into their words, their gestures, and their moments. They are, before reality, like primordial humans before the rocks, the trees, the light and the winds full of gods.

Should the projections and astronomy, though, compose for them an ensemble of revelations by which they ought to be so deeply troubled? There is a "Splendid Select Palace" in the town, and often, traveling showmen set up a little tents in the Place de la Mairie in Sénecé itself. There, for a few sous, one can be stirred by the tumultuous rides of Rio Jim and the melancholy buffooneries of Charlot.[21] But what comparison is there between those petty stories and the myriad unfurlment of authentic images of the world? And what comparison between the sidereal splendors delivered to them by the telescope in the meadow, Carmenton's phantasmagorias and what they can have learned about the cosmos and matter at school or from the popularizations in the newspapers?

Finally, even more than the strangeness and magnificence of the white panel, it is them that are new! Those same spectacles, if they would have diverted them before, could not have left a profound imprint in their hardened and blocked minds, heavy with turmoil and servitudes, nor shaken their sensibility, fixed in the few age-old rituals conditioned by that turmoil and servitude. Whereas, at present, the leisure given to them by mechanical transformations has given them the time, the taste, almost the obligation to talk about things at length, with an applications and a warmth in which their unconscious need for action, the unemployed surplus of their physical energies, is dispensed, which compensates for the unacknowledged disillusionment left by the free and excessively frequent enjoyment of traditional pleasures.

---

[21] Charlot was the nickname by which Charlie Chaplin was known in France. When silent movies were provided with French scripts they often underwent transformations, so the pioneering Western feature film starring William S. Hart, *The Bargain* (1914), was retitled *Le Serment de Rio Jim* in French. That reference suggests that the present passage might have been written in 1914, a few months before the outbreak of the Great War, although Hart did remain known as "Rio Jim" in France for some time thereafter. Charlie Chaplin also made his debut in Keystone Studio films in 1914.

For them, tavern games and amusements, hunting, fishing and flirtation, retain so much rudimentary poetry and hereditary excitement, in spite of their satiety, that they remain the categorical definition of what pleasure is. And they do not perceive that in the shadow of their outdated prestige, other fêtes are in preparation, which, without being reckoned as joys or called by that name, are gradually coming to substitute for the old attractions.

Descartes meditating the organization of the *Discours de la Méthode*, and a farmer calculating the purchase of a harrow, would both say that they are thinking. The mind, preoccupied, expresses with the same word two operations whose seat is perhaps the same in the farmer and he metaphysician, but whose object, dimension and materials are incalculably different.

One of the two thought processes is a kind of pandemonium, in which, present, in play and spanned in each of its vibrations, are the most subtle general elements of human nature and the known universe, the sum of the spiritual and temporal experiences and acquisitions of intelligence and science; that thought process runs from one pole to the other and from the commencement of the ages to the distant future; in the same flash of time it judges, weighs, encompasses in its stride empires, continents and systems of ideas that have governed for fifty centuries, and from that innumerable concert, that immaterial unfurling of things, works, beings, facts and noumena, that thought process, from that same vibration, extracts and creates an unprecedented notion that will be the skeleton or the blood of laws, new modes for the universality of human reasoning.

The thought process of the farmer, like those balls of glass that reflect and stretch the garden, will contains a small number of immediate images: the wheat, the tool-shed, numbers... If the cerebral carriage of these images, as slow as the plowshare traveling over the sod, calls itself thinking, and if that invisible work moved by the circular motion of a horse at a mill emerges from the mind, what name does the vertiginous meditation of Descartes require?

Is that not a caricaturish homonym? The truth is that the mind, and thought, only enter authentically in the ultimate analysis into the intellectual adventure that functions in circumstances very rare and singularly severe for the multitude; for there is only automatism and servitude while no irresistible revelation or irresistible necessity has triggered in the individual the heroic decision, the courage and the pitiless honesty to revise for himself the elements and states of his judgments, his sentiments and his actions.

The metaphysician, in saying that in order to attain the truth it is necessary once in life to undo all the opinions that one has received and to reconstruct from the foundations all the systems of his knowledge, is saying that the individual requires nothing less than that honesty, courage and heroism to conduct his investigation through the mass of images, conventions, habits and directions that surround and bathe every aspect of his amassed actions, sentiments and even perceptions, as high, permanent, inevitable and penetrating as the terrestrial atmosphere over his limbs and his lungs.

That investigation, however, is of the same order as those mythological exploits at the terminus of which a hero or a saint, triumphant over weight and duration, rises above that terrestrial atmosphere into the august regions where God is to be seen; it is the great work of knowledge, of discernment and of victory, alone, which elevates the individual to the human condition.

The trigger had been pulled; mind awoke in Sénecé, the gift of the mechanical miracles, of bringing the universe nearer, of an upheaval in every fiber of being and of the sensation of the dense and old notions of necessity and effort, space and time. It was a stammering awakening, akin, on the psychic level to the gesture of the naked man sculpted by Rodin, arbitrarily dubbed "The Bronze Age."[22] The man is stretching his limbs vertically in a heavy manner; it seems that a thousand tiny fibers are tightening, a thousand capillaries quivering and swelling in the numb thickness of the tissues, the spine emerging awkwardly from its horizontal paralysis...

Between that vacillating stretching of the mind in Sénecé and the metamorphosis attempted by Denis, how many false gestures there would have been, creakings of joints rusted by age-old automatisms, how many stumbles in the heavy succession of years and generations...if the experiment had not, in his plan of acceleration, had not anticipated stimulating that birth, spicing the culture-broth...

Simultaneously with the material liberations, he counted on the work of women, and two incisive factors: the excitement of their coquetry and the concrete instinct of possession that makes them urge men to realizing activities.

One small incident is to be the departure point of the feminine intervention: the hazard of a child's drawing in a school exercise book, which the teacher brings to the château one day, laughing. The latter is a friend of Draguin, who got him the appointment at Sénecé. The drawing is by little Savinien Mannevy, the miller's son. Scrawled in the margin of a geography exercise book, it represents, as well as might be expected, a bizarrely-dressed woman, and underneath it, the child has scrawled "Lène."

---

[22] The bronze statue in question, dating from 1876—which was controversial because the sculptor was suspected of casting it from a live model—was originally titled *Le Vaincu* [The Vanquished], but Auguste Rodin changed the title for an unknown reason to *L'Âge d'Airan* [The Bronze Age]. The suggestion was made that he intended an allusion to the demoralization of The French following the Franco-Prussian war, but Rodin never confirmed or denied that supposition, any more than he ever confirmed or denied having taken a cast of the living body of the model.

A few days later, the young sketcher is informed that Madame Aury has had a dress made in accordance with his design. He is in the process of playing tag in his garden when the chatelaine arrives. She has come to pay him a visit and to ask him, with perfect seriousness, whether the dress is as he imagined it when designing it. Alarm and ecstasy of little Savinien at that splendid apparition, which seems to have emerged from his ingenuous pen!

"The next dress as pretty that you design," says the apparition, "I'll have made for your sister Albertine."

Leveil, who has accompanied Lène, questions the astounded children. "What about you?" he says. "Do you also amuse yourselves drawing beautiful images? Toys, furniture for your houses, adornments for your sisters? The teacher will choose the most successful, we'll exhibit them, have them made at the château and give them to you."

A double maneuver.

A deluge of more-or-less ludicrous projects soon rains down on the teacher. The adolescent girls do not hesitate to assist the imagination of their little brothers and sisters in the hope of a dress of a jewel; fathers design caskets, furniture, pendants, in order that the suffrage of the château, after having honored their children, might come back to them well and truly worked, in real and heavy precious metal.

One item of jewelry—a hazardous stylization of an image of the screen, a flower from a garden in Java—having been much admired at the château and executed for Lène, the child who is its so-called author blushes under the felicitations and lets it slip that it was the work of his father. *Bang!* The event enters like a lever into Denis' strategy. Leviel goes to find the father and, at the same time as he offers him, for his wife, a replica of the piece, declares that he is a great artist, and engages him to realize his ideas himself. The château will furnish him with the metals, the crucibles and all the necessary materials.

Scarcely has the turn taken by the child's indiscretion become known than the truth is liberated everywhere. Many good Sénéçois own up to being manufacturers of art, naïve debutants but already impassioned.

Wives and daughters excite their husbands and their young men incessantly to extract ideas from their compact brains and graces from their gross fingers. Here and there an art is sketched, strangely rudimentary, but which instinctively seeks inspiration in its surroundings, subjecting, in massive and despotic impressions the original forms emerged from mechanical upheavals that have been substituted in many places for age-old aspects.

A similar domination of new images is only possible in a very restricted milieu such as a village. The gaze and intelligence of city-dwellers reflects the interpenetration and coexistence of millennial works and modern figures. An entrance to the Metro opens opposite the Louvre, aircraft overfly Notre-Dame the Escurial and the Coliseum. Seeking its elements in its surroundings in Sénecé, art finds an ambience so new that one might mistake it for another planet. The mind senses profoundly modes of life requiring more subtle and looser gestures. The eye is filled by giant machines, familiar engines with a thousand muscles of metal.

Meanwhile, there are still the trees, a river, the sky...

Is it really certain, here, that that tree, the water of the Courtoise, the light of the sun, and the sun itself, are as they seem to be? The telescope and the microscope have filed the vision of the Sénéçois with science and doubt. What they see with their natural eyes, the eyes of their memory decompose, populate and recreate.

As a Georgin, in his little glazed studio in Épinal, translated candidly the signs and images of his time, these new primitives submit to and transpose the spectacles that surround them. They are led, while imagining and fabricating primitive items of furniture, small objects to decorate the house and children's toys, and designing dresses and ornaments for women, to create lines that no longer owe anything to original rituals or ancient needs, or even, sometimes, to the direct conception of things.

Now, here and there, a few hands born for the harrow and the plow, applied to genteel works, the majority with a propensity toward certain objectives once superfluous, a more numerous curiosity, a mental kaleidoscope of universal images...are those the elements with which Denis will recreate humankind? It will be necessary for the images on the screen to become insatiable temptresses, like those which summoned him, as a child, toward a positive embracement of the world; it will be necessary for the curiosity to become an irresistible determination to know, an unparalleled lust to possess by knowledge; it will be necessary for the tentative art to become an amorous, sacred and inextinguishable mission to enrich life and the world.

By contrast with his own adventure, in which superlative passions were unleashed in him by the very attractions that he proposes to the Sénéçois, it is first necessary to give birth in those slow peasants to the force, the enthusiasm, which by their own exaltation with provide them with these exalting attractions. It is first necessary to give birth in them to the faculty of exaltation—in a word, passion, insofar as it is pure dynamism; passion, the primordial fire, the blood of action; the passion without which all possibilities remain dead letters, nebulous whims.

What does the alarm call that awakens them matter? What does the spark that excites these beings matter? In order for the experiment to pass from the first creaks of the mind, widened eyes, petty works and indecisive leisure activities to recreative desires and actions, it is necessary, like the electric fluids streaming through the compact mass of their glebe, that passion should excite and exasperate their nervous batteries, flow like a fever through their fibers in all circumstances. Seeking to expend itself, it will find the paths opened by Denis; seeking to satisfy itself, it will find the materials heaped up at the foot of the endeavor.

IV

A picnic at the home of Joris Krontgen, a Dutchman become a Parisian, an avant-garde artist passionately discussed.
He was, alongside Bernard Leviel, one of those who felt with
the greatest acuity the unusual enrichment brought to all the
arts by the great mental and scientific revisions germinated in
the early years of the century; one of those for whom those
revisions had, in a sense, snatched the penitential hood from
the planet, and for him the light with which it shone, in its
course through the heavenly spheres, was now that of a virginal visage.

The picnic is held at the country house where the painter
spends the summer, a few leagues from Paris, in the heart of a
forest, on the edge of Trigny, a little village on the banks of
the Marne. Everyone arrives with provisions as the day is de-
clining and they establish themselves on the grass of the lawn.
No constraint, no dissonance. They are laughing and mischie-
vous, like idle children, the musicians and painters, sculptors
and poets, some illustrious in the fashion of Krontgen, others
satisfied more discreetly with the delights of an elite. There is
Ravot, whose symphonies serve as the basis for an entire
school of modern music. There is Hellin, the young engraver
who, a few months earlier, had put the light of his audacious
xylographs into Verhaeren's *Débacles*.[23] There are artisans
like Thalburg, who has rediscovered the secret of the blues
and burning reds of Medieval stained glass windows. There
are debutants too, warmed before any other fever by bathing in
the radiance of their elders.

On one of the trees in the garden a large placard is fixed,
jovially illustrated by Krontgen. It is the program of the fête

_____

[23] Emile Verhaeren (1855-1916) was a Begian Symbolist poet;
Les Débacles, originally published in 1888, with a frontispiece
by Odilon Redon, is a study in harrowing despair—not the
only ominous indication contained in this chapter.

140

that will follow the picnic—an elastic program leaving plenty of room for the initiative of the comrades. It is content to announce fireworks at nightfall; a bar with a "continuous flow"—of coco, lemon squash and cocktails—in a corner of the garden; country games; Ennoia,[24] the celebrated chiromancer, expressly brought from Easter Island, will provide oracles in the hut ordinarily reserved for the gardener. The placard also makes mention of an orchestra recruited from the village itself. People can dance if they wish, to the sounds of an accordion, a trombone and a flute. Finally, anticipated in the course of the night is a "Grande Prométheide" by Denis Aury. Those who read the list question one another; Joris, when consulted, replies: "It's a surprise." Denis and Lène have comes with Leviel, who is accompanied by a tall brunette.

The picnic has scarcely begun. Joris, striking the first empty bottle with a knife, sings an old Dutch song whose refrain is curiously accompanied by the knife and forks. Ludmile Arloff, the interior decorator, sitting next to the poet Alain Mariat, sings in her turn, in Russian, one of those ballads in which the massive and desperate anguish that is the core of the Slav soul runs beneath the truculence. Mariat in not really listening, only having eyes for Lène, separated from him by a group of diners. Lène is wearing a dress of golden cloth with fleecy, hyaline white sleeves—"the cream of snow," Joris said, when welcoming her.

Hoisted on to an empty crate, Krontgen announces in a resounding voice: "Those who..."

"Bravo, Krontgen! Glory to the host!"

Krontgen continues: "...Have not brought their percolators are informed that there is coffee at the bar."

---

[24] Given the earlier reference to Flaubert's *Tentation de Saint-Antoine*, this Ennoia presumably echoes the one featured therein as the companion of Simon Magus, memorably featured in an illustration to an 1896 edition by Odilon Redon.

Diners have risen to their feet; the groups are disintegrating.

Mariat has drawn close to Lène.

"What a beautiful creature you are, Madame," says Ludmile Arloff to the brunette accompanying Leviel. She is a young woman, tall, with bold and grave features. The Russian has taken her arm.

Lène and Mariat have remained a little behind.

"Ludmile is very smitten with your friend," the poet says to Lène.

"It will be easy for Madame Arloff to see Edith MacLeara again; she lives with us in Sénecé. She is keen to work with Denis Aury as a secretary.

"MacLeara? But..."

"Her father was the president of the Irish Republic at the most troubled moments of the Independence. After having resigned, he knew rather hard days, and Edith, finding herself poor, has boldly come to seek employment in France. We were lucky enough to be alerted by one of our friends..."

"The luck is primarily hers," said Mariat. "It's enviable to involve one's life with you two. I've been to Sénecé once..."

Shrill and absurd music burst forth a few paces away from them. Behind and against the villa, a floor has been placed over the sand of the garden. The accordion, the trombone and the flute, installed in a little kiosk, have conscientiously launched into a polka.

Hortia Griano, Krontgen's mistress, with the face of an empress beneath her graying hair, approaches Denis. "Shall we open the ball, Aury? Come on, Mariat, Lène, you too..." She draws Denis away.

"I don't want to dance," says Mariat. "Unless you...?"

"They don't need us. The example has been quickly followed..."

The floor is invaded by couples, who set about imitating the heavy gaucherie of country dancers. Others attempt to adapt the mimes of the tango to the naïve music.

"I've been to Sénecé once," Mariat resumes, "taken by Thalburg when he was ornamenting the windows of the gallery leading to the big hall. Do you remember?"

"Of course."

"Yes, your Irishwoman is lucky. I've never forgotten the impression of my brief visit to Sénecé... Enviable, as I say, all those who live in your atmosphere... I'm not only thinking of the most beautiful of chatelaines, but the harmony of your château and that of all the things that are going on around you...around the couple you form, Aury and you," he adds, after a brief hesitation. "I recall three ravishing maidservants...."

"My young maids."

"They looked like princesses..."

"Perhaps they have royal ancestors. They're foreigners. Did you know that certain young women of good education but without significant resources—Danes, Rumanians, Slavs—who want to see the world and to learn, in order to supply their needs in the country that interests them, don't hesitate to obtain places as domestics?"

"In truth, no."

"That is, however, what certain young foreigners willingly do, and those that we've baptized Jade, Ambre and Corail are of that species."

"Where the devil did you unearth them?"

"It's Denis who found them, a long time ago. They ought not to regret having encountered him during their sojourn in France."

"And must no longer have the desire to pursue their pilgrimage across the world."

"I think so. All the more so as domestic labor, in our home, is no longer anything but a phrase. Electricity does all the hard work."

"So that your princesses have been able to become princesses again..."

"Almost. Once their facile tasks are accomplished, Ambre takes pleasure in assisting our friend Leviel. She prepares his colors according to his recipes, accompanies him, penetrates his ideas, refracts them with a fresh and limpid intelligence. Corail assists our friend Draguin with his laboratory experiments, passionately interested in the magic spells that he weaves in his little glass palace..."

"And Jade?"

"That one," the young woman says, laughing, "has found her happiness in adoring me, my gestures, my perfumes. She would gladly remain sitting at my feet all day, laughing at my laughter, breathing through my breast..."

"How gladly I'd trade her blissful livery for all my literary glory, forever!" exclaims Mariat, whose voice, through the emphatic affectation, has a hint of plaintive melancholy.

"Truly!" said Lène, courteously, who has perceived the sadness in the voice. They have arrived at the extremity of the garden and slowly follow a path along an iron trellis that separates them from the forest. The music from the ball reaches them in snatches: the acidic piping of the flute, the wheezy bellowing of the accordion. Flirting couples pass them in the shadows. Other are confusedly perceptible against trees, stifling the laughter that dissolves around stolen kisses while large gilded leaves quiver around the clusters they conceal.

After a few steps in silence, which take them back in the direction of the villa, Mariat says gravely: "The book I'm preparing will be entirely under the influence of the few hours during which I was your guest."

"How charming," says Lène, politely, "and what an honor!"

"I'm not content with it. I'm struggling with the impossible in every poem. I seemed, in your home, to have approached an instant of incredible union with the most perfect signs of happiness...I don't mean such as it's imagined, for the sentiment that has incessantly paralyzed my inspiration is that your reality begins where the imagination, even that of a poet, stops..."

"That's very...eulogistic," says Lène, "but I don't really understand."

"The imagination has only ever been a sort of projection outside of us...in symbols, in songs, in adventures...of that which we cry in our fibers as well as in the innumerable pullulation that we call our soul. But we, with all our soul, are submissive, even taking account of the craziest, most splendid escapes of the spirit, to a certain number of conditions common to the generality...."

"Which means?"

"Samain escapes by means of his imagination his quotidian life as a bureaucrat: 'His soul is a child dressed for a parade...in which exile is reflected, eternal and regal...' Verlaine, between two hospitals, turns to Watteau's beautiful listeners, or the Virgin of good people throughout the centuries. 'O Virgin Mother, Immaculate Mary...white through the wing-beats of the angels,' etc..."[25]

"What are you getting at?"

"This: that I sensed in your home that the ordinary conditions of your life escape the habitual...common...rituals. Your gestures, your ambience, the things and people with which you surround yourselves escape assimilation and comparison...to put it better, the reserve of images, ideas and sentiments in which the poet, even in the finest exaltation of his imaginative faculty, can draw his terms. With the result, in brief, that it would be necessary to live your life in order, as a poet, to use it as the pedestal of a poetry that borrows nothing from that reserve, where Samain's Escurial and Verlaine's Mary are: a poetry creating its ideal world entirely founded on that reality, your reality, which is for those who look at it from outside—even me, a poet—itself and ideal. There."

"I see," says Lène, laughing. "But it's very simple. I invite you to come and finish your book at Sénecé."

---

[25] The quotation from Albert Samain is from "Mon âme est une infante," except that Mariat substitutes "*Son*" [His] for "*Mon*" [My]. The quotation from Paul Verlaine is from "Un conte."

He plucks a few leaves from a bush and rolls them between his fingers. Then he laughs nervously. "That's an idea! Thank you..."

"In any case," Lène adds, "you doubtless won't be alone. In a little while you'll all know about Denis' great project. If the enthusiasm for which he hopes is produced, many artists will come to Sénecé to assist us in our attempt...but I don't want to spoil the surprise..."

"I won't go," he says.

Lène stops dead, astonished.

"The book entirely inspired by your joy would be sad. Listen...something would prevent me from savoring, from living as would be necessary, the life that I sensed out there. Instead of seeing in you only the ideal figure, the emanation, in a sense, and the animating force of all the harmonies that compose that reality, so rare..."

"I'm only one of those harmonies," says Lène. "The animator—the creator—is Denis."

"Perpetually exalted by your presence, your being..."

"No, Mariat. I too am his work."

"Too modest. You don't know? Are there no mirrors at Sénecé?"

"Is that what you have to say to me?"

He hesitates, and then, precipitating his sentences: "Out there I'd be choked, miserable. A spell cast over my eyes, my soul, which would forbid me to raise myself to the contemplation, the reception, broad and pure, of you and things. A savage tension in my arteries...all the egotistical tyranny of desire..."

Lène laughs lightly. "What prevents you from releasing your desire?"

"All sorts of reasons...because it would tarnish, subjugate my spiritual, esthetic impressions to the riots of my blood...and also because that desire would be vain. You're in love, you're admirably beloved. You're invincible..."

"No."

He looks at her, with severity and stupefaction. Momentarily, he searches for face for both the irony that he supposes and the signs of a possible perversity. The visage is clear, cheerful, singularly placid, with dilated pupils. The man is confused.

"You...you scarcely know me," he stammers. "This evening's confession, immense for me, for you nothing but a...let's say a bramble in your path. Do you think that I can compete for you with a man you call the creator...a struggle, in the fashion of primitives...that I could take you from him...?"

"And carry me off to your wigwam? No, not that. Conquer me. Others than you have desired me, Mariat. Conquer me...Denis permits."

"I don't understand."

"Can you imagine that he wants only to hold me with a love perpetually renewed? A love that chooses him incessantly, selects him above all those who might attracts me..."

"The pretention of any lover. I don't see what that has to do..."

"It's that love that he wants isn't a blind and reckless adoration. On the contrary...filling my eyes with all sumptuousness, surrounding me with all the pleasures of the world, he wants to appear to me not as the man to whom I owe all the blossoming that I might attain, but as the man most worthy to be the one to whom, with my eyes incessantly more wonderstruck and clairvoyant, I bring that blossoming."

"A proud pretention, I admit...."

"So, the freer I am, and the more splendid the gift, the greater his victory is, in the measure of that splendor and that liberty."

"Ah! May I be frank?"

"Of course."

"Your greatest splendor seems to me to have for its primary goal that of giving him the testimony of his. It's a pretention of immense pride rather than that of love. It resembles a little, in the moral domain, the sentiment that, for instance, drives a banker to cover a demoiselle with ever more costly jewels in order that she can testify to the opulence of the wallet that adorns her..."

Lène laughs. "You're wicked, Mariat. There's something else to comprehend, for a poet."

"Go on."

"You were seeking just know to know what ideal could depart from our reality. I'll tell you what animates and constructs that reality: an ideal that Denis has set above us, and him, and even our love..."

"Which is?"

"And idea that, as a poet, you might perhaps think sufficiently poetic: that of being in the expansion of all its potentials of joy. Denis has attempted, in himself and in me, to bring that ideal to life. And I am for him the evidence, not of his splendor, but of his idea..."

Mariat sketches a skeptical gesture.

"Yes, Mariat...and to such an extent, with so much sincerity and faith, that he is ready at any moment for the tournament with whatever causes me to marvel, whatever might surpass him, in the name of a joy that might be other and vaster than his. To that joy, he accepts, he would want me to go. That is why I can be conquered. I am not the demoiselle that the banker covers with jewels...I'm the companion and the stake in a perpetual ascension."

"Let's go back to the light and the dancing," says Mariat. "And forget all my follies."

They take a few steps.

"I've judged for myself that you were an exceptional being..." He adopts a negligent tone. "If you were not one of those, I would think, of a love like that of Denis Aury, that your lyricism idealizes it strangely...and that behind that sort of consent to losing you, there is...someone who could tolerate such a consent."

"Which means?" asks Lène, a trifle sarcastically.

"My first impression...a lack of veritable love."

"Truly?"

"I mean exclusive love... The man who lives the life of the beloved individual absolutely, carries that individual within him like the fire of his blood, can no longer accept the thought of being separated from her, the thought of seeing her snatched from his heart... Yes, veritable love is more ferocious, less encumbered by ideas. If a moment comes when your cavalier has to choose, to let you go...ah!...if he loves you, you'll see...the idea...!"

"I don't know," says Lène. "Those moments have come—or, rather, they could have come. It's me who always felt Denis' superiority so forcefully that the adventure stopped short."

Mariat dies not reply. They have reached the ball. Denis is not among the dancers. The Irishwoman, twirling with Ludmile Arloff, brushes the couple and smiles at Lène.

"That Edith MacLeara is beautiful," said Mariat.

"Isn't she?"

"Look," says the poet, abruptly, "You are indeed going to find me very...wicked. The presence of such a secretary next to Denis Aury..."

"My dear Mariat, I'm the one who brought Edith to Sénecé, who placed her with Denis..."

"Curious!"

"Even more curious than you think. I had an urge to gamble. I too wanted to amuse myself in my turn, to risk myself in the same tournament, which ought to oblige me always to be more beautiful, more attractive, than anyone else..."

"Well," says Mariant, sarcastically "it seems to me that it must be a trifle wearing to have keep watch on oneself like that, to worry continuously about possible competition..."

"Yes, for someone who doesn't have the resources to renew herself, to surpass herself, as one of the authors of one of Denis' Bibles implies..."

"We're in the heart of Nietzscheanism, in fact! Is that serious?"

"For someone who has those resources, there is no competition, no effort. One of Denis' familiar comparisons: each of us is in a garden in which the seeds of all flowers are planted. It's sufficient for a little sunlight to strike each seed for it to germinate. You understand, Mariat: no competition, no effort, in order that something should incessantly be germinating within us, if everything that happens in our lives, in our love, plays the role of sunlight within us..."

A crowd at the far end of the garden is bustling around the gardener's shed. One by one, people go in to see Ennoia, who, her evening dress covered by a cloak painted with pentacles, is sitting at a little wooden table. A pale blue paper lantern illuminates the table with a diffuse light, propitious to the pilfering of occult powers. The window of the shed was blocked by a metal sheet that indiscreet individuals soon removed; there is no prediction that has not been overheard by some jeering head leaning toward the curtain. Mocking comments are addressed to anyone who remains too long with the prophetess.

Not far from the lair, those impatient to know the future cluster around Vuermoz, the animal painter, who is known to be steeped in hermetic philosophy and an expert chiromancer himself. With his back to a tree, he gravely deciphers by the light of a lantern the futures attested by the lines of the left hands offered to him for want of Ennoia, too well-patronized. At times, a match or the lighter of one of the audience-members helps him to scrutinize lines that are particularly complex.

It is Edith MacLeara's turn.

"Read that her statue will be made within three months, by me," said Pierre Huvion, the sculptor, to Vuermoz.

"I only say serious things," replies the painter, placidly.

Huvion protests.

"You promise ten statues a day, and only make two a year, slacker!"

"Madame's beauty renders my promise as inescapable as an edict from Fate itself!"

"You next, Denis!" says Edith, when Vuermoz lets her hand fall. She has just perceived Denis among the idlers with Hortia Griano.

"I don't believe in it!" says Denis.

"You're wrong!" Vuermoz protests.

"I make my life, and it's the lines that follow," says Denis, mildly.

"Oho! Well, give me your hand. I'll see what you've altered in the original plan."

Denis holds out his hand.

Vuermoz looks at it and immediately: "Your will...a great faculty of emotion..." He looks more attentively: "A host of intersections...the light's poor...it's necessary to examine scrupulously...."

"What have you seen?"

Vermuoz has gone pale. "Actually, I can't see well enough..."

Someone strikes a match, but Vuermoz has let go of Denis' hand.

"Ah, Comrade Prometheist, I was looking for you...are you ready?" asked Krontegen, arriving at that moment.

"Let's go," says Denis. He follows the painter. The latter says, in his phlegmatic voice: "You'll have difficulty making yourself heard. It's beginning to warm up in the gray matter..."

"Excellent," says Denis. "Where do I operate?"

"In place of the trombone, the flute and the accordion, whom I've sent to get a bite to eat. Wait a minute. I'll announce you with a few fireworks..."

Rising up to either side of the floor installed for dancing, golden flares have filed the garden with a fantastic light and brought the most distant guests back toward their sumptuous fire: the couples that the harsh light has revealed, Ennoia's audience, Vuermoz' clients and those in the bar. Denis has before him a crowd full of murmurs and jokes, scattered in disorder over the benches, sitting in the Turkish fashion at the foot of the kiosk, or sprawling in the grass. Huvion and Hellin have climbed into a tree, in the leafy branches of which lanterns are swaying perilously overhead. The last fireworks cut out burlesque shadows, and their staccato light dances over Denis, standing in a slightly theatrical pose in the kiosk.

"Prometheans!" he cries, suddenly, in a thunderous voice that immediately commands attention. What thaumaturgical farce is the lord of Sénecé bringing to the warm and jovial flower-bed?

"Prometheans!" Denis repeats, caressing the captivate audience with a soft and gentle voice. "There is no one here, who, on hearing that name, does not think themselves summoned personally! I'm talking about the part of you that, whatever to place, the time or the circumstance, maintains its passion aimed at the incessant flow of things, as Prometheus extended his desire toward the clouds in which the fire of Zeus was hidden. I'm talking about that which, within you, always present, burning, insatiable, makes of artists, sensitive, resonant, ravishers!"

Tumult.

"Bravo!"

"Flatterer!"

"What's the surprise?"

"My exordium is preparing it for you," Denis continues. "I have deliberately chosen this picnic, where so many artists are assembled at the same time. Why the word *Prométhéide*? It's because I want to appeal to ardent antennae, the inextinguishable sensitivity that is sacred to you. Why make your works, artists, if not because the eternal force that sent the titan to steal fire in order to give it to humans drives you to enlighten, to enchant, to augment the world with that same fire, revealed and encapsulated in your art? What do you expect, as the supreme goals of your works, if not that they flourish, in the desert of the ages, like oases of peace and light where travelers plagued by all the simooms of humankind might pause? I am bringing you a work that corresponds to those goals...and which no longer requests of you the brush, the chisel or the pen but that which guides the brush, the chisel or the pen. I bring you human beings themselves, and deliver them to you, on whom you may act, not by the trickery of our works, but by the direct shaping by your passionate and subtle humanity of their humanity in genesis."

A pause.

"I bring you a race before which each of you will be akin to the lord Lord God before the primal clay. But I have prepared the clay for you, comrades! Let us correct the enormous error of the Scriptures. It is not true that the old Lord God made humans. It was a hybrid creation that emerged from the famous handful of dust. What the diabolical or jovial Creator breathed into it was not humanity but the illusion of humanity! Clay that believed itself upright, capable of love, of joy, of dreaming...that was the farce of the sixth day!

"Have not the great majority of the descendants of that clay remained eternally incorporated in that earth, narrowly regulated by the massive laws of the earth? Is it not the case that what its illusion names its dreams, its joys, its amours...and its works, its troubles, its wars...are sticky with mud? It is that monster of which I have taken hold, comrades. Such as Jehovah made it, and such as he abandoned it...at present, I bring it to you having worked upon its matrix...I have washed it, raked it and scoured it of the thick laws that begrimed it. The monster, in my hands, has become chaos again, like the clay before the generating breath, but that chaos is that of the dreams and the joys of the clay, and within the primordial illusion is stirring. Your work will be to make the mirage of Adonai a reality. Will you who know the sign, you who, among the spoiled clay of Adonai, hold and manipulate the fire of Prometheus, help me to extract, from that magma, the real human being?"

Indistinct murmurs. Denis cuts the air with an abrupt gesture. "Enough prosopopeia! This is the adventure, comrades! I invite those of you who wish to do so to come and stay and Sénecé. Residences, simple but pleasant, will be offered to each inhabitant, lunches, snacks and dinners at the château. The pretext for the invasion, in the eyes of the indigenes, will be a series of fêtes that I'm preparing, about which we'll talk again out there. In reality, my design...is to lodge the males in houses rich in daughters, the women in those where boys are more numerous. Very easy, your work, comrades: it will be sufficient for you to be there. It's from that that I expect flavorsome perturbations. And it is thus that you will blow into the clay that I mentioned just now.

"I want to put my haggard Séneçois in immediate contact with your tastes, your visions, your actions, made of choice, space and originality. Such will be the spells that you will cast without effort, such are the keys with which you will open to my unbalanced dullards the notion of a possible, real and different humanity. But what will that notion be, if you do not give it force and life by the passions that, it goes without saying, you will trigger.

"Men with voices of fire, honey and benzoin, men with eyes rich in so many contemplated splendors, to merit a glance from your opulentissimal eyes, the daughters of Sénecé will feel obliged to call upon the arms of seduction and grace that I have prepared for them, and which are still trembling in their inexpert fingers...

"Women of all sapiences and all delicacies, the boys, in order to please and conquer you, will have to put to work the talents and gentilities that I have rendered possible to them, but which are not yet for them anything but the alphabet of a language devoid of poetry, the scattered beads of a rosary that awaits its god...."

Muffled protests, hesitant at first. Someone shouts: "And what about those who are married?"

"At your risks and perils, the escapade!" Denis ripostes. "But let's not distort its character. I'm asking you to be, by means of the indispensable unleashing of passion, the animators of a race toward superior goals, labors and desires to which I have already given a creative virtue. It's that task alone that occupies us: that is the *Prométhéide!* Passion is only one element of the adventure, the boiler of the machine, not the work. As for...accidents of the labor, I appeal...to your honesty. And if one of you is smitten with one of my Séneçoises, or one of the local lads…my seigneurial blessing on the couple!"

3

I

Juste Jubier, a reporter on the staff of the *Grand Journal*, got off the train at Crennes. It was necessary to travel eight kilometers by road to reach the village, and a further kilometer and a half to reach the château.

Monsieur Aury will surely have sent his auto for me, the journalist thought.

He was disagreeably surprised, on going through the gate, to find that there was only one automobile outside the station, into which the other passengers from the train climbed. They appeared to Jubier to be local landowners or well-to-do tourists.

As for the auto, it was no ordinary vehicle! As large as an autobus, what one could see of the interior made one think of the sumptuous modern drawing rooms that architects design. First of all, Jubier perceived violet cushions ornamented by gold trim, negligently scattered, and the banquettes—at least twenty seats—were gray velvet with floral patterns. Each spacious place was separated from its neighbor by a panel of bright wood, delicately carved, it seemed…it was necessary to go closer to discern the characters of the flowers represented therein.

More astonishing still was the exterior. The bodywork was painted, with bizarre pictures. Juste could make out fields with hayricks, a forest with masses of trees, a village with its houses, and the fields and hayricks, the forest and the trees, the village and the houses, were inflected and inclined, painted sideways—in sum, as if seen by a drunkard…or, if you like, as if being traversed by a fast-moving auto…

Although amused, Jubier could not remain there indefinitely. He thought about taking the first train back to Paris, in order to give this Monsieur Aury a lesson in politeness.

"Are you going to Sénecé? Aren't you getting in?" asked an extremely chic gentleman with white suede gloves who was standing beside the immense auto. He added: "It's the station omnibus, and transport is free."

"I'm expected by Monsieur Aury," Juste replied. "I'm astonished..."

"If Monsieur Aury hasn't sent a car, it's doubtless because he wants you to go through the village on foot before arriving at his house. You won't regret it, Monsieur. This vehicle will drop you off at the entrance to Sénecé, in front of the Deux Collines café. I'm the owner of the café. Get in, if you please."

That elegant chauffeur a village café-proprietor? It is appropriate for a good journalist to accord a certain confidence to the unexpected, and Juste had all the more reason to expect the unexpected here because the purpose of his reportage was, as well as interviewing Monsieur Aury, to make a visual study of the village about which extraordinary rumors were beginning to circulate. The President of the Council—the *Grand Journal* had revealed—had recently told a few close friends that the Government was keeping a close eye on what was happening in Sénecé; that a wealthy landowner there was amusing himself by putting his fortune in the service of his generous ideas, and was carrying out a rather original experiment there...

All that was known, in any case, was mere gossip, doubtless exaggerated, spread by tourists. The *Grand Journal* had decided that it was worth the risk of sending a reporter. Juste's mission was to penetrate as delicately as possible the personality of the philanthropist, estimate at their true value the eccentricities of Sénecé, and extract a sensational article from his expedition.

He climbed into the auto. The café-owner with the white gloves got in behind him, closed the door and sat down at the steering-wheel. Scarcely had the vehicle moved off than he said to Juste: "You've never been to Sénecé?"

157

"Indeed no," said the journalist, "but I've heard mention of the village in the home of the President of the Council."

"Perhaps you're a député, Monsieur?"

"No, I'm…"

A journalist at work ought not to reveal his profession to just anyone, for fear that people might immediately envelop him with circumspection, as a snail retracts its horns and withdraws into its shell. It is only in the milieux of the theater, letters and the magistracy that a reporter sees manifest around him the power that he has of printing a name—the same phenomenon of attraction that draws flies toward a dung-heap. In the majority of other social categories, people, however vain they might be, still prefer silence to the risk of seeing a curiosity attracted to them of which they cannot know in advance whether it will be sympathetic, mocking or overly inquisitive.

"I'm a friend of the Presidency," Juste said. "And I write in the papers from time to time."

It goes without saying that there cannot be any question, for a reporter, of lying about his identity. That would be using the method of the police. It is sufficient to handle the revelation of his estate with prudence and delicacy, in order not to alarm people and to give the impression that the estate in question is not incompatible with sensitivity or intelligence.

"If the newspapers knew their business," says one of the passengers, "they'd have sent us reporters a long time ago. Sénecé is a place that doubtless has nothing like it anywhere else in the world."

"But that's precisely…," said Juste

"Let the reporters stay where they are!" said another passenger. "The best thing is to leave us tranquil in our corner. What would be the point of exciting a heap of poor people by telling them what's happened in Sénecé? No one could imitate us. There aren't two Aurys in the world."

"It appears, in fact…," said Juste.

"Look," said the first passenger, pointing at a box that he had set down beside him on the banquette. "There's a microscope in there that I've brought back from Paris. It's one of the best. The State laboratories don't have many as good. Poor scientists! The merchant mistook me for an American chemist. Scarcely anyone but Americans have the means to buy apparatus like this. What would he have said, that merchant, if he's known that he was talking to a butcher? A butcher from Sénecé, it's true..."

"Monsieur is...?" asked Juste.

"Yes, Monsieur. Raymond Alfred, Place Jacques. You don't find many butchers who have the means—and the leisure—to have a passion for biology. We're all at that point, in Sénecé. Except for a few fossils deaf to all progress, everyone has his interest, some in the sciences, others the arts... For my part, I've got a taste for biology. What a marvel, Monsieur! What a source of excitement!"

"Ah! Monsieur..," Juste approved, politely.

"And what horizons, Monsieur, the contemplation of the infinitely small opens to thought! Monsieur Bailhard here, who occupies himself with astronomy, sees in the movements of the most formidable planets, movements absolutely parallel to those revealed for me by a molecule..."

"Science is full of surprises," said Juste, prudently He turned toward the passenger named Bailhard. "Monsieur is an astronomer?"

"A grocer, Monsieur. The Bailhard grocery, father and son...but for some years..."

Monsieur Bailhard launched into a strange speech in which the study of the stars was mingled with the sale of alimentary goods. While listening, Juste studied the attire of his companions with amazement. Raymond Alfred was dressed in a white flannel suit, whose trousers, turned up in the English fashion, allowed a glimpse of dead-leaf silk socks emerging from fine morocco-leather shoes. His white gloves were negligently turned back at his wrists. As for the grocer-astronomer, he could have been called Monsieur le Comte de Bailhard since birth and would not have worn more casually his costume of beige sports jacket, narrowed at the waist, and gleaming silk shirt with the collars turned down over a grenadine scarf secured by a pearl pin.

All the other passengers were as elegant as the amiable café-proprietor-driver.

Are all these Sénéçois millionaires? thought the journalist.

The road descended gently, and Sénecé came into view beyond the spinneys and the large meadows traversed by the Courtoise. The village seemed to be a cluster of multicolored bell-towers, flowery terraces and scintillating cupolas. Two hills rose up at the entrance to Sénecé, or, rather, who enormous dazzling massifs of bright flowers; one seemed, at a distance, to be wearing a red mantle, the other, all yellow, gave the impression of being enveloped in velvet the color of the sun.

"The view is delightful," said Juste.

"The hills, eh?" said the café-owner. "One, they were two frightful mounds, bare and rugged, like two surly guard-dogs at the threshold of the village. Now they've become two sprightly bonjours. It was an idea of Monsieur Leviel, the painter, whom you'll doubtless see at the château. The hills were remade, as one replaces faded bouquets on a mantel-piece. Everyone lent a hand. You should have seen the machines rounding off the rugged crests, others turning over the ground, piling up the earth...and all of us, bringing seeds, watering, weeding, pruning...the red hill is planted with purslane, columbine and sage, the yellow one with gorse and two kinds of marigolds. It's nice, isn't it? Anyway, here we are..."

The vehicle drew to a halt with a soft hiss of the brakes. The passengers got down, saluting Juste, who returned the gesture.

"Come into the café for a minute," said the driver. "Take a little something—it will give you the stomach for your astonishments."

Juste had the impression of finding himself confronted by a copy, on a reduced scale, of the Restaurant de la Cascade in the Bois de Boulogne. The façade was all glazed. On the threshold there were four large steps of red-tinted milky stone, not unlike agate. Inside, the furniture, the counter and the walls were a dazzling white, like that of porcelain, ornamented with red arabesques, soberly distributed. The tables were made of vast plateaux resting on feet as broad as columns.

"I have a little Burgundy wine that will please you," said the proprietor. "Permit me to let you taste it."

He went behind the counter. On the wall there were several rows of buttons, of the same red as the stone of the steps. The café-owner pressed one of the buttons.

Juste had leaned on the counter. Suddenly, a few centimeters from his elbow, a rectangle in the counter folded back like a shutter, giving way to an emergent slab bearing a dusty bottle and a glass.

"Oh...ah!" stammered Juste.

"It's amusing, isn't it?" said the proprietor. "The button acts electrically on an arm in the cellar, in front of the rack of bottles corresponding to the customer's choice. The order of the buttons on the wall corresponds to the disposition of the different liquids. There's a whole set of mechanisms that bring the orders to the tables, where they arrive from inside the columns forming the feet."

"Very ingenious," said Juste. "But isn't it a great deal of trouble to achieve a result simple enough to obtain manually?"

"In truth, Monsieur, that's the way things are done in Sénecé. Small or big results, it's all the same. I don't say that I'd have any great trouble going to fetch my wine from the cellar, but when it's a matter of rolling a barrel, bottling its contents, or cleaning the establishment, for example, it's very agreeable only to have to press one of these buttons, here or there. Then again, there are a lot of little mechanisms that are just whims, luxuries, One makes them to amuse oneself. One seeks, one invents. Everyone puts his self-esteem into having ideas to liven up his work. Here, taste this Burgundy for me..." He turned toward the control panel on the wall again.

"You'll get your gloves dirty uncorking this venerable bottle..."

161

"Not in the least. I shan't touch it. Sometimes we do with our hands things that we once had to do for work, but it's uniquely for distraction, or for physical exercise."

While he was speaking a white annulate tube as stout as an eel descended slowly from a round opening in the ceiling and oscillated in front of the counter. The café-owner seized it and fitted it to the bottle by means of a kind of metal sleeve at the extremity of the tube. There was a hiss, the sleeve carrying away in an internal vice the cork that had just been removed.

"There's no more to do than drink," said the proprietor.

The bottle was perfectly clean, its dust having been removed as if captured by the sleeve.

He filled the glass. Juste picked it up and sniffed it with the sudden respect inspired by the amber color of the liquid.

"It's a Montrachet...very drinkable...," said the proprietor.

"What a bouquet!" said Juste.

He took a sip, rolled it around his mouth, closed his eyes and smacked his lips "If I were the king of France," he said, flippantly, "I believe I'd make it my *ordinaire*."

"It would be sufficient for you to live in Sénecé," the other replied. "It's one of our habitual wines."

Several questions were jostling in Juste's skull. From their entanglement one emerged: "Is everyone in Sénecé rich, then?"

"Very rich. The majority of the machines that do the work were originally furnished by loans of such long term that the purchase price is amortized without being perceptible, or as good as. They've simplified, augmented and improved the quality of production in such proportions that it's retained in advance, either by the town or by shareholders, at prices above the norm. Hence the tidy profits for our producers. They'll soon be as rich as rentiers...but what am I saying? They already are rentiers, or as good as, since their work is done without them. Where do they spend their money? On luxury goods? The pleasures of the towns? The goods they can send for. Bailhard, the grocer, Raymond Alfred, the pastry-cook

Lauvin, Madame Gorgère, who was one a fou-sou mercer, me...we can afford all the finest and rarest—and we enrich it ourselves, that trade. As for the pleasures of the town, we have them here. I dare say, in fact, that we're a hundred years ahead of those that the wealthiest Parisians can offer themselves..."

"You're joking!"

"We move, Monsieur, we're up to date. The Sénéçois go to Paris when they want, and further afield...but they come back! They don't find the material advantages of Sénecé anywhere else, nor the moral atmosphere, which is also in advance by I don't know how many..."

Juvenile laughter sounded nearby.

"That's my daughter laughing with the maidservant," the proprietor said. "You'll see a fine specimen of a demoiselle."

He went to open a small door opening into a garden. "Thérèse!"

Juste scarcely had time to perceive beyond the door a kind of firework display of flowers, a dazzling multitude of species. A young woman had appeared. What! Was that the daughter of a village café-owner, a country girl? An actress could not have been more perfumed and made up, and what attire! White muslin embroidered with silk, girdled with a silver tress; the arms, neck and shoulders bare, a silver torsade surrounding the short-cropped hair; the feet shod in little white leather boots, creased at the top in the Russian style.

"I have to take the omnibus out again," the café-owner said to his daughter. "Keep this Monsieur company for a moment." To Juste, with a smile that seemed ambiguous to the reporter, he said: "Excuse me."

He went out. Immediately, with the casual ease that frequentation of the most various milieux and the habit of adventures give to a journalist, Juste said: "I'm amazed, Mademoiselle. I didn't expect to find such perfect elegance and grace in a village. I'm a Parisian, and I rub shoulders on a daily basis with the most exquisite enchantresses of high society and the theater, but I don't think I've ever seen...undoubtedly there's some kind of social gathering today at the nearby château? Or doubtless you're a Parisienne visiting your father. Haven't we met before in Paris?"

"I don't think so..."

"Aren't you in the theater?"

"Well, like all the young women in Sénecé, I amuse myself by acting from time to time..."

"Ah! The young women? There's a theater here? What do you put on? Du Flers and Cavaillet? Or the classics, perhaps?"

She laughed and said: "Do you think so? We perform old songs or rounds, arranged by a great musician, Monsieur Ravot, a friend of Monsieur Denis..."

"Ravot! Really! Damn!"

"In the rounds and songs, one represents the subject instead of simply singing. It makes for delightful spectacles. We perform in the square and the fields...anywhere the place can serve as a setting. At present we're rehearsing a song you surely know. '*We were ten girls in a meadow/All ten of us to marry...*'"

"*There was Chine...There was Dine…,*" sang the journalist. What can one do with that?"

"Splendid things. Everybody's working on it. Some are designing the costumes, others inventing the accessories, others performing. The bed in which the son of the king takes La Dumaine will be magnificent. All in gilded and sculpted wood, surmounted by four immense plumes of peacock feathers. Savinien Mannevy, the miller's youngest, has designed it. The king's son, mounted on a white charger covered with a silver sheet will come out of the forest on the edge of the meadow where we're plying. To finish, a cortege of lords and knights, is costumes of all eras, will escort the king's son and La Dumaine all the way to the village, so those who can't come to the performance will see the best bit anyway, without having to disturb themselves."

"That's admirable! I write in the newspapers from time to time, as I was telling your father. I'll come back from Paris expressly and take a photograph. And I'll write a nice article about the fête. When is it? Which Sunday?"

"Why do you expect it to be on a Sunday? In Sénecé, we have all week to work of fêtes, and which serve for fêtes..."

"A pleasant land! And the heavy tasks, in the meantime. Even admitting that machines...perhaps there are slaves?"

"There are machines and apparatus, yes. As for slaves..." She laughed. "I'll introduce you to mine. I was rehearsing with her just now when Papa called. She's playing the lovely Suzon in the song. I'm the Duchesse de Montbazon."

She went to the little door and called: "Berthe!"

A second young woman appeared. She was as richly ornamented as Thérèse, clad in a shiny royal blue smock secured at the waist by an amethyst belt, similarly powdered and bareshouldered, her feet bare, in dainty blue buskins with violet laces.

Juste was beginning to feel troubled.

"Mademoiselle...," he said.

A maidservant! He felt suddenly very agitated. What the devil? He would take the time to find out how it came about that a serving girl could be dressed in that fashion, in the middle of a weekday afternoon, and how it could be that the daughter of a café-owner...and also how...there were too many *hows* and *whys* to satisfy, since he had emerged from the station. He would put them in order later. The father was going to come back at any moment. And then, Juste would have to go... It would not be said that two such beautiful creatures had passed within his reach...especially these creatures, so singularly made-up, half-undressed...

He thumped the counter lightly and said: "Mademoiselles, you can't stay in Sénecé. Such as you are...your old songs, that's very nice, but before an audience of Séneçois...you must come to Paris. That's where you belong. I have friends in real theaters. And then...let's see...I don't have much time today. We need to meet again. I envisage a heap of things for you..."

"Monsieur," said Thérèse, "if you had an auto outside the door, you'd be proposing to abduct us..."

"Undoubtedly!"

"You're not the first, Monsieur," said Berthe. "A lot of tourists pass through this café."

Well," replied Juste, slightly put out, "that proves that there are people of taste among the tourists..."

"We please you?" Thérèse demanded.

"I'm absolutely seduced, and..."

"That's always nice to hear," said Berthe. "Which of us to do like the best?"

"But...," stammered the journalist, "you're both so delightful...."

He heard himself babbling and pulled himself together. Oh, the hussies! Were they deliberately mocking him? He'd seen others... A Juste Jubier... The *Grand Journal*... Paris...the wings...Enough good fortune behind him, thank God...

"Don't bother," said Thérèse. "There's no need." She assumed an expression suggesting that she wanted to be serious. "Tell me, Monsieur," she said, "What would you have offered, to the one you would have chosen?"

"But...Mademoiselle...," said Juste, nonplussed. "An...enthusiastic amour...sentiments..."

"What is it that you put into your amour?" Thérèse demanded. "Tendernesss?"

"Certainly! A tenderness that doesn't exclude..."

"Passion," said Berthe. "Male passion, mad kisses."

"Yes," said Juste, who was beginning to feel disorientated.

"An art of caresses…," Thérèse continued.

"Oh, I should say so!" Juste exclaimed, and thought: *What are these young women?*

"Banal, your amour, Monsieur," said Thérèse. "That's all that you have to propose?"

"If I were the king of Golconda, I'd throw all my treasures at your feet. You'd walk over carpets of diamonds. But all in all, my situation, my relations, for want of millions…one has a good time with me…balls, theaters…"

"Caresses, money, balls…that's not the amour for us," said Thérèse. "You have to take all that to the old women of Sénecé."

"What do you want, then?"

"Wait until you've seen other Séneçoises than us," said Thérèse. "You get excited easily."

"My poor Monsieur," said Berthe, "merely by walking through the village, all the young women you'll encounter will drive you mad. You won't arrive at Monsieur Aury's alive."

"Why not?"

"We're far from being the prettiest, the most elegant…"

The café-owner came back in.

"Papa," said Thérèse, "this monsieur is very smitten with the two of us; he wants to take us to Paris, but we've advised him to make a tour of Sénecé before abducting us…"

"Aren't they lovely girls?" said the café-owner, joyfully. "But you're not drinking," he added, looking at the bottle, still full.

"*Au revoir*, Monsieur," said Thérèse.

"*Au revoir*, Monsieur," said Berthe.

"Mesdemoiselles…"

They disappeared. They could be heard laughing. Juste took out his handkerchief and mopped his forehead.

"I confess…I've never seen…I don't understand."

"Monsieur Aury will explain it to you," said the café-owner, blithely. "You're not at the end of your surprises."

"I need to hurry to the château. Don't think for a moment that I seriously wanted to abduct those demoiselles… A few amiable remarks."

"Don't apologize, Monsieur," said the café-owner. "You're not the first."

That remark aggravated the journalist for a second time. "And you're not afraid, for your daughter?"

"Afraid?"

"Pretty and well-dressed as she is..." Juste, seething with both incomprehension and chagrin, exploded: "After all, damn it, your daughter's a woman! Amour is something that still exists, even in Sénecé."

"Undoubtedly. But our daughters have an idea of amour that isn't the same as before."

"Before?"

"Before the arrival of Monsieur Aury and all the great changes."

"Zut!" said the journalist. "I need to have all this explained, starting with the a b c...but whatever it is, setting amour aside, before a daughter like yours, any normal man would experience..."

"Ah! Well, yes. You want to talk about sweet talk, gallantries..."

"Desire, in fact!"

"I understand very well. In truth, our children like to please, and the boys here, as everywhere else, are sensible to their charms...but the boys and girls alike have other preoccupation and pleasures that divert them from the road to which desire lead...that desire..."

"What pleasures?"

"Well...the efforts that our lads have to make to shine in the eyes of the lasses, in the arts, in inventions—in sum, by some talent or other. Our girls were, it must be said, dazzled once by artists from Paris. To reach the heights of the memories that they left behind...but wait. In return, the boys expect from the girls the finesse and the grace that for which the female artists who came at the same time left them a taste. The result...how can I put it?...is that the desire you're talking about fragments, on the way, into all sorts of desires, satisfactions, in which the eyes, the sense of smell, the soul...yes, Monsieur, and pride too...which take their enjoyment and find sensualities there...I'll go so far as to say just as vivid, just as pleasant, and those that in the rest of the world one finds in..." He laughed. "In friction... You know what I mean..."

"I'm wondering what time I'll arrive at the château," said Juste. "If Monsieur Aury's waiting for me... But it's really his fault. How much do I owe you for the bottle?"

"You haven't touched it. Permit me to make you a gift of the few drops you've drunk."

"Thank you. Anyway, I expect that we'll see one another again. At the rate things are happening in your village, I think I'll be obliged to come back several times, if I want to write an article that won't send the reader to Bicêtre."

Informed as to the route to take, Juste set off across the fields that extended for several hundred meters before the first houses of Sénecé. He had not taken fifty paces when he perceived an old peasant in one of the fields, with dirty trousers, a soiled straw hat and coarse features. The man was pushing a plow that three horses were pulling with great effort.

Well! thought Juste, astonished. *So there are still plows, horses and men without white gloves in Sénecé! The café-owner wanted to put one over on me! Of course! It would have been too ludicrous.*

He went to the edge of the field and shouted: "Hey! Monsieur!"

With a "Hoo! Hoo!" the old man stopped his horses.

The reporter asked the way to the Aury château.

The peasant shrugged his shoulders and went back to work, muttering.

Juste went into the field, marching on tiptoe to avoid the stains of the greasy ground, went to the man and repeated the question.

"Eh? Straight ahead. You can see it perfectly well, that way, after the village. No lack of people there to show you the way." He turned away and shouted: "Hey up!" at his horses.

"You don't seem to like strangers," said Juste.

"That depends," the peasant replied. "For those going to that evil man's house, I don't have any tenderness. They'll find enough of it in the village. Hey up!"

"I'd like to have a few words with you," Juste persisted. "I have business at Monsieur Aury's house. I don't know him. I've been told all sorts of things about him. Why do you call him an evil man?"

"I've nothing to say to you."

"Come on, old chap, don't be like that," said Juste. "Have a cigarette. I assure you that you'd be doing me a favor. I've been told that Monsieur Aury is an admirable man. I've been told that In Sénecé no one works with his hands any more, but here you are with your plow like all worthy peasants everywhere..."

"Worthy peasants! They don't exist in Sénecé anymore. There might be half a dozen like me, who don't want to abandon the land—the others are all messieurs! Oh, God have mercy! Your Monsieur Aury has brought evil to Sénecé. People who were honest cultivators, father and son, spending the good Lord's time playing music, looking at insects through opera-glasses of some sort, and many other stupidities. The lads, the lasses...the youth is lost...one doesn't dare go through the streets any longer, for the shame of it...And on top of all that there's that lot at the château, Monsieur Aury's whore and the rest...who show off to the children in costumes that would have had them locked up in my day..."

"Thank you," said Juste. "I see that I was right to be on my guard. Thank you. *Au revoir*, old chap."

He held out his hand; the other took it.

"There's no government. The Republic, liberty, is permitting saracens like that to ravage the land. You can repeat that at the château if you like. I've nothing to expect from them. Hey up! There!"

Amazing! Juste said to himself, when he had resumed his route. *I believe it's going to be amusing.* He hastened his pace.

A few minutes later he reached the first houses. The high street opened in front of him.

He stopped, his eyes dazzled, as when the gaze is struck by a reflection of the sun from the silvering of a mirror. From the paving of roadway and the stone of the sidewalk, the faces and roofs of the houses, there was an innumerable explosion of variegation, an avenue, a multicolored corridor of flamboyance, an immense page detached from a book of Russian images, a cathedral close whose stained glass windows reflected to infinity the forms of slabs and pillars, vaults and walls. The bewilderment was such that Juste put his hand over his eyes, uttering a sonorous oath. His own exclamation restored his aplomb. He stood still, examining his commotion.

Am I in a fairy tale, in an enchanted village?

Here, uniform stone, framed by arabesques and mosaics; there, perfectly regular paving stones, each of which had a different glaze, whose assembly formed a figure, like those formed by children's building blocks; the roadway with its polychromatic sidewalks alongside, evoking the bright fabrics of Persia or India. As for the houses, some of them were painted from the threshold to the attic in flat colors, interrupted by the different colors of the doors, shutters, curtains or flowers climbing the walls; others were decorated with frescoes, like old Italian houses.

And it was not only the torrential rush of colors that held the reporter pinned on the thresholds of the extraordinary street, but also the bewildering diversity of the houses. Few among them had conserved their original architecture beneath the adornment of mosaics or frescoes—the design common, save for regional characteristics, to the general run of village houses. Many seemed to have been reconstructed on new principles, in a style that seemed, at first glance, jarring and eccentric...

The spectacle, in its entirety, was hallucinatory, giving the impression of a gigantic petrified carnival.

Juste, steeling himself against all amazements, went forward. Seen at close range, the houses, the paintings, and the mosaic designs, had something gauche and primitive about them, as if they were the work of rudimentary artists, but they also had, in many parts the delightful discoveries of the naivety of primitive arts. A desire to ornament, to inscribe grace or gaiety with the minimum of detail, seemed to have directed the architects...

But who could those have been, except the Sénéçois themselves? That soon became apparent to Juste. Indeed. Here and there, inside houses, through open doors and in the doorway, people could be seen, some equipped with brushes and pots of paint, others armed with chisels, working on embellishments to the stone, woods or ironwork. Juste would never have thoughts that the vulgar collars of sheet metal retaining the various pipes along the walls could be the pretext for ornamental decorations. It sufficed for them to be painted with a line of color contrasting with that of the pipe or the all, chiseled with a flowing arabesque... The colored head of a nail became a golden dot, a vivid flower, a star. The hinges of doors, the grooves, even the joints, played their decorative role in being emphasized by a streak of color.

A young woman went by, deflecting Juste's curiosity from the strange esthetic of Sénéçois edifices. Her stride scarcely extended, for she was walking in sandals. A scarlet silk tunic left her cleavage exposed, molding her breasts tightly; tightened at the waist, it descended in two long flaps over a black velvet skirt. The red sandals slyly darted a flame at every step. The mocking warning given to him in the café echoed in the reporter's head: "My poor Monsieur...you won't arrive at Monsieur Aury's alive."

A desire gripped Juste to follow and overtake the young woman, and then to stop her, in order to contemplate, when she went past him again, the rude quivering of her breasts in their ardent sheath more terrible than nudity...

While he was hesitating, other young women went by, and his hesitation was suddenly resolved. He remained rooted to the spot, his senses petrified.

Not all of them were beautiful, no doubt, and a few had a certain rustic heaviness in their gait, but they were all dressed in such a manner that the eye, overloaded by the richness of the fabrics and the audacity of the arrangements, could not linger on any displeasing detail. A singular combination of new research and the resurrection of illustrious graces, images by Perugino, Luini and Raphael, added to the wondrous surprise of the journalist. Some, in dresses of bright cloth covered in hand-painted flowers, espoused the body with pleats and soft undulations, evoking the most sumptuous figures of painters, and two went by whose beautiful hair was crowned with torsades of pearls and enamels like those with which Botticelli had ornamented so many of his heroines. Another, meanwhile, was dressed in a kind of surcoat of blue cloth, with ample pleats, covering a sulfur waistcoat, such that Juste exclaimed to himself: *Impossible! They have a branch of Poiret in Sénecé!*

Suddenly, a debate began timidly in his consciousness, concerning the nature of the sentiments that had immobilized him at this point in his expedition. Had he been stopped solely by the desire to inform the readers of the *Grand Journal* about the strangeness of Sénecé, and more particularly, Séneçois feminine fashions, or was it by an entirely personal delectation, which, overflowing curiosity and duty peripherally, if one could put it like that, was taking over the emotive centers in a redoubtable fashion?

He put an end to the debate by remembering that he was expected at the château. Certainly, Monsieur Aury ought to have sent a car for him...and any delay could, in sum, be excused as having been caused by the lord of the manor himself...but to interview Aury was to have the key to the fabulous village. It was to have the means, on the return journey, of knowing how to talk to these young women, and what their vulnerable points were... The gibes of Thérèse and Berthe still sounded in his ears. Gallantry mocked fears the laughter of beauty...

He went on. Glimpsed through gaps between houses, gardens blossomed behind wooden fences painted in cheerful colors, some sculpted. There was always the same firework display of species, the same floral eruption as in the garden at the Deux Collines, which he had only seen for an instant. The young women in flowery dresses whose had passed by a moment before, and those he could see in the distance, seemed to prolong these gardens, mingling them with the ongoing life of the village.

Charming! Juste thought. *But does no one eat in Sénecé. Thus far, of butchers and bakers, not a shadow. Of course! They have the famous pills predicted for evolved humankinds! That's the secret of the cuisine that permits the beautiful Thérèse and her slave, to be made up like Monico's boarders at three o'clock in the afternoon...*

He kept up the monologue as he hastened his steps.

So it's not astonishing that the butcher of the autobus devotes himself to biologism and the grocer to the contemplation of the stars, But...the Montrachet? Holy flattery!

Expressing his uncertainty in that jovial fashion, he arrived in a large square, and his questions were satisfied. He perceived a baker's sign immediately, a butcher's, a fruiterer's and several taverns. The coquetry and luxury of the shops in question offered an abundance of temptations to linger, but he was firmly determined to put off all curiosity until his return from the interview. He did, however, have time to observe that the loaves displayed in the baker's window were uncommon in shape, and that their vermilion crusts were ornamented with figures in relief.

All the same, he said to himself, *sculpting bread really is a matter of having time to waste...*

II

"My poor dear, there's another coffee spoiled," says Cahoche, putting down his cup. "Look at this mass of grounds at the bottom."

Madame Cahoche shrugs her shoulders despondently.

"The cook must have shaken the filter to make it pass through more rapidly. Ring. I'll take a little alcohol. A drop of brandy will help the dregs of the coffee go down."

Madame Cahoche rings. "If you want good coffee, there's plenty in Paris. As long as we're in Sénecé..."

Cahoche takes *Le Temps* from his pocket, tilts the shade of the little electric bulb illuminating the table and goes to sit down in a rattan armchair that the light has revealed, at the foot of a chestnut-tree. The garden is silent, heavily calm. A moth collided with stubborn regularity with the pink-clad bulb.

A made appears, fairly young, with the lumpen face of a Bretonne.

"Here are the keys to the sideboard, Carmélia," says Madame Cahoche. "Bring the liqueurs. With a glass, of course, for Monsieur le Maire."

The maidservant mutters: "Of course…a Maire doesn't drink from the bottle…"

"A dirty breed," says Madame Cahoche, when the maid is some distance away. "Oh, you're making me endure a fine purgatory!"

"Are you starting that again?" Cahoche remarks, dully, without interrupting his reading. "For a cup of coffee…that's a big deal!"

"The coffee's only one of a thousand domestic details that are killing me by inches..."

"Are we going to rehash the same discussion again? You always look at things on the dark side. If you knew, as I do, how to adapt..."

"You! Of course, you're the most cynical…"

"Shh…shh…," says Cahoche placidly, nodding toward the maid, who reappears.

"Why two glasses, Carmélia?"

A slow tread causes the sand of the garden path to crunch. A shadow appears behind the servant.

"It's the curé…asking to see Monsieur. "He arrived at the back door, through the kitchen…"

"At this hour, Monsieur Malusson? Through the kitch-en?"

"Yes, my dear Madame. I've come over the fields."

The curé comes forward. Cahoche has risen to his feet.

"What's the matter, Monsieur le Curé?"

Monsieur Malusson comes into the lighted area. His face is pale, his hands tremulous.

"I beg your pardon... An abominable crime..."

"Leave us, Carmélia," says Madame Cahoche to the maid, who is listening, as if rooted to the spot.

"Take this chair, Monsieur Malusson," says Cahoche. "Wait while I pour you a little cordial. What's happened?"

"I've put up with a lot," says the curé, "but this is the last straw. It's finished. Since this morning, I've been shut up in the presbytery, not wanting to see anyone, not daring to go out. I waited for nightfall. I came over the fields. All day I've been in a state of shame, affliction, to the point of not knowing what to do. Monsieur le Maire, it's necessary to take severe measures, with a...definitive energy."

"Against whom?"

"Oh, if I knew who was responsible...!"

"I've been away from Sénecé all day, came straight back to dinner. Not up to date with anything. Have a little drink, Monsieur le Curé, and tell me what it's about."

"It's enough to amaze the most perverse imagination. Monsieur le Maire, there's no longer a single Christ in Sénecé. Last night, Our Lord has been decrucified from all the calvaries!"

"What!"

"Early this morning, I went to visit the widow Antonet, who hasn't been very well for a few days. Arrived at the Rue de l'Epieu, I turned, as usual, toward the Christ in the niche beside the Chauvions' shop. Disappeared! It's a shock...but I'm always expecting, and without repose, so many things! I couldn't suppose, however... I go past the Crassois pond. The Christ is gone from there too. I begin to feel my blood running cold. I make a detour. I go across the Carrefour Saint-Herbelet...there too! Everywhere, the poor old cast-iron crosses, stripped of the good Lord. One can see little spider-webs, all shiny with dew, over the holes where Our Lord's hand and feet were fixed the day before. One might think they were tears...oh, it's frightful! Finally, from calvary to calvary, it must be said, here I am in the Place Jacques, where the big cross with the wooden Christ was standing only yesterday. A crowd...they stand aside when they see me...embarrassed faces...sniggers, too...old women looking at me with terror...and what do I see?"

"Lord!" exclaims Madame Cahoche "What did you see?"

"Instead of our Christ with extended arms, with the great bloodstains that I had repainted last year, a new statue, brand new, of Our Lord in a white robe, but with his back to the cross, his arms detached, extended toward the ground, toward the people...in one of his arms, a sheaf of real wheat...at the end of the other, in his hand, a bunch of grapes..."

"Damn! A symbol..."

"An unspeakable sacrilege! Our true Jesus is still bleeding.... All that was done at night. You can well imagine that it requires accomplices. An organized sacrilege! The statue is rather crudely made. The sculptor can doubtless be found in the village...but those who removed the Christs from the little calvaries... Well, it's necessary to go back to the source...to the organizer..."

"And your suspicions?"

"Come on, Monsieur le Maire! Your great friend. The one you've never wanted to touch..."

"Permit me, Monsieur le Curé...you need evidence..."

"You're joking! You don't think that it's been abundant, since the first day that Monsieur Aury took up residence. Alcoholism, idleness, luxury...the devouring torrent before which the unfortunate Séneçois, completely abused, haven't ceased to open the floodgates!"

"Not so fast! Many consider the progress due to Monsieur Aury to be a great benefit."

"Permit me in your turn! No one has ever heard me say that it's necessary to criticize progress. I'm a man of my century. Monsieur le Maire. Machines...have their advantages, which relieve the creature of the harsh effects of the original sin, but on the condition that the liberty they give serves for the maintenance and fructification of virtue, the refinement of the soul..."

"Well, that's what they've done."

"What!"

"Virtues different from those you praise, obviously... We have a village of thinkers and artists...as that monsieur wrote in the *Grand Journal*, who has cast a luster over Sénecé, circulated in two million copies...eh? Last night's prank..."

"Prank! Blessed Virgin!"

"...Is a kind of ransom, for the state of the village that earned us that beautiful article..."

"That beautiful article? What has it earned us?"

"I'll grant you that it hasn't changed anything fundamental...a few tourists, a certain number of businessmen curious to see whether there's money to be made..."

"Not a few vagabonds..."

"Who hoped to live here as rentiers and didn't find the opportunity. Some have gone into the factory, others have gone to get themselves hanged somewhere else. That doesn't prove anything. The article ought to have revolutionized the world...if it had been done properly. Between ourselves, the journalist didn't understand anything. It passed him by. You too, Monsieur le Curé, haven't understood. You can't understand...but I do."

Madame Cahoche sniggers.

"Denis Aury, at the very beginning, explained his ideas to me. They were so extraordinary that I thought it a harmless utopia..."

"Oh, yes indeed!"

"And then, I believed. Madame Cahoche is like you. *Oculus habent*, as you say, *et non*..."[26]

"Indeed! I have seen very clearly! Atheism, profligacy..."

---

[26] The interrupted quotation, *Oculus habent et non videbunt* [They have eyes but do not see] is from the Vulgate Bible, psalm 113—psalm 135 in the English Authorized Version.

"Myopia, Monsieur le Curé! It's merely a moment of evolution...the seething of eggs before they can become omelets. If you look a little way into the future, and judge all the results that have been obtained without prejudice, you'll see Sénecé as a miraculous success!"

"That's a success that I shall never see. I understand that there's no aid to be expected from you, Monsieur le Maire. I'm leaving, to shaking the dust off my feet in the village, fief of Satan."

"Would you like some advice? Let it be known that you'll leave the church closed until the guilty parties have been denounced."

The priest starts. "Oh, no!" he protests, naively. "What an idea! I have enough trouble already retaining a few good souls who still come..."

"What do you want me to say to you, my dear Curé? Imitate the Holy Father in the Vatican. Drape yourself in your spiritual royalty. Stay in your church. Consider the village as the pope does the Quirinal. You'll always have one compensation. Christ is still crucified in your church, and for those who come to it. That's the main thing. How do you expect me to help you? I can search for the guilty parties, on the basis of the degradation of public monuments. As for the state of mind that led them to it...we're in a Republic. I don't have any right over beliefs. If people have put wheat and grapes in the arms of Jesus in the Place Jacques, they could have found that themselves, without the need of any direct inspiration from Denis Aury. It's a simple enough symbol, and in the logic of the state of mind that's turning them away from the church. The good Lord had himself crucified for their salvation. Now they've found their salvation, the good Lord no longer has to suffer on their behalf. He can rejoice with them, like a brother, in all the good things of the earth. What is it that they go in search of at church? Perhaps they find that what you tell them is made for the unfortunate, and that happiness is on the other side of death than the one displayed by you: the side before..."

"Adieu, Monsieur Cahoche. I pity you. The village will have a terrible awakening. God sees further than you, and although his designs are impenetrable, they always triumph. Adieu, Monsieur Cahoche..."

"You haven't touched your little glass, Monsieur le Curé," says Madame Cahoche, with a profound sadness.

"I beg your pardon..." He drinks, mechanically. "Au revoir. I'll go out the back way. I don't want to encounter anyone..."

He draws away, his discouraged tread rattling the pebbles.

Madame Cahoche bursts forth: "You're a bad man! That's all that you could find to say? And your admiration for Denis Aury...it won't do, Cahoche! You're ridiculous, with our progress and your ideas. As ridiculous as you are in seeing me suffer by remaining in Sénecé. Your big words, which you've heard at the château! As for what keeps you here, knowing that the least of the peasants knows more than you do, and the least of the peasants is better off and better dressed than your wife, what keeps you here, like a hungry dog at the door of a butcher's shop..."

"Enough!" says Cahoche, rudely. "You're boring me. I'll go have a chat with Denis Aury with regard to these Christs. Let's not say any more about it."

"Content, eh? An opportunity to go and see your beauty!"

"You're making up all your absurdities. I don't stay in Sénecé for Lène Aury. You're incapable of understanding the superiority and the disinterest of the...philosophical curiosity that attaches me to the village. Pour me a glass of Armagnac."

It was, in fact, not entirely because of Lène that Cahoche was clinging to Sénecé, in spite of a host of inconveniences—among others, those that the regime of a village where domestic service was no more than a memory caused the intimate life of the Château d'Harcors. At the very least, the functions attached to that phrase presented themselves under the particular auspices that had bewildered Juste Jubier in the person of the amiable Berthe. Cahoche, who could not, with the same entitlement as the peasant, draw upon Aury's generosity, but was not, on the other hand, rich enough to make the Château d'Harcors the same kind of palace with a thousand electric mechanisms as the Maison Aury, was still obliged to have recourse to valets and maidservants, and, for want of finding any in the locality, to seek them elsewhere.

Recruitment had become increasingly difficult as the eccentricities of Sénecé had become more pronounced. The domestics at Harcors, far from being able to play the usual role of château flunkeys among peasants, found themselves reduced, with regard to the Séneçois, to pitiful individuals, to antediluvian laborers. They could put their pride in their pockets under emollient purses swollen by enviable wages, but they could not support for long the overly complex fashion in which amour was conceived in Sénecé, which meant that the flavorsome compensations of dalliance with the indigenes were forbidden to them.

Cahoche, careful of his belly and by no means insouciant in regard to his comforts, judged the grievances of the servants' parlor as well-founded as the complaints of his wife, but he passed over them, as if shielded by a certain delectation that outweighed all the domestic disturbances. Certainly, there would have been enough to fix him in Sénecé in the burning and breathless state in which he was held by his breathless desire for Lène Aury: a kind of muted lust, a kind a masochism, in experiencing, when he found himself in Lène's presence, both the fury of that desire and the restriction of the impossible. However, he was compensated for his chimerical suspension by a kind of continual tickling of the senses, a salacious bliss into which the vestimentary fantasies of the Séneçoises plunged him. That was the secret delectation which, on the margin of Lène, attached him to Sénecé.

The abstract sense of the evolution of the village had not touched him, no matter how hard he pretended to have understood. In reality, too important a landowner, too full of himself, to have put himself in the school of the indigenes, to have undergone their candid reactions, he had, fundamentally, remained intact. The elegance of the Sénéçoises affected the same centers that stirred in the bourgeois spectator of music hall revues. But here for him, the revue was performed relentlessly, in the street, in the houses, inserting into everyday life the stage on which the girls filed past, quivering, in a state of diabolical undress. He lived in a strange disposition of complex satyriasis and torpid wellbeing, and when the accumulation of his admirable heart threatened to turn stormy, some pretext took him to Paris, where specialized demoiselles took on the role of lightning-conductor for him.

On some evenings, when the sky above Sénécé was low, the château-dwellers amused themselves by projecting images on the clouds. The powerful apparatus that had previously, on the screen in the pasture, awakened true images of the world and the internal reality of things, there permitted the most bizarre of farces. There were frescoes, colossal by virtue of being immeasurably magnified by the distance, or polychromatic images in stained glass, representing religious or historic scenes: a mixture of lithographs from the Place Saint-Sulpice, old posters from Épinal, reproductions of classic masterpieces, and also paintings by Sénéçois artists, not a little proud to be taking part in the gigantic exhibition! A phantasmagorical farce: the clouds, as they moved, deformed the immense pictures. In accordance with the shadows and the hollows in their course, it seemed that the scenes swelled up or shrank, swirled in spirals or scattered in multicolored flakes: Jesus and the Father seated in Paradise; some scene from the twenty thousand heaven of India; Philippe-Auguste at Bouvines; the coronation of Napoléon...

On other evenings, the terraces of the château burst forth with great firework displays, a treat particularly esteemed by the Sénéçois. Many of them did not disdain to design and build the frameworks for the displays. Draguin was ingenious in discovering powders. What labor and thought went into shows of such brief duration! The marvels they dispensed lost their ephemeral character for individuals who gradually came to measure time more by the intensity of their emotions than its horary dimensions.

One day, Leviel said: "The airplanes might play a role. Let's cover their wings and bodywork with phosphorescent variegations. They'll fly up in the midst of a firework display, seeming to carry it with them and continue it in space..."

"Why not rather," said Draguin, "a magic lantern on the clouds? They could rise up to assault the gods."

"In fact," said Denis, "why not bring the same gods down to earth. What if I were to enact the ascension of Elijah? What if we were to reproduce the chariot of fire that Jehovah so courteously sent to his prophet?" He turned to Draguin. "Difficult?"

"Well...risky, with the petards and the roman candles that you'd have to take with you to play the part of the chariot of fire..."

"You mean to do it? My love!" cried Lène.

"Yes, damn it. Well, with the aid of projections that can inundate me with all the fiery colors we like, and rockets flying high enough to frame me...we can try?"

"In that fashion, we certainly can," said Draguin.

Bounding wild beasts with limbs of lightning in jungles of topazes, rubies and emeralds; flocks of magical birds, of which every wing-beat is prolonged in a stream of gems; cascades of silver and nacre; bombs bursting on the ground into geysers of diamonds...

Suddenly, as if springing from the flamboyant parade, an immense form of fire, roaring and throbbing, rises up obliquely into the air. On the wings and the body of the aircraft followed by the incandescent beam of the projector, painted flames seem to be writhing. Long rockets launch forth in pursuit of the monster, overtaking it, exploding in sprays of gold and sapphire.

"Elijah!" cries the delighted crowd, to whom the play has been advertised.

The airplane turns in the fantastic crater hollowed out in the darkness by the lights that escort it, rising up; the rockets can scarcely reach its altitude; only the projector sticks to it, like a gigantic oar to a canvas boat.

The cries of the spectators and the detonations of the rockets are such that the roar of the air embraced by the propellers is inaudible.

For a moment, the golden beam allows the prey that it is setting ablaze to escape. It searches, hesitant and awkward, seeming to totter in space.

A kind of red tongue, a ball, and then a tress of true flame, which becomes entangled in falling vertiginously to earth. A mad clamor. A brief yellow column mingled with dense vapor in a distant field.

The fastest arrive at the foot of a smoking chaos of wood, canvas and oil, which sizzles, with stinking blisters.

A few paces away, illuminated in snatches of light that the wind extracts from the blazing wood, is something human, dislocated, bloody, and frightfully mute.

PART THREE

1

I

Cahoche was going through the village at a slow pace toward Telluire wood when, level with the Lauvin bakery, his ears were solicited by an unusual sound: the moans and gasps of children, punctuated by coarse laughter and exclamations, in which he perceived the voice of the baker coming from the room behind the shop. The Maire drew closer, and as soon as he had crossed the threshold, recognized the grunts of a child busy kneading. He smiled furtively, and opened the door of the bakehouse.

"Bonjour, Lauvin. It's a long time since that song was heard. You've gone back to this, then? The machines are broken?"

"Bonjour, Monsieur le Maire. It seems strange, doesn't it?"

Lauvin is bare-chested, his belly and limbs covered by an old apron, and his arms coated up to the elbows with dough. Two children, similarly half-naked, also have their arms plunged into it.

"It's pure chance, a funny story," said Lauvin. "My Jacquot, as you know, makes human figures and all sorts of animals with the dough, as well as anyone. This morning I find him and his little comrade—this is Guignier, the child of a workman at Courtoisans, who has a taste for the arts...so, Jacquot was modeling very nicely the   lumps of dough the machine had prepared, as usual, and was showing Guignier his manner of working. I don't know what went through my head

185

as I watched them. I started saying to myself: 'It's all very well to interest oneself in the pretty things one can do with the dough, but there's the dough itself...when it was necessary to knead, first, a simple plain loaf before being baked, it was much more difficult than these kids...'"

"That was in the old days," said Cahoche, slightly ironically.

Little Lauvin looked at the Maire gratefully.

"Jacquot said that, just like you," said Lauvin, "having the air of taking his Papa for a fossil. Then I said: 'It had its good side too, that difficulty.' And, while talking about the hard labor that it was necessary for a father and son to do with their hands, there I was rolling up my sleeves, opening up the old rusty kneading-trough, and cleaning it, and then adding the yeast, and turning it over, adding the salt, and laboring away, and finding a strange contentment in it, believe it or not. All the more so in seeing that I hadn't lost the knack, that finding my hands in that lovely great mass, which resists you, and hollowing it out, stretching it, fluffing it up like some sort of fat, white, amorous cat...with all due respect to the children...such contentment, Monsieur Cahoche, that shortly before you came by, to put myself at my ease, I undressed as in the old days, and made the kids undress too. When you came in I was inculcating them wholeheartedly in the old methods...not so stupid! These lads. who virtually came into the world in a time when the bread made itself on its own, as if it fell ready-baked from the moon, are beginning to get a taste and rediscovering the charm of the old work..."

Lauvin's voice softened. Cahoche looked at the children, running with sweat.

"You think they're getting a taste for it? They don't appear to be."

"It's warning them up a bit, to begin with..." Lauvin scratched his head. "And then, you see, Monsieur Cahoche, to tell the truth, I wouldn't be sorry if my Jacquot were to become a baker, if necessary, such as there are everywhere else but Sénecé. One never knows what might happen. Since the accident...many things that we'd never have thought of.... In the times of Monsieur Denis, there was a kind of whirlwind, in which one never found the time to reflect, nor to collect oneself. I've wondered often enough whether my machines might not explode in my face one day..."

"No! What an idea!" said Cahoche, with a smile that seemed to be suspended over a rather vague protest.

He took out his watch.

"I'll leave you, Lauvin. I have a few small visits to make..."

He shook the baker's hand, left the shop and resumed his slow march toward Telluire. Thoughts were agitating within him, which, so long as he was in the village, tightly enclosed within himself, never reached his mild face. As soon as he had entered the wood, those thoughts burst forth, in the form of an energetic sweep of his cane bestowed on a bush, which broke five or six young branches. Then the Maire straightened up, and accelerating his pace, strode on briskly, whirling the stick. As he went past he lashed the trees, the most singular trees in the world. Telluire wood, too, had been subjected to the enterprise of the Séneçois artists. Crowns were trimmed into the silhouettes of birds, into strange shapes, phantasmal individuals. The trunks had been engraved, the bark exaggerating the grooves as it aged, into sometimes-monstrous arabesque.

At a bend in a path that Cahoche was following, Frignot was sitting on a tree-stump with his rifle between his legs, stuffing his pipe. He stood up precipitately.

"Bonjour Frignot. What's new?"

Frignot slowly leaned his rifle against a tree, put his half-stuffed pipe back in his pocket, taking his time, and said: "A great deal new today, Monsieur le Maire. Monsieur will be here in a few days."

Clinique du Dr. Lugnault

My love, my joy, my light, I wish the words of this letter could spring forth and shine before your eyes like the fabulous diamonds when the fisherman in the Thousand-and-One

187

Nights opened the casket that he had drawn up from the depths of the sea. It's from much darker depths that these words of delight and victory rise up toward you! *De profundis chamavi as te, Domina!*[27] The most unexpected, the most complete of miracles has been accomplished. Not only has my life been saved, but—the cure alone would have been worse than death, if it had been that of the monster that the stupid adventure, in smashing my body, had made of me—that life has given me back myself, almost intact, thanks to Lugnault's genius. All that invention, served by an admirable science and generosity—to the point that science and generosity merit the name of love—all that an extraordinary prosthesis can reunite and create to reorganize disrupted lines and arm vanquished limbs, Lugnault has sought, attempted and achieved. I have returned to all eyes as I was, or nearly.

For as long as I was that human thing, numbed, ringed by death, my soul folded back in unconsciousness, as my body, after the accident, was folded in the sheet in which it was brought back, you have wanted to approach me, to see me, to fill your eyes with the most atrocious image. As soon as Lugnault, after waking me, proffered, at the same time as the verdict of life, the hope of the miraculous prosthesis, I resolved at that very moment that no one would see me again until the day when I had recovered my own image and my being of before the fall. Forgive me, my beloved Lène, for having so severely deprived you of the poor tender pleasure of coming every day to my bedside, to scale the complex and difficult stages of my resurrection. Apologies to Pierre, to Louis, to Bernard. I wanted that severity, in the name of a greater, finer happiness, worthy of us. I wanted those to whom, after believing me lost, expectation had been returned, forcefully, to be able gradually to recover, during that interval, from the horrible image stolen from the shroud of unconsciousness, that of what I was, on the ardent and luminous

---

[27] From the depths I have cried out to you, O Lady!—an adaptation of the opening words of psalm 130 (A.V.)

roads of my life, constructed and designed such as you loved it, such as it was known to all of you, to whom I know that my warmth of love and joy of living communicates warmth, joy and confidence in loving and living.

I am coming back. In a few days, I shall tell you the exact date. Hazard will doubtless determine that it will be around the same day, if not the same one, when I reappeared at Sénecé in the overall of the electrician Amédée. Then, I had a marvelous empire, and the plans of a more harmonious and vaster life that had ever been, not just attempted, but dreamed. No shadow over the radiance of my work, my great dream, no riposte, no treason of reality. No! For I could not measure the stupidest of incidents and its catastrophic consequences. But it is not by a spark from a rocket, striking the precise point of a wing where a few drops of fuel had spilled, that the innumerable splendor of the world and the innumerable human faculty of joy, have been give the lie! One swallow does not make a summer? One flower that sheds its petals does not unmake a summer. Around and beyond me and my blazing airplane, life, the world, humanity, continued, continuing to be what they are...what I have seen, what my faith and my love have recognized that they are.

I am coming back, my beloved, rich in my inviolate beliefs, ready for all our delights, able to pursue my creative work. I have understood from your letter that I shall have a few small thrusts of the tiller to make, that the accident and my long absence have disturbed minds somewhat, have hindered the inventive audacity, so necessary, of Pierre and Bernard, slowed down the production of the factory. All that will be quickly restored to the right track, since I shall be returning as the same pilot. And you, I that I shall see you again, and that you too will have remained the same, the visage of my faith, the proof of my verity, the living light of my work.

Lène, life is beginning again. Doubtless a few gestures will be difficult for me, or even forbidden, but what will those few be for someone who has recovered, in finding himself upstanding again, his lucid awareness of so much happiness, and so much happiness still possible! Lène, soon I shall be before you again, with my love and all my strength of love, my joy and all my strength of joy.

Nervously, Cahoche digs a hole with his cane in the soil, greasy beneath the dead leaves.

"So I was there," said Fringot, "when the letter arrived. Madame put it into her corsage without reading it. She put her arms over it as she were an animal shielding her little ones, and went up to her room to shut herself in on her own. Good. I had an idea what there was in that letter, because they talked about it all through dinner, and from the servants' parlor one can listen through the shaft of the dumb-waiter—enough to know that it contained mountains and marvels, that we're going to see Monsieur again; in brief, that everything is going to start again, and more so, as if nothing had ever happened."

"Incredible!" said Cahoche.

"Something curious to mention to Monsieur le Maire, and which I think he'll be able to explain better than me, is Madame's reaction. When she came down from her from she had a bizarre expression. One can't say angry, but...more afflicted...embarrassed, anyway. On the other hand, one took account that she was immensely happy about Monsieur's return. I haven't the capacity to put all that together..."

"Immensely happy?"

"That's not saying too much."

Cahoche silently filled in the hole that he had made, by pushing the surrounding leaves into it with the tip of his cane, and then he scattered twigs over it.

"Let's not get carried away. Whatever there was in the letter, it's not possible, not admissible, that the Denis who comes back to us will be the one to whom we..." He hesitated, looked at the frowning Frignot, lowered his head and murmured: "...Submitted."

There was a silence.

"Well," said Frignot, "it's necessary to admit that he disturbed things rudely..."

"Rudely," muttered Cahoche.

"Revolutions like that aren't made for peasants, nor for people like the majority of us. Right from the start, I began not to understand things any longer. I wasn't useful for anything any longer. It wasn't a life. If one's only been with poachers, one doesn't know any longer what's permitted and what's forbidden. Authority, fraternity...without which there's nothing but...a salad!"

"A salad," said Cahoche, slowly, his eyes fixed on the ground, "that it will be necessary to eat again, if everything recommences."

"Wait a minute, Monsieur le Maire. I haven't finished yet. As you've just remarked, it isn't admissible that after such a catastrophe...and yet, to believe Monsieur's letter, it's as if he's cured and, so to speak, as good as new..."

Frignot took his stuffed pipe out of his pocket. "With your permission, Monsieur le Maire?" He lit it.

"They let Madame go on, during dinner, making plans. They didn't want to contradict her or displease her. Afterwards, when she'd gone back to her room, the messieurs went into the park. I was there. I asked them very softly: 'Is there news of Monsieur?' Then they shook their heads."

"Ah! And then?"

"To summarize it briefly, it appears that what they know directly from the doctors doesn't square entirely with Monsieur's hopes, and, as you say, that it's necessary not to get carried away."

Cahioche could not repress a "*pfft...*" of relief.

"All the more so," Frignot went on, "as to putting things back fully as they were when he was here, it'll take work...lots of work, for a man enclosed, if I've understood, from head to toe in apparatus..."

"Ah?" said Cahoche. "Poor Aury, so vigorous, so fortunate in his health..."

"Yes, the poor Monsieur," said Frignot.

The two men kept silent for some time.

"One can see a little further ahead," Cahoche began. "When he's definitely reinstalled here, after a certain time, it's to be presumed...oh, immensely happy, I understand that very well!...today...it's to be presumed that Madame Aury's sentiments, in his regard, won't be absolutely the same."

Frignot stopped smoking, and did not move a muscle. He listened with the greatest attention.

"She has a need for happiness in her blood...and him, with his theories...he's done all that was necessary for that to always to go at full tilt, whatever happens...I can't see her playing nurse for the rest of her life, eh? Happiness...happiness, that's a big word...there are all sorts of it, happiness. Yes. Well...well, that's enough for today. Tell me, Frignot..."

Cahoche plunged his hand rapidly into the interior pocket of his jacket, took out his wallet, and removed several banknotes.

"Take this...for today."

Frignot simply took the bills and put them in his pocket.

"Perfect," said Cahoche. "It's going to be very tense. It'll be necessary to be more solidly in accord than ever. Delighted with your little tips. Nothing will change when Aury comes back?"

"No."

"If you put aside what I give you every time, it'll be a nice nest-egg. I don't mind that. The day when..." A flush of blood in the cheeks; a tremor of the arms. "In brief, that day, we'll get out of Sénecé. We'll meet again in Paris. You'll have what you need to be a rentier for live. If it's not enough, I'll round it out. Agreed. There are all sorts of happiness, eh? You can offer yourself in Paris... And all the colors of the rainbow."

Frignot picked up his rifle and passed the strap over his shoulder. "Agreed. No need to talk about it again, Monsieur le Maire."

II

It was, in fact, on the precise anniversary of Denis first coming that the latter reappeared in Sénecé. He was sitting in the auto, open, beside Léne, radiant and maternally attentive. Facing them, Draguin and Leviel. Next to the chauffeur, an unknown man with a fat, rather delicate face, with a gold pince-nez, about thirty years old.

Denis, pale, his sitting up straight, his arms partly folded in front, his clasped hands supported on the handle of a cane, was smiling, looking all around with sustained and joyful attention. He communicated his impressions to his companions without leaning toward them, keeping his neck and torso stiff. When someone pointed something out to him, he turned his whole head. A high-necked pullover covered his neck all the way to the hairline, and in front to the chine.

The auto came into Sénecé by the main road between the two hills. Many Séneçois were assembled there. The men raised their hats gravely as soon as the auto was in sight. As it drew nearer to the hills, all around the base, studded with fresh flowers, young women dressed in brightly colored dresses the colors of the flowers, which blended in with them at a distance, separated from the massifs where they were waiting. They came forward. The auto stopped. They surrounded it, and filled it with flowers taken from their belts.

Under the odorous hail, Denis, leaning heavily on his cane, lifted himself up slightly and shouted: "Bonjour, the earth in flower that is coming to me!" Then he sat down again with a dry click. His eyes scanned the hills, running from the foot to the summit, and his eyelids fluttered slightly.

Leviel had followed his gaze. "You've been warned," he said, in a low voice, as the vehicle moved forward slowly. "You wanted frankness. We said to them: no fuss, no joy on command. You're not welcoming a minister. Your sentiments, naked. Those who have reasons for not rejoicing at this return, those who have changed their opinion about Aury's work, our friend hopes that they'll express themselves without constraint. He's coming back to work for the truth, and for the reconstructions that it will involve."

"Good."

"We didn't want to give any indication. Those young flowers on the hills found that by themselves. However, you'll have noticed that the hills themselves, toward the top, are less ornamented than before. Scars, cracks…they've fallen somewhat into neglect. You'll see other instances of backsliding..."

"I don't fear any. I expect cracks more serious than the ones on those hills. What does that matter. I'm here!"

In the high street, a certain incoherence: Séneçois at the windows, on the doorsteps, shouting: "Vive Aury! Bonjour M'sieur Denis!"—and houses that are hermetically sealed.

"The Bafferts have left Sénecé," said Leviel. "Judging themselves rich enough—thanks to you, of course—for life in the town, they've put their house in the hands of the notary in Crennes and left everything behind."

"Strange calculation. The town will ruin them quickly, and only offer them poor old joys. They had better ones here."

"In your time, Denis."

"You've let them get bored?"

"We've done our best, but..."

"But what, demiurge of new forms?"

"The enthusiasm is no longer there...anywhere. We'll talk about it presently..."

"Look, Chaleix…," said Denis.

The cobbler, sitting at his door, clad in his black apron, sticky with old resin, as hammering a shoe with all his might. When the auto goes past him he strikes harder, exaggerating the effort and the noise, his nose obstinately lowered over his leather.

"He was a monsieur," said Denis, softly. "His machines did it all, and he studied butterflies..."

"His machines have rusted," murmured Draguin, "and he delivers his shoes wrapped in the pages of his treatise on entomology."

"Lauvin also neglects his machines," said Leviel, "and he's teaching his son bakery again."

"It's necessary to say," added Draguin, "that the factory has been obliged to raise the price of current..."

"Oh?"

"The deposits aren't being discovered as easily. We'll talk about that with Géard. He's waiting for us at the château. Look, there's good old Chauvion..."

In front of her house, Mère Chauvion had constructed a little shrine. On the altar, between two big leafy bouquets, was a big picture reproducing the sacrilegious Christ of the Place Jacques, carrying the wheat and grapes. The head of the Christ had Denis' face. Savinien Mannevy was standing some distance away. He advanced toward the auto, his hat in his hand, and said: "Bonjour, Monsieur Denis. It's me who painted you in Jesus' place, but it was Mère Chauvion who had the idea of the shrine."

Beside the altar, turning to watch the auto pass by, old Madame Chauvion was on her knees, and she raised her joined hands toward Denis.

"I've heard it said in very distinguished places," said the painter, "where chiefs of industry, editors on newspapers, division heads in the ministry pronounce it coldly: 'No one is indispensable.' It's exactly the same opinion that's expressed, in other terms, by concierges, at the bistro, and by companion plumbers: 'One man's as good as another.' Damnably revelatory remarks. They betray not only a strange absence of any faculty of evaluation...let's say a trifle lacking in introspection...but above all, an indisputable mediocrity of taste. It's exactly as if they were saying: 'If didn't have Beethoven, it would be a misfortune...but haven't we got Gounod?'"

"What are you getting at?" Denis asked.

They were all sitting in the big hall. One might have thought that it was one of their casual conversations of old, one of their almost everyday meetings, in which the forms and actions of their life, extended toward the fullest joy, were elaborated in subtle duels and surges of ideas.

Géard was grave. Draguin stood up, pacing back and forth, his hands in his pockets, visibly anxious. Leviel seemed to want to drown an embarrassing argument under a flood of words, as the simple or the culpable do. Lène smiled at Denis, showing him a face that was confident and placid, and yet was observing the slightest detail of his movements with a passionate acuity. He was at his table, his legs extended, his forearms resting on his armchair, listening, offering his friends an appearance of unshakable serenity, and delight in being there.

At times his gaze encountered the marble Bacchus, and lingered upon it. Then his thoughts appeared to escape the conversation. Lène, her heart suddenly clawed, glimpsed one of those moments. She thought she saw a new Denis, a face in which a kind of defiance shone over a brief rictus of suffering.

"What am I getting at?" said Leviel. "At the simple truth that you're absolutely indispensable. That everything that has emerged from you can only be maintained by you, that it's sinking without you: the factory, Sénecé, all of us..."

"I don't admit that. A stupefying, indecent confession, unworthy of you three and Lène. Pass for new Sénecé, a kind of extra-natural plant, without roots, which has only received its aliments from outside. If the nourishment stops before the plant has been able to put down its own roots, it comes unstuck, uprooted by the first storm..."

"Exactly," murmured Draguin.

"Eh? The roots were beginning to take hold. Savinien Mannevy...the girls who imagined the polite welcome on the hills, and all those that I'll gradually get back...But you! Your own wealth, independent of me, I counted on them to continue me!"

A silence.

"So?" Denis said, good-humoredly, "no Elias has picked up the mantle and the miracles of Elijah?"

"But, you must understand...," said Lène.

196

"Old chap," Leviel interrupted, "we were all completely devastated after the accident, as you can imagine..."

"That within you which loved me could weep, could be downcast...but that within you which loved my work should have separated after the accident, which only struck one individual. That within you which was your own power, love of life, beyond me, ought to have overcome..."

"That's precisely the point," said Draguin, stopping abruptly beside the table. "Our powers, our wealth..."

"We perceived that we owed them to you, Denis," said Leviel. "That's the great confession. Without you..."

"You!" Denis exclaimed. "My fathers!"

Draguin continued: "Our twenty years, at which you drank, are far away. What would have become of us, by ourselves, if you hadn't rendered them to us and relentlessly vivified them? Our meeting, back then, at the U.P. du faubourg, our conversations...you think you're our debtor? But why did you come to us? There's an admirable phrase in the Scriptures: "He that seeks me has already found me."[28] He took a few more paces. A profound emotion was audible in his voice. "Those conversations, the grapes that they provided and that you pressed, would probably have been nothing but words, if you had not had the wine within you. You know the old aphorism of the occultists: 'The initiate will slay the initiator...' On the contrary, it's to you, whom we initiated into the rites of the superior life, to you that we owe having been initiated in our turn, and far beyond what we had given you. We brought you the rites, a few arcana...you enabled us to attain the supreme secret, and to live it...to love..."

Denis closed his eyes for a moment, and sketched an inclination of his head toward his hand, as if to collect himself, but the head remained rigid and it was the hand that rose slowly to the forehead.

---

[28] Although based on the gospel accounts of Jesus, it was actually Blaise Pascal who formulated the nearest equivalent to this dictum.

His eyes covered, Denis said: "It's necessary that I accept what you say, of which the facts prove the gravity to me."

The hand fell back, the fine familiar gaze sparkled. "But no, no, my friends! You're chastizing yourselves unjustly. What could I have done myself without you, and without Lène? How do I know? It's our alliance, the combination of our enthusiasms, our perpetual enrichment by one another..."

Géard and Leviel had stood up. With Draguin, they approached the table, shivering, their arms extended toward Denis, suddenly redeemed, enlightened by a verity even simpler than the one affirmed a little while before by Leviel: a verity that had until that moment been veiled by their grief.

"Of course!" Denis went on. "If it had been to one of you that the accident had happened, would the mutilation of the strong and harmonious being that we form have been any less? Speak, Lène, Bernard, Pierre, Louis!"

They looked at one another. The four attitudes remained assent and gratitude—but s shadow descended over the four faces and the first verity was reintegrated into their hearts.

"Let us all be reborn together, then!" exclaimed Denis. "To work, brothers! Louis, prepare your books, with the fissures laid bare, develop for me by tomorrow the plans of which you've thought, dreamed, the possible remedies, and don't be put off by those which seem the most madly audacious. We, Pierre and Bernard, are going to take up Sénecé on the evening of my deadly acrobatics. As for you," he said to Lène, "as for us, what point is there in weighing down with words that which was resuscitated with all its light in the very instant that our eyes met again?"

They are alone. Here and there, in the hall, on the carpet, the table, the divans, are the welcoming gifts brought to the château that morning, before Denis' arrival, and throughout the happy day. Many flowers, some strange, issued from the gardens of Sénecé where invention had continued to be employed, others from the fields, but of unusual colors and dimensions, grown in meadows where electricity had intensified the activity of the soil. Naively damascened cups, painted ceramics, embroideries, a fine cane, patiently carved at the pommel and the tip...

Draguin, Leviel and Géard have left Denis and Lène. Scarcely had they stepped into the long gallery than Lène got up, went to Denis, who has not quit his armchair, knelt before him, placed her head on his knees and looked at him with the dilated eyes of adoration. Her head experienced an unexpected contact, encountering something hard and leathery. The impression has not touched her consciousness; it is the flesh that is astonished, where it instinctively expected the elasticity and warmth of flesh beneath the garment...

The consciousness is entirely in the adoring eyes.

"My master, my beloved, it's not true that any of us is your equal. You're our heart. Oh, wicked man, who didn't want poor Lène, trembling with joy and pity at every contact with your linen, to do a little in that which saved you..."

"Your dear image, my love...the thought, the desire to see you again, were in my every minute...in everything that saved me."

"It's necessary to forgive us our distress. It's necessary to forgive me for not being able to surpass myself in the name of a joy...from which you were absent..."

"But my dear love..."

"I know...I know what you want to say: Joy in itself, abstract, isn't it? Its reality, outside you, who represent it, who are its evidence... Oh, as if anything, anything at all, outside you, could exist... Joy, I know, like a religion that continues after the death of the god, which is amplified by his death...No, my dear Denis. We aren't ripe yet...none of us. We're still too saturated by all the old ideas of sadness. Too many old fibers in us, habituated, all ready to resonate with dolor. Joy...your joy...it's too new to act without you..."

Denis held the beautiful plaintive head in his hands. Those hands were burning, and she trembled

"The other annunciators," Lène continued, softly. "No! I've had time to reflect...you really are one of them, my love!

The others took account of human misery. When they were gone, everyone could easily take account of their words, at every instant, each recovering in the verities of his weaknesses, his fragilities, and the life charged with supporting those verities. But you...you've denied evil, suffering, weakness. It's true, when you're there, that everything is beautiful, fortifying, made for happiness...a happiness that appears quite natural to beings as you see them...but it's also true that without you, things begin once again to show their baseness, their pettiness, that they are what we have always been allowed to say that they are...and that one is not, before them, made for the marvelous mirage..."

"It's not a mirage."

"Look, my beloved....I won't talk about the assiduities of the grotesque Cahoche...that's not serious. But our friends...not all...some of those you reckoned most highly...but I'll tell you... For the moment, oh, how happy I am!"

Parting the grip of the hands, Lène stands up, holds herself upright, proudly, ready for a kiss. Denis tries to stand up in his turn. A weight retains his legs to the floor. He lowers his arms rapidly, applies his fingers to the sides of his knees; the double click of a mechanism is heard; the limbs bend. Denis pushes back the armchair, and as he stands upright, the double click is repeated. He takes a step, his limbs stiff; Lène, instinctively, has taken a step back to allow his movements free play.

His arms extended, his face illuminated, he goes to embrace her.

Suddenly, cutting off the movement abruptly, one of his legs abruptly buckles. Denis totters Lène utters a cry and moves toward him, her features suddenly contracted by anguish and pity.

"Nothing! It's nothing!" Denis, white-faced, straightens up impetuously, as if to refuse that anguish and that pity. The apparatus that encloses him upsets the instinctive equilibrium of his body. An irresistible weight drags him toward the side resting on the failing limb. Denis waves his arms, clutches the air, loses balance and falls to the floor with a frightful cry.

A moan, a gasp, immobility.

Lène throws herself upon that heavy, sprawling mass, grips and lifts the arms, puts her arms around the chest. Her hands, her face, her breast are pressed against the fainted man, bumping into a frightful armature everywhere, bruised thereby. She undoes and tears off the garments, sees thongs, corsets, sheaths, linked together by steel rods, studded with screws, nuts and bolts.

"Madame, Messieurs," said the man in the gold pince-nez, "your affection must lend itself to a lie. Madame, in her emotion, whose is perfectly explicable, has undone Monsieur Aury's garments and has seen the apparatus. Now our invalid is sitting in his armchair, and his effects are almost back in place. I ask you, when he has recovered his senses, not to make any allusion to what you have seen."

He readjusted his pince-nez with a mechanical gesture.

"Please take into consideration that Monsieur Aury has taken me from the clinic and attached me to him personally, exclusively for the office, particularly complicated and meticulous, of dressing and undressing him. That signifies, I know, that he does not want to be seen at those moments by anyone but me.

"But Monsieur!" said Lène, desperately. "I'm his wife…!"

"Forgive me, Madame. I'm dealing with individuals who are too intelligent for me not to call things by their name. I believe that I have understood that it is for Madame, before any other, that my orders have been expressly formulated."

Lène made a gesture of aggravation, and mastered herself.

"Might these falls be frequent?" Draguin asked.

"No, Monsieur. In principle, they ought not to occur. The apparatus is absolutely marvelous. Assuming that a bolt was poorly tightened, Monsieur Aury, who, with a practice, would immediately have readjusted it with a slight touch of his finger through the garment, made a mistake. That isn't what made him lose his balance, but rather some gesture…an overly abrupt contraction. His faint is due to the brutality of his fall, which has, as you can imagine, provoked a general shock to the organism, still very fragile, at least with regard to the skeletal system, and more particularly the axis vertebra, which has suffered a lesion. It would only have required a small tremor at that point, although the axis, in the normal gesticulations of our invalid, would be protected by the solidity, proof against anything, of this minerva."[29]

He turned down the neck of the sweater slightly. "You will notice that this apparatus, which we call a minerva and which encloses the cervical vertebrae narrowly, has supports made of pure steel, under the projection of the chin and the occipital protuberance. By rigorously forbidding the inclination of the head forwards or backwards, it protects the axis perfectly—except, of course, in the case of a massive fall like the one to which it has just been the victim…"

"So that dear head," said Lène, her eyes full of tears, "is condemned to a fixity…"

"It retains complete liberty of lateral rotation, Madame…" With respectful compassion, the man continued: "Come on, Madame, it's necessary to be reasonable. Take account of the fact that a masterpiece has been realized, and that when Monsieur Aury has become a little more accustomed to it, he'll be able to regulate his gestures himself, to avoid jerks, and those that remain to him will be permitted to become gradually more natural. He's carrying contraptions about him far more complicated and tyrannical than that minerva. There are the ones that permit him to move his arms almost perfectly, without which they'd be completely limp. Remember that the humeral heads were absolutely crushed. As

---

[29] A minerva was a particular kind of printing-press, now obsolete, although some still exist and remain in use; the designer of Denis' artificial exoskeleton has presumably adapted the term analogically from the machine rather than borrowing the name of the Greek goddess of wisdom directly.

for the legs...do these messieurs know what pseudoarthrosis is?"

He did not wait for a response. He spoke forthrightly, while retaining all his compassion. "The two femurs were fractured. When bony graft does not take, or is not sealed, a cartilaginous segment subsists between the broken part...that's the pseudoarthrosis...which is to say that, without the apparatus, if our invalid were to stand upright, his thighs would buckle at the location of that segment, as if there were an elastic gap there..."

Denis stirred, with a dolorous sigh. His eyes opened. Instinctively, Draguin and Levil advanced to mask Lène, whose face expressed the most frightful distress. But Denis' gaze sought her out.

In an instant, she had recomposed her features. She came to Denis and put her arm around his neck.

"You slipped, my love...and you were stunned. I was frightened, and I called for help. We put you back in the armchair, with Monsieur..."

Denis turned his head toward him. "It's necessary to call him Paulin. That's good...Paulin Charras is a worthy fellow, who knows exactly what it's necessary to do... Lugnault was kind enough to deprive himself, for my sake, of his best assistant...but yes, Paulin, yes, the best... He'll be here, in the house, for a host of small troubles that might be produced in all these machines that maintain by bones and my muscles. Who put me in the armchair?"

"Me," said Draguin, precipitately. "With Monsieur Charras..."

"You must have felt with your hands...it's heavy. There's at least fifteen kilos of it. I'm now a weighty man, eh? My poor, dear Lène, I understand that you're afraid...but it's nothing. I'll only have to be a little more careful, for a while...a habit to acquire..."

His eyes flickered. It seemed that a new consciousness was animating within him. "Come here and look me in the face. Do I look as if I'm depressed? Look deep into my eyes.

You'll see that they're tranquil, with the same light as ever. Think! A little screw that comes loose won't shake the entire edifice. I told you in my letter that certain gestures would be difficult for me. A great many others remain to me, thank God! What's needed to continue our happiness, our festival of life! I wrote to you... I was so excited at the idea of coming back, of living again, of seeing you again...now, after that stupid slip, you probably believe that I exaggerated, in my excitement... You'll see…you'll see…whether I exaggerated..."

2

I

A new group of drinkers came into the main room of the Jerry. Two women, one excessively bejeweled, giving the impression somewhat of a former country tavern-keeper who had suddenly become a millionaire; the other was Lène, clad in white velvet retained at the shoulders by two sapphire clasps. Four men accompanied them.

As soon as they appeared, one diner stood up as if launched by a catapult, extended his glass and howled: "Hurrah! Vive Méran!"

The music, the dancing and the conversations stopped. All the disparate clients of the sumptuous restaurant got up, held out their glasses and cried: "Hurrah!"

The leader of the orchestra said a few feverish words to his musicians, and the Marseillaise burst forth. A maître d'hôtel advanced, bowed profoundly and escorted the new arrivals to an empty table. The nearest female diners snatched the bouquets from the vases ornamenting their tables and threw them at one of the newcomers, a handsome fellow of medium height, blond and broad-shouldered, with a clear and cheerful face.

One young man, precipitately quitting the distant corner where he was eating, approached him as, after having responded to the cheers of the audience with a merry salute, he was waiting for his companions to sit down.

"Monsieur Méran, I'm Juste Jubier of the *Grand Journal*. Tell me something—no matter what. I'll telephone the item immediately. Tomorrow morning, you'll have given immense pleasure to two million readers."

"Oh! Well, indeed...telephone to the *Grand Journal* that I'm content, very content...and that I'll be eating with a good appetite."

"Perfect! May I add, as from you, a little word...shall I say patriotic?...appropriate?"

"Of course."

"A thousand thanks! I didn't see the match, but no one was talking about anything else when you arrived. The first round, then...the American on his back...your straight left?"

"Indeed." Méran sat down and unfolded his napkin. "Will you have something with us?"

"Thank you...I'm in company...and I must go telephone. Just think, this evening, those people who paid a thousand francs for their seat...and it didn't last two minutes...."

"One minute twenty-seven," said one of Méran's companions, a fat man with a radiant crimson face. "But a punch like that represents fifteen years of work."

"And victories!" Jubier exclaimed. He disappeared, running to the telephone.

"It could have been even briefer...," said another of Méran's three companions.

"Damn!" said the fat man.

"...And more elegant. Méran, so gracious in his strength, was nevertheless a little troubled..."

"You're very kind, Monsieur Aury," said Méran. "On your lawns I had nothing in front of me but a balloon..."

"And then, it's the costume that's ugly," said Lène. "Those padded shoes cutting the leg. Why not fight barefoot, as when you were training at the château? Isn't that right, Hirchitz?"

"You artists don't have a say in it," said the fat man. "That's fine for rehearsals. But the moment the piece is played, with a million and a half in receipts...*cedant arte poignae*, as one says in Latin."

"In Latin...the ring...my dear Lamps...," said Hirchitz.

"I put it in my own fashion. What does it matter, if it's understood? Hey you," he shouted to the maître d'hôtel, with whom Aury was discussing the menu, "no bisque for the national hero!"

"This evening, Ponpon?" said Méran, pouting like a schoolboy. "I'm not fighting again for three months. I'll have time to digest the bisque."

Juste Jubier reappeared. "It's done. A real piece of luck for the paper that I happened to be here. I made you say something very good...a polite word about America. We need them for the oil." He noticed Lène. "Forgive me...I only had eyes for our victor. Have I not had the honor of being your guest...Madame Aury? An unforgettable day. I didn't succeed, in an article that was too short, in expressing my enchantment. And Monsieur Aury?"

Lène extended her hand to the journalist. "I remember perfectly...but don't you recognize my husband"

"I'm unpardonable," said Juste Jubier, suddenly embarrassed. "How are you, Monsieur Creator of Men?"

"A little less well than on the day of your visit."

"It doesn't show..."

"You're very kind. You didn't recognize me..."

"Oh, but..."

"Don't apologize. I only recognize myself in mirrors with an effort of memory."

"An accident?"

"That's right. But it's ancient history. You can see that it doesn't prevent me from being a Parisian, from time to time,"

"I'll have the greatest pleasure in seeing you again," said Jube, who having once extracted from Denis, and just now from Méran, the substance of articles that he could devote to them, was in haste to get back to his supper."

"So," murmured the boxer to Lène, "while all France and America had their eyes fixed on me, it was about the padding in my footwear that you were thinking?"

"Does that shock you?"

"On the contrary, it's marvelous. It's very feminine. I mean..."

"Go on."

"That to take an interest in such a detail, there's scarcely only a mother...or a *friend*."

"I am your friend."

"Not in that sense…I mean *friend*…mistress."

"Well, as you see, no. It's sufficient to be a friend."

Méran poured, and shook his head

"What's the matter, my boy?"

"Nothing…it can't be explained like that…it's too delicate."

"Thank you, my dear Madame Lamps," said Lène to the bejeweled tavern-keeper, who was dividing the flowers on the table with her.

"Look," said Hirchitz, "my sketches from this evening, while Méran was functioning…" He passed a pad to Denis.

"Let me see, please?" said Lamps.

"Of, do that again…," begged Méran, in a low voice, as Lène set a glass down on the table that she had raised, amusing herself by reflecting the light of the room's huge chandelier in the golden wine.

"What?"

"The glass…your arm raised…"

"Monsieur is a painter too?"

"What do you think? It's for your breasts…oh, that's pretty," he said, with candid enthusiasm. "The velvet stretching…it's as if you were naked…"

"Would you like to shut up!"

"Would you like to know what I was trying to say to you just now?"

"I'd like that. You don't scare me."

"I said that it was necessary to be a lover, a mistress, to have noticed…"

"My poor little remark touched you so deeply?"

"Let me finish. You said that it was sufficient to be a friend."

"Of course."

"Well, who's to say that I'm not right, if the simple friend has in her…perhaps without knowing it…the sentiments…of a lover?"

"Impossible."

"Sentiments that, one day or another, or one evening...one evening when I've won a splendid victory, would come to be expressed..."

"What, here? Just like that?"

"Oh, no need to say much...a word...a little glance... a sigh..."

"Well, keep watching."

"You're playing the tease. Come on, I've seen the way you look at me, out there at Sénecé. I know that you're an exceptional woman. But between us...me, I can't play games. Do you think there aren't thousands who, this evening, if I raised my little finger..."

"You don't say!" Lène mocked. However, the coarseness of the gallant made her draw away slightly

"Aha! That's him, Méran, champion of the world?" Lamps guffawed, Hirchitz's pad in his hand. "Look..." He passed the pad to the boxer.

Méran contemplated a tangle of volutes and spirals, cut by imperious straight lines.

"It's true that if Papa saw that he's have difficulty recognizing his son."

"It's not you," said Hirchitz, "it's your movements—or, rather, the system of lines that they create in space."

"But these sketches...are to make a statue of me?"

"Of course. I shall fix your movements in the marble, as others might strive to fix your shoulders, your biceps, your fists."

"And his head," exclaimed Lamps, "so that future centuries can say: 'There's the famous Méran!'"

"Portrait are the concern of photographers, my dear Lamps; there are as many of them as one could wish, once and for all, and in all the museums..."

"That's theories," said Lamps. "It doesn't mean anything to me. I'm not in the club."

A pellet of bread struck Hirchitz on the cheek. He turned his head swiftly. At a neighboring table behind him, a woman made a sign that the projectile came from her. He looked at her and recognized her. He interrogated her with his gaze. A discreet hand gesture invited him to approach.

"Don't worry, my dear Monsieur, it's not to ask you to pay for our supper. I'm Mademoiselle Brionne, of the Renaissance, and my friend, Gerda Hetchine, the violinist."

"I've had the honor of applauding you, Mademoiselle. What do you want with me?"

"Simply to know the name of the lady in white at your table. I can only see the profile. She hasn't one turned her head this way..."

"Madame Aury."

"Aury...that doesn't tell me anything at all. Her first name?"

"Lène."

"Ah! You see...it's surely her," she said to her companion, a strangely thin, boyish woman with coarse features and short-cropped straw-colored hair.

"So what?" she said, nonchalantly.

"Well! It would be very odd! And what does she do, your Madame...Aubry...Aury?"

"She's a chatelaine. Aury manufactures radium. Very rich. I believe she loves him, in spite of his being infirm."

"Necessary to believe so, if it's for him that she left the theater...pfft! That's what on calls letting go! Thank you, my dear Monsieur. It's very funny. Try to get her to turn this way a little, in case there's been an error..."

"Understood. Very glad..." He returned to his seat and said to Lène: "Do you know Brionne?"

"Brionne? The actress?"

"Yes."

"Hmm...yes...I did know her...a hundred thousand years ago."

"Damn! You and she are very well preserved. Well, turn a little to your left. She's over there, and wants to be certain that it's you."

"Why?"

"Don't know."

She turned.

"Garain!" cried Brionne. "Bonjour! What a surprise!"

"Your colt's smitten with the chatelaine," the lady with the abundant jewelry said quietly to Lamps. "Watch him. If they'd fooled around out there, it wouldn't have been serious, but I think she didn't want to know. The boy's got all worked up, and is going to get down in the mouth...and lose weight."

"Impossible. If he'd wanted to, he'd have had her. Hup! Just like that. Take it for granted. Being who he is, and knowing how to talk to women as he does. Don't make anything of it. It's not the disdain of any woman that will thin him down. The opposite, rather...if I don't keep an eye on him. I don't know one of them who wouldn't have honor and glory in swooning in the arms of the man whom the whole world envies France."

Hirchitz had changed places with Lène in order that she would be nearer to Brionne. He had drawn nearer to Aury and was talking to him.

"Fundamentally, the critics...and the others...the eternal recopiers, don't see any more clearly than Lamps. They betray their gross blindness in less simple terms... It's abstract art...the intrusion of the metaphysical into the plastic, if, instead of hitting them in the face with a statue of a boxer with arms, a torso, a head, one translates the lines of force. But damn it, isn't it the plastic, those lines, and nothing but the plastic? To a more subtle degree, that's all."

"This is what it's like frequenting night-spots," said Brionne to Lène. "Me, I'm up to here with it. So, you don't leave your château and never see the revues? Do you remember the comrades? It's a long time ago...it was nice: little Laillard; Antoine's bellowing when he was putting on the...the...I don't know any more. There were turning tables and a revolver shot in a spotlight, in the fifth..."

"And your prince?"

"Still. He's very proud of me. I got into the Renaissance without him...just me, my talent. Anyway, the public welcome proved it. And what press! A good old boy, the prince.

One only sees him once every six months. And you? The great romance? To have renounced the theater! That made a few girls happy. It's silly to have quit. You were well launched...such that I, Brionne, was keeping a close eye on you. One can say that now. I watched you coming up, up... perhaps I wouldn't have been at the Boulevard if you'd carried on..."

She looked at Lène silently. Her eyes were gleaming. "You're very beautiful. It's done you good, the romance. Happy?"

"Very."

"Marvelous! Marvelous that you can be happy...happy, finally, truly, outside the theater. That's always seemed impossible to me."

"I've learned to think absolutely the opposite."

"Too late to ask you for the recipe. And what brings you to this dump? And with our national champion, his manager and Mère Lamps? Méran was talking to you very closely...all the pullets here must have envied you."

"Do you...?"

"Oh, me...men...here's mine," she said, bluntly, putting her arm around Gerda Hetchine's neck.

"Like that, one's fixed," said the violinist.

"It's Hirchitz who brought us here. You know him? You talked to him."

"Not at all. It was to know your name. Who is the fellow? Very amiable."

"You don't know Hirchitz? The sculptor..."

"Haven't a clue, my beauty."

"He's the leader of a school...the initiator of a new statuary..."

"Another cubist! Me, you know, I'm very *Artistes Français et Nationale*. Hirchitz...that's a name I've never read in *Théatra*. He mustn't be very famous."

"Yes, but not for..." She did not finish. "Aury has made a friend of him. He's offered him a studio at the château..."

212

"Very chic! And Méran, has your man also offered him a training room at the château?"

"Precisely. A room, the park…"

"Really—how odd! If it's nice where you are, perhaps he'll offer me one too…a rest cure, wallowing in the grass. What does one have to do?"

"It was arranged for Hirchitz and Méran by mutual friends. We've had, and have at present, many interesting people out there. Aury likes to surround himself with all the eminences of the age…"

"Damn! My dear…"

"…And of all genres. From sportsmen, like Méran to great minds like Burgand…another name you can't have seen often in *Théatra*."

"I believe she's teasing me, the chatelaine," said Brionne to her companion.

During the movement that the actress made in leaning toward Gerda Hetchine, Léne's eyes went to the little watch on Brionne's wrist.

"I beg your pardon," said Lène. "A word to my husband…"

She learned toward Denis behind Lamps' back, which separated them, and tugged his sleeve gently.

"Darling…"

Denis was watching with Hirchitz the dancing of two near-naked Hindu women, the star attraction at Jerry.

"It's late, my love," Lène murmured. "Exceedingly… Don't forget that Lugnault's coming to see at noon tomorrow. Tomorrow—which is to say, very soon…and you need to sleep."

Denis blushed slightly. "I'd forgotten. Thanks. In a minute. Understood."

"That's your husband?" asked Brionne.

"Yes."

"The hero of the romance?"

"Yes."

There was a silence.

"I can say what I think?"

"Speak."

"He must have been very handsome, your husband...and something even finer than handsome..."

"Yes."

Brionne looked at Denis squarely. "I can see that in the eyes...the nostrils. Only..." He hesitated. "He already has white hair. And you...you, you're dazzling...you still look twenty-five. And then...why is he holding himself stiff like that?"

"The consequences of a fall," said Lène. She added, slightly trenchantly. "I still see him with the same eyes. He's an incomparable individual. I adore him."

"Cash," said Hetchine to Brionne. "That way too, one's fixed."

"And then," queried Brionne, avoiding responding to Hetchine, "all these...eminences, as you say, in your home...what's the point of that?"

"In the times before the accident, it was...let's say by spontaneous attraction, between us and the artists, the great men... Now it's like a need, for my husband, to involve himself in their intimacy, to see them live, exist, create... Oh, he returns in large measure what he receives from them. His vision, broad, ardent... Méran, for instance owes to him having added to his science the elegance, the harmony, that his admirers and artists recognize in him..."

"I'm not joking," said Brionne. "If you invite contemporary eminences...my place is entirely indicated, out there. When can I come?"

"I'll write to you," said Lène, evasively

"If I let you go...," the violinist remarked. She lit a cigarette and blew the smoke toward Lène.

"We're leaving," said Denis, "if Mademoiselle Brionne will permit..."

A maître d'hôtel, summoned, moved the table aside. There were introductions.

214

"Anyway, we'll meet again," said Brionne. "I'll expect your letter, my dear."

In the shuffling of chairs and the movement toward the exit, Hirchitz found himself next to Lène. He whispered: "While talking to Brionne you made admirable gestures. Without seeming to, I drank them in, literally. That velvet—at certain moments, made you naked..."

"So I was told a little while ago. But you, it's as a sculptor...."

"No," Hirchitz cut in, brutally. "it's as a man."

"Can we drop you off, Hirch?" asked Denis, while shaking hands with Lamps and Méran.

"If it's not taking you too far out of your way to go past the Avenue de Villiers..."

"It's on the way to Bellevue. We'll go to the Bois via the Boulevard Péreire..."

When they were alone in the car, Denis took Lène's hands and drew her toward him.

"Thank you, my love, profoundly..."

"Why, seigneur?"

"For having thought about Lugnault coming."

"But of course..."

"Yes, yes. In that milieu of lights, dancing...through the declarations, not difficult to see, of Méran...your surprise, your gaiety of finding an old comrade from a past that was very dear to you...you retained, present, concern for me, for that meeting...and the tenderness of your voice when you reminded me of the time..."

"But it's quite natural. Méran's declarations...poor boy! As for that image of my first life, the life of another...a Lène that you never encountered...I don't want you to thank me at all. That would make me think that you could have supposed me capable of forgetting the meeting with Lugnault. What an idea! That was much more important to me than the Jerry, Méran, Brionne..."

Dawn was breaking when they arrived at the villa at Bellevue. Everyone was sleep. The chauffeur opened the gate himself. On the landing where their bedrooms were, Denis opened a door and saw Paulin Charras snoring wholeheartedly in an armchair.

"Don't wake him," said Lène.

"It's necessary..."

"No, it's not," she said, attempting to hide behind a smile the sudden emotion that burned in her voice. "The poor boy. If you'd like me to try...I assure you..."

"Darling...," said Denis, with a tender reproach. Abruptly, he shouted: "Paulin!! Het, Monsieur Charras!"

The medical orderly woke up and came to his feet.

"Bonsoir, my love," said Lène.

She extended her forehead. Her eyes were misty.

Denis saw those eyes.

"Bonsoir, my love," he said, simply.

II

Having gone past the stocks of radiferous stone, in large heaps, and then the electric crushers, Denis passed the workers occupied in collecting and bagging the pulverized mineral, responding with his hand to their salutes. Further along, in the vast barrels, the uranium ore was treated with alkalis, which were slowly disintegrating it, covering it with gray foam. Beyond those barrels were the first buildings of the factory, with the immense horizontal clay filters, like interminably stretched accordions, and the vats of acid. Under the filters, traversed by running water, trenches collected the liquid rich in the uranium salts, the soluble elements that the water had extracted, and took it to the vats. Around the filters, workmen, after the passage of the water, were clearing and scraping the uranium residues from the filtering partitions, which they heaped up in piles of ochreous sand.

Denis went through the halls, in which the dimensions of the filters and the vats gradually diminished, and which were lined with bowls of a sort on pedestals, where the crystallizations were carried out. At the far end of those halls he reached a laboratory in which a young woman in a white blouse was finishing obtaining, in a little bowl, the pinch of radium bromide, one gram of which was the final product, the two-millionth part, of a series of triturations that requires eight hundred tons of water, four hundred tons of mineral, a hundred tons of acid and ninety tons of solid chemical products. An open coffer, with stone walls lined with a layer of lead several centimeters thick, contained on one of its shelves a few minuscule glass tubes full of white powder. They were tubes of pure radium. From those in the shadowy corners of the safe a green-tinted phosphorescence emanated. Adjacent to the safe was a glazed door, which Denis opened.

"You came in the back way?" Géard asked.

"I wanted to come through the halls and observe the attitude of the men when they saw me arrive unexpectedly. Your Renkoff is here?"

"He should be waiting in the antechamber."

"Perfect."

Denis sat down in a large armchair facing Géard at the vast desk. The morning sun threw bright beams through the high windows that formed three sides of the room.

"You came through the stocks? What do you think?" asked Géard.

"Not as large as I expected."

"There was a radiogram from Madagascar on my desk this morning. The Ambatofotsy deposit is exhausted."

"What was it?"

"Ampangabite—one of the best uranium ores. Here..." He handed Denis a yellow pebble with sharp angles.

"No compensation elsewhere? Norway? Tonkin?"

"Not for the moment."

"Not even Utah?"

"Nothing."

"What are the prospectors doing? Their last reports?"

"Justifications. Nothing to say." He tapped the table, began: "The truth is…," and fell silent.

"What?"

"Well, old chap, they're worthy fellows, knowledgeable, hard-working…but back in the day, you'd have set off in the airplane, dropped in on them, and your presence…"

"Yes. I asked Lugnault if I could risk it…"

"What? Put yourself at their head, traversing torrents, climbing peaks, camping in the bush…"

"In any case," Denis said, "Draguin has something extraordinary in the works, which will render the prospectors unnecessary. If the experiments are successful, we'll obtain a host of substances equivalent to radium, with all the properties of disintegration. In fact, he's working on the hypothesis that the radium isn't its own source of energy but the channel for an exterior energy…"

"Norman Lockyer's theory. You know what energy? Nothing less than that of the condensation of the universe…"

"Yes."

"I know the hypothesis. A study of it recently appeared signed by Jean Labadié. How can Draguin hope to find the utilization or the equivalent of that energy, which is that of the very creation of the world? To hope, as the same Labadié wrote, to mimic astral temperatures and pressures, figuring in millions of degrees and atmospheres?"

"But forgive me, old chap, if one could capture or transform the energy itself…"

"That seems to me, until further notice, to be a trifle colossal…and chimerical. I'd advise Draguin to hurry up and construct his accumulators or transformers, because, in the meantime, apart from the thinning out of our deposits, there are trials going on in America with the carnotites of Colorado—which, if they succeed, will bring the price of bromide tumbling down from eight hundred thousand francs a gram to less than two hundred. A hundred and eighty, to be precise."

"You think so?"

"I don't think it'll happen tomorrow morning. I'll draw up an exact report..."

"There is, presently for sale, bromide worth eighteen million in the safe."

"Let's keep an eye out for storms, Denis. Those eighteen millions are the most solid part of our capital. If, while it lasts, our prospectors continue to fail... And when I say the most solid, that's on condition that the Americans don't bring the price down...and even then..."

"What else, Cassandra?"

"The workers, Renkoff. I think we should keep the safe hermetically sealed, unassailable, when we're not here. A rush of blood to the head...a concerted revolt..."

"You think them capable of that, after all I've done for them?"

"Do you want to see Renkoff?"

"Yes, and to settle it. I've only come for that."

Curious, thought Denis, abruptly. *Where the devil have I seen that face before?*

He rotated the seat of his armchair and faced the workman standing, cap in hand, a few feet from the desk. Overalls stained with crusts of ochreous sand. About fifty years old, a large moustache and a sharp gaze beneath bushy eyebrows.

"About two years ago," Denis said, "an article in a newspaper attracted a certain number of idlers and adventurers to Sénecé. They didn't stay long. Those who did stay, after having lingered for some time, felt incapable of adapting to our local mores. In fact, here, promotions go, and only go, to those who demonstrate invention—in sum, individuality. They were presumably people who had doubtless not succeeded in making a living elsewhere in the world, since, instead of going back there, they preferred to offer themselves as manual laborers to the factory. Which is to say, where, apart from the wages being higher, the work remained little different from what there is elsewhere, only demanding physical automatism.

You were among those who, in that fashion, were taken on at Courtoisans."

"That's correct, Monsieur."

"No. It's correct that you let it be thought, in introducing yourself here, that you weren't capable of anything better. In reality, you're intelligent. You would certainly have been able, by remaining in Sénecé itself, to find yourself an occupation, distinguish yourself and participate in the material and moral advantages of the village. You disdained those advantages in the name of the revolutionary mission to which you've devoted yourself. It was to accomplish that mission that you came to Sénecé after reading the article. It's for that reason that you've subjected yourself for two years to the brute work of raking the filters."

"I don't know what you mean, Monsieur," the man replied. "I do my work like everyone else."

"Don't waste our time," said Géard. "If I've summoned you, it's because we know what's going on."

"Scraping the filters," Denis went on, "doesn't prevent you from talking to or indoctrinating your comrades. A delegate of the communist party, you maintain a correspondence with it. Your theme was, at first, in broad terms, that of the non-collaboration of the classes. Because of the high wages, and because the men here are treated with an almost fraternal cordiality…and, above all, because the moment they manifest any tendency superior to what I call physical automatism, they are, from the first to the last, at liberty to quit the factory and become—are even aided to become—citizens of Sénecé, with all the associated privileges…for all those reasons, the theme of non-collaboration didn't take hold.

"You found something else: the idea, as clever as it's simple, that the workers at Courtoisans, as well as the Séneçois in being satisfied with the advantages I've given them, are increasing by their activity the social suffering of the rest of the world…with the result that, enjoying the delights of Capua, they're turning their backs in a cowardly fashion on the great proletarian struggle. That concept succeeded with a few. I'm the enemy, the inducer of sleep. There are the timid beginnings, here and there, of sabotage. Production is slightly down.

"In brief, it's necessary that all that stops. So I'm purely and simply throwing you out."

"Purely," said the man, "I don't doubt...but simply?...no."

"What!"

"Admitting that your reprimand were justified, shouldn't I, when I'm called to the Director's office, be afraid...perhaps beside myself...at having been betrayed? I've come. I'm not afraid. That could prove that I'm innocent..."

"Or that you think you're very strong. You're relying on the solidarity of your companions."

"That's right. It's pleasant to chat to intelligent people."

"You know, Renkoff, that pleasure is...the collaboration of the classes."

"No. It's a skirmish, putting on airs...that's of no importance. What's serious is what you said just now. The satisfied, licking their lips in a little corner, while the host of the wretched are dying of starvation all over the world."

"You're sincere?"

"I've devoted my entire life to the fight against that monstrosity."

Géard looked at Denis impatiently. Denis calmed him down with a small hand gesture.

"You have an education?"

"Not much. It bored me."

"But you have eyes. Then, all that I've attempted, realized, in fraternity, at the factory, in liberation, in beauty and elevation, at Sénecé...results that I estimate to be unique in the world...none of that moved you, influenced you?"

"All the cries of distress from everywhere else were ringing too loudly in my ears for me to hear your laughter and music in Sénecé. Too many millions of fleshless arms before my eyes..."

"Idiot! Poor blind man!"

"Hey!" said the man, menacingly. "I'm being polite, me. It's not because there's *Director* written on the door, you know..."

"Blind to what's behind the laughter, the music, the gracious joys of that liberated people What are you doing bringing us your gross humanitarian alcohols? You've mistaken the palates, my dear chap! You haven't understood of your own accord that this is the future of your revolutions...not only the threshold crossed of the city dreamed of by your coreligionists but the garden of that city! You haven't understood of your own accord that this is the chrysalid of the humanity toward which your grim conquests are aiming: the living image of what your children will stand up one day as irresistible evidence before the tyrants and the blind!"

Renkoff, a trifle bewildered, remained mute, shifting his weight from one foot to the other. Géard, surprised at first and the increasingly irritated as Denis prolonged a conversation that he thought futile and rather ridiculous, suddenly found himself completely disconcerted by the tone of furious exaltation in which the tirade had been pronounced.

"Why," Denis went on, in a calmer voice, "humanitarian as you are, haven't you dug a little deeper into the humanity here? You would doubtless have discovered a secret with which you could have continued, if you insisted, to preach your upheaval of the world. In Sénecé, the words rich and poor, in the name of which you militate with so much zeal, no longer have their old significance. Before the secret of Sénecé, the rich that you want to demolish, with all their gold, can be beggars. Haven't you suspected it, with your nose in the garden that I've enabled to grow? The secret that people respire here will flatten your dogmas of battle, my red captain, and your weapons, the currents, the appetites, the rancors that unleash crowds. The secret of Sénecé is the liberation of the self by the self, in the name of the verity of joy, which can only be attained by intelligence and love."

"Too abstract, your truth. Too complicated, your secret, for ordinary people to understand. Until all the world resembles Sénecé, the humanity that I belong to will continue to groan. That's what I'm working for."

"And you're plotting to break my back. A scientist searches in his laboratory for a cure for cancer. He finds a formula, a serum, experiments carefully. Translation of your way of seeing: if the scientist can't cure al the cancer-sufferers in the universe at a single stroke, destroy the test tube!"

"I don't say..."

"That word, empty of meaning, that you have incessantly in your mouth: humanity..."

"Empty of meaning?"

"That massive generalization, makes you act like La Fontaine's bear with its paving-stone. Over the head of the Future, something flutters. You hurl your slab. It's not a fly but a bee, full of honey. You mistake Sénecé for Capua, when it's a laboratory. You think I'm putting people to sleep? I'm Christopher Columbus."

He raised his right hand with the intention off thumping the table. A thin metallic click sounded. The arm fell back, heavily.

Without seeming distressed in the slightest, Denis put his left hand to the place from which it had come, leaned on his sleeve, and flexed his right arm with satisfaction.

A troubled silence surrounded that exercise. Géard, his hands clasped, cracked his knuckles nervously. Renkoff, his head bowed, twisted his cap between his fingers.

"And now," said Denis, "I know where I've seen you before. Have you always been called Renkoff?"

"What a question!" said the man.

"You haven't changed, Mazou. You're still traveling with the same phantom, rattling its chains in your ears, as you were more than twenty years ago. You thought that there was a body in the white sheet, you bumped into it, you stopped. Blow, and the sheet is empty. The phantom in question is called humanity. There are as many humanities as there are human beings. That's the truth, as soon as one emerges from a primary classification, the sense of which is only interesting to zoologists. Whoever truly suffers from poverty can operate in themselves the revolutions that you desire. No need to take the species, history, the regime, or capital at birth. The union that your people say makes strength—the strength of a battering ram, not human strength!—in reality defeats the profound strengths that everyone can find in himself, and which he neglects, relying on that of others. The man who overcomes his flaws, his own weaknesses, the ignorances that oppress him, will see the Great Day dawn. The meaning of the word humanity is modeled on the person who pronounces it. When I knew you—a long time ago—in the infancy of my thinking, it was in sharing the theories and ideas that you propagate that I, too, saw the phantom... I got past it, and beyond it, I encountered the individual."

"That's hard to believe...," groaned Renkoff. "And where is it that we knew one another?"

"We were neighbors in the workshop, at the lathes in the Bergniot fanctory."

"Bergniot...ah...wait a minute...I can only remember a bizarre apprentice...I'd forgotten all about him...and to recognize you...!"

"Why do you call yourself Renkoff?"

"Russian names help the propaganda. Oh, so that's it...it's you, the petty bourgeois from the factory...it doesn't astonish me anymore that you talked the way you talked. I rest on my positions. You would have seen...if you'd been born poor. All your doctrines are the claptrap of the rich. Your...experiment at Sénecé, what does it prove? You've begun by ridding of your guinea-pigs of what, everywhere else, prevents the first gesture, that of the liberation with which you've tried to dazzle me!"

"I wanted to go quickly here...to edify a proof. In reality, the idea of possible joy can suffice on its own, in everyone, to raise the strength that will liberate them!"

"Get away! If you were like me, born of an unknown father and a vegetable-seller..."

"I've been a worker, like you, a proletarian, like you. It was at that moment that I created myself!"

"You...a proletarian? So what? Your great sermons. There would have been many things to say, looking at you closely. All the same, you're exaggerating, Monsieur Aury. Sénecé isn't paradise yet. As for you...your creation? And the money and Papa's nice château, which fell to you ready roasted? In the final count, where has it got you? With your millions...your factory...look at you!"

"Enough!" cried Géard, exasperated. "Get out!"

Denis had a strange smile. "Leave it," he said to Géard. With a kind of sarcastic calm that chilled the engineer, he added. "Just think...see how curious it is. The article in the *Grand Journal* brought us, and left us, all told, as a positive effect, the worthy Renkoff. And the worthy Renkoff, after two years spent amid what I believe, what I want to be, precisely, the concrete proof of the idea that he finds too abstract...instead of being enthused by an ensemble of indications already sufficient...shrugs his shoulders disdainfully, sniggers triumphantly at the weak points of a demiurge at work...still inevitably imperfect. And on top of that, throws mud at the spirit of my work, at my physical disability. And the most curious thing of all, you see, is that the man who talks incessantly in the name of humanity, Renkoff, that image of a uncomprehending, hateful and destructive humanity...is a far more authentic humanity that the one of which I speak, the one of which I've dreamed."

Géard, completely out of patience and gripped by an imprecise anguish, sketched a protest.

"But yes, yes...it's marvelous. Listen, Mazou," Denis said, with the same strange smile. "What if I were to offer you millions, and the factory? No joke...I'm lucid and of sound mind. Stamped paper, a pen, our two signatures. There's everything we need on this desk. What will you do, with the factory, with my millions, and Sénecé? Answer me. Go on...this isn't to test you. Are you going to continue to exploit my radium and have the filters scraped by your brothers in misery? Or

225

are you going to give my millions to the party...or will you, with the château, form here...well, a center, a college of revolt...a nursery of missionary brothers, chose rabble-rousers capable of making all the proletariats of the world rise up at the same time...?"

"Sometimes...," Renkoff began.

"You're amazed. You wouldn't have had that idea? It's tempting, that college? Go on, I can see that you aren't up to it. You're letting me talk instead of leaping on the stamped paper and the pen. So? Do you want to leave? Of your own volition? If I kept you on, would you continue to debauch my workers? You know, I can always close the factory if I'm irritated. With my millions...the millions I offered you...you know that I have the advantage, that I'm the stronger. Go on, get out," as Géard said. "Go, Mazou...I won't keep you. You can go back to your filters. I'll think about it...in case you decide to stay. Go on, Mazou..."

"Keep him, do you think?" Denis said to Géard, when Mazou had gone.

Ready to explode with all the indignation and amazement he had accumulated, Gérard was nailed to silence, as much by the utterance as the unhabitual sound of the voice, both stifled and mocking. And behind it, as if in the back of his throat, in his chest, there was a supplication...

Mastering himself and simulating joviality, he asked: "What do you want to do?"

"I'll doubtless astonish you by telling you...I'd like him to continue his agitations."

"Bah!"

"With the secret hope that his words, falling into the heap, will one day force the ears of a young, indecisive and passionate individual...who, with his blood boiling, but not knowing how to expend the fever...with his heart ready to devote itself, but not knowing yet to what cause...will embrace those ideas of revolt and destruction, make them his own, fan their flames, and be really capable of hurling crowds at the old world...."

226

"What's got into you?" said Géard, softly.

"It's...that it's true that life is badly made...that my proud tirades, just now, were just sounds...the echo, as if foreign to my present being, of my beliefs and my excitements in the time when my strength and my health hid the world and life from me beneath their own marvels."

"You no longer believe..."

"There are moments when I'd give everything...yes, it wasn't entirely a comedy...the factory, all my wealth, when I'd accept to find myself naked, and prostrate, before a being animated by a true faith...a mirage of construction or a fury of destruction. But destruction would be better...and more useful.

"Do you know, Géard, what I was thinking in offering the factory to Mazou? If he had been more knowledgeable, I would have told him, to tempt him, that the laboratory is marvelously equipped for a certain number of amusements... Superlatively reforming amusements... That by provoking the abrupt dissociation of a single atom, one could blow up the planet... Draguin told me the other day that two physicists in Chicago have attempted that kind of explosion by discharging a hundred-thousand-volt condenser through a tungsten wire.

"To abolish the time factor, and succeed in a single second in the disintegration of an atom that will take twenty centuries to do it of its own accord...and by the same stroke disequilibrate all the surrounding atoms, and others, and others, and all those that form the universe, in consequence. What a tango, for a second! And, suspended I don't know how in I don't know what space, to wait until the atoms, in re-equilibrating, had formed a new universe, consciousness and the earth, in which the truth that I have given was palpitating..."

Géard was so pale that Denis stopped, and noticed the distress that was contracting his friend's features. He burst out laughing.

"Oh, my poor friend! You believed it! You believed it! What stupid things I can say! I was dreaming aloud...one of

those sinister dreams that besiege me when I'm too disheart-
ened, vanquished...by the blessed fifteen kilos of my steel and
leather. You have no idea...a host of petty rancors accumulated... And also, all these stories...the exhausted deposit, America, Mazou surging forth from my youth and has seen Sénecé
without one of his ideas receiving the slightest ray of its sunlight...

"Enough specters! I'm awake again now. Keep an eye
on me, Géard! I'm prey to a frightful drama, sometimes too
heavy... This apparatus that I have to put on every morning
before I commence living...the loosenings, the tightenings, the
thousand little pressures by which they remind me at every
minute of my servitude...and above all what they bring with
them of renunciations, of treasons, of a hoist of gesture that
my instinct of action, space and enthusiasm drives me sponta-
neously. The drama Géard, between my damned body, which
draws me toward bitterness, discouragement, a pessimistic
vision of things...and my will to hold up, above the waves that
grip me, my treasure, the cup of Bacchus, the clear certainty
attained in the full light of me being...

"Help me...save me from myself, Géard...in my
name..."

III

Lène slips into the completely dark room, advances with
precaution, bumps into a piece of furniture; a bulb lights up in
the ceiling. Denis, woken up, has pressed a switch next to the
bed within reach of his extended hand. A cry: "Lène, damn
it!"

The bulb goes out. Lène has had time to see the sheet
from which the tipped-back head emerges, designing a kind of
limp form.

"Out! Yes!" she murmurs, her voice breathless. "Forgive
me. I'm not trying to go against your will. I have something
important...serious...to tell you. And I need darkness to say it
to you."

"Lord! What is it?" asks Denis' voice, calm again.

"I have an immense difficulty. I know too well, in broad daylight, with what smile you'd stop my confession. In order for you to hear it, in order for me to have the courage, I thought that the night...the night that hides our visible being... I can't see you. You have no need to oblige your gaze to light up with its perpetual flame of joy, or to oblige your forehead to serenity. And me, I'll have no more need to show you a face full of smiles...and the tears that it masks from you, that you'll never see..."

"Your words are disconcerting. What a Lène in distress they reveal...and what strange image of me are you making?"

"Denis, let's liberate ourselves from this barbaric comedy. Let me penetrate the secret of your suffering. Share that secret with me as you have shared your joy. Let me into your true soul. Don't place before the woman you've so magnificently loved and completed, the parade of a shame, a pride, more monstrous for me than the verity of your body, even if it's worse than the images constructed by my despair..."

"I don't understand...either what you're saying or what you want..."

"My love, my treasure, my adored...let me henceforth lean over that poor body, where there is not one place, whatever horrible traces and scars it bears, not one place that does not belong to my lips. Let me dress that dear body myself with its cruel armor. You'll see of what gentleness, what skill, my love is capable. Oh, you'll see... I've thought about it so much. It's as if I were doing it already. The places that my hands will manipulate will become like my own fibers, and you'll feel their warmth running through yours. Each of the eyelets of your corsets, your sheaths...like a small round kiss...I would be all alongside you, present against you, and your pain, at every moment..."

"My tenderness, what presence do you want, there, in comparison with that which you have in me, and which not for an instant, since the very first day, has never ceased to be incorporated into my fibers? Why are you pitying me? I don't know what nightmare has gripped you. What is this true soul into which you want me to welcome you? There is no shadow in my perpetual soul. Because a few petty annoyances afflict me from time to time…a lace that comes undone, or a recalcitrant spring…you've been able to suppose…? In truth, the sum of these petty annoyances, if they were a hundred times worse, would not justify a single tear from your eyes. You have wept? You, Lène?" An aggressive anguish dries up his words. "But you talk to me about those laces, those eyelets, as if you'd seen my apparatus?"

"I've seen nothing! You hide it so well! Your Charras is such a good guardian! But it's so easy to suppose…Like everyone else, I've seen…catalogues…"

"Lène, my darling, what you're asking me, sheltering in the darkness, selecting an hour when, deprived of my armor, you think me delivered to my weakness, delivered by it…as if my strength were in a leather corset! What you're asking of me, once again, I refuse."

"Denis, I beg you!"

"Understand, then… Oh, certainly, at first…yes, a pious, maternal tenderness…but soon, insinuating within you, taking hold of you, the tiresomeness of such work, which is, expressly, the chore of a mercenary. No, what I refuse, is that inevitable moment…and for myself, I don't want to see your dear hands on these miseries…"

"I assure you…"

"I also refuse to cede to a desire born of the imaginary torture to which you abandon yourself, of believing me to be unhappy. My weakness, entirely physical, the spectacle that I'm avoiding, of my disgraced body, are only minor details, unworthy of your concern, in the ever-harmonious rhythm, the innumerable communion with the beauty of the world, which is the verity of our life. Our life…a galleon around which buzz like mosquitoes the few little defects of my armatures, my ephemeral irritations…mosquitoes! Is that worth talking about? And…oh, oh…weeping over?"

The voice trembles, an anger resonating within it.

"What can I do with your pity? A copper coin to Croesus! And then... and then, I don't accept it...I don't want any more of that sentiment to reside in you. Even if it's one of the faces of our love, erase it, for love of me! No, no more backsliding into mental states with which we've finished forever! Here, in my own realm, no more theological alms! Our charity, our pity, is the solar spectacle of joy, forcing misfortune and weakness no longer to extend a questing hand, as before, but the desire and the intoxication of taking the spade or the pick in one's hand with which one plants and reaps one's salvation in oneself! I, the king, the dispenser and the example of that superior charity, should accept from the queen what she offers me...the merciful sadness that she draws from I don't know what old hidden purse, what disaffected crypt of her being? Impossible! A hundred times impossible!"

"Come back to reality, my beloved king. You're intoxicating yourself with an illusion that the simplest facts cruelly denounce. You know full well, my Denis, that you're no longer absolutely the same...that these grand words are too often belied by gestures..."

"Belied! Is it you who is saying that? Belied, for someone who stops at the most immediate appearances! The gestures that have become impossible for me, I make them, I see them, transferred, prolonged outside my vanquished body. All these elite beings with whom I surround myself—they're the ones who accomplish them. They're my arms, my legs, my impulses... Am I not in the victorious temerity of Méran's fists, in Hirchitz' creative fingers? My gestures! Seek them in Sénecé, in the young strength that I stimulate, gaze at them in Draguin's eyes, poring over the theft of universal energy..."

"None of those bearers of you is you. In none of them is that accord, that marvelous complicity in every instant, of sensations and emotion...which becomes love. You talk about Hirchitz? A fine example! Listen, then. That one—you suspect that he desires me, like most of the others—would you believe what that creator, that custodian of a little of your soul, has found, has done, to overcome my resistance?"

"Tell me, to see..."

"Surrounding it with vague tirades in the name of joy, beauty, etcetera, he has not hesitated to speculate bluntly on your incapacity..."

"Imagine that!" says Denis voice, sarcastically.

"But you have no suspicion, yourself, of these base sides to those who surround you. There, however, among these base sides that show themselves to me, are the maneuvers of one who sustains your beauty of the world, one of those artists whom you once called the mage-kings, the Prometheans!"

Denis' voice is grave. "It's you who haven't been at the height..."

"Oh! Indeed!"

"The ugly violence emerging from Hirchitz in the face of the prey that he thinks you have become...that violence comes from his organic humanity, that in which he's a man like other men. But in what, in him, is inalienable, in the artist, in the creator, he remains nevertheless the mage-king, the Prometheus. It's that part of him which is the true Hirchitz. The rest doesn't interest us. It's voluntarily that it's necessary to omit from him all the points that aggregate the common run of men, in order to know what distinguishes him and raises him above it."

"But what if, before me, your mage-king casts off his crown and red robe, and shows himself in the skin of an ape...and that ape overheats?"

"Throw his robe over his nudity, his royalty over his baseness, like the sons of Noah..."

"You're good! The surprise, the disgust, breaks my arms.

"Love ought to mend them."

"Love Hirchitz?"

"No. Love, quite simply. Love people and things...in whatever fashion is appropriate to what there is in them of the beautiful, the superior, to which one goes quite naturally...or let it be love that dictates the gesture. In this case, the re-dressing of Hirchitz."

"His desire would have rejected the cloak!"

"Or, ashamed of the nudity that he had shown, that desire, obliged to become that of the king dressed in his red robe, he would have risen to the authentic grandeur of the true Hirchitz."

"And then?"

"Then, in the elevated regions where the true Hirchitz is king, other objects of love and passion solicit him…and if he had continued to covet you, it would have been so magnificently, and over so many rivals…"

"What? Do you see where this is leading me?"

"In the most splendid moments of our love, my love, I have not spoken otherwise. You were always free to go to whoever conquered you over me."

"You're still the same, then? Ready for the journey?"

"Yes! Do you doubt me?"

"No, but me…delivered to myself, incapable, without you, of discerning the true beauty of individuals and things, incapable of a love that wants to replace things, in spite of them, on the plane of their excellences…that love which is not of our humanity!"

"But I'm close to you!"

And suddenly, Lène cries: "No! No! Not as before…"

"What do you mean?"

"That you're lying to yourself. That what you've just said, for Hirchitz, is sublime…but it's no longer with the voice of before, which you lit up with evidence. You too, now, see the shadowy face of things. Do you believe, then, that I haven't noticed your sniggers, your impatiences…"

"Bagatelles! Nervous reflexes. Those brief abdications aren't my true self. I want to remain the embellisher!"

"You no longer believe, Denis."

"Yes, with all my faith. And for you, for you, the symbol of that faith…you, thanks to whom the splendor of the world remains certain to me, when my own belief is near to darkening!"

"Then it's me who arms you with that pride that I've come to implore! Why would I no longer be the same, the passionate companion of that which, in you, behind the pride, is suffering?"

"Impossible, my beauty! You're made for true beauty! And that suffering is ugly."

"Everything is beautiful, which is you! What if that ugliness, from which you're keeping me apart, for me, because of me, were to become beauty too?"

"We'd be back to the deification of wounds, making misfortune sacred! No! So long as I'm alive, you will only see of me that which is my true self, which is joy…and via me, outside of us, the true beauty of the world, numerous enough that before it, all the little personal disgraces are compensated, effaced, forgotten."

"As soon as I escape your ensorcelment, I see that beauty covered with a host of black spots and defects! What you're hiding from me can't be worse!"

"I want to remain the ensorceller."

"What if you cease to be?"

"Then it will be because you have found my master, my vanquisher."

"And what if I, too, am only one of your mirages? A poor woman, if left to herself, a skylark, capable of mistaking glass beads for diamonds? Denis, I'm afraid for myself, on my own."

"I haven't abandoned you!"

"Your illusion no longer possesses me, in which I sense your desperate will stiffening! Oh, I beg you, let's set aside all these phrases, now vain, in which your blood no longer runs and your muscles no longer harden! Consent to our own reality, let's submit to it, let's look at it with the same valiant gaze! Accept the love that I'm holding out to you with all my lacerated forces, which your consent, with a single word, would cause to be reborn...as alive, as radiant, as those you once created. Denis, return your entire being to me! Let me touch your body, let me adore your wounds."

"I shall kiss your mouth, Yo…ka…na...an!"[30]

"Denis! Wretch! What can you be thinking?"

A silence.

And suddenly, the voice, simultaneously mocking and tender: "My dear love, let's put all this off until tomorrow. The night is favorable to the most absurd phantoms. Listen. Tomorrow, if, tomorrow, in broad daylight, you can repeat this lea, after having looked me in the face…and plunging your eyes into mine...well, then we'll see. But at present, it's decidedly as I tell you. I'm a little fatigued, uncomfortable. This every evening, the worthy Paulin was treating the devil of a scab…it stabs me, at times…and I'd like to sleep, in order not to think about it any longer. You understand, my darling love..."

IV

"…Which doesn't alter the fact," says Brionne, "that I've just had a sharp lesson in modesty. The journey was worth it just for that. Funny! Say, you don't accept nuns here?"

"It depends," says Denis. "Why?"

"A supposition. I abdicate Paris, the theater and its pomps, and take my retreat here."

"Paris would pursue you here, my sister. Our lunch today had nothing monastic about it, and those who were there came from Paris, where you could find them again."

"I believe I'd need something of a novitiate in order to venture alone into that Paris. The one in which I circulate bears no relation…what enthusiasms, your eccentrics! I'd never have thought that one could talk like that about luminous beasties…the…you know, the ones that circle overhead

---

[30] The quotation is a slight modification of the text of Oscar Wilde's *Salome* (1891), originally published in French, although it is possible that Denis and the author actually have Richard Strauss's 1905 operatic version in mind, where the line is reproduced in the libretto.

like little colored lamps…it gives one a yen to ask for the address of the jeweler. And that tall thin fellow from the Sorbonne, who tranquilly puts numbers on the passions. Are they like that all the time, your guests? I might be demolished elsewhere. A question of atmosphere. Unusual! An entire lunch without a word about the theater or clothes! The generals, the gossip about sex, politics...as if they didn't exist! And I wasn't bored for a minute... Quite frankly…a conversion, I tell you."

"Delighted," says Denis.

"The downside is that I have the impression that I'm going to find all of my habitual society idiotic from now on. So much the worse for me. I had to come...

"It was for the poor…," says Lène.

"It's true that you've given me fifty louis for my orphanage… You can see that it's always useful to do good works! The real truth…is that I was burning to see how things were in your place, and as you didn't write to me...." She looked at Lène. "However, my pretty..."

She bites her lip lightly. There is the same rapid gleam in her gaze as at Jerry. Denis has noticed that gleam. "In brief, I remembered that I was collecting for the kids for the 'Footlights,' and that you were rich…it's kind of you to have replied to my letter, to have invited me, and to have divined that I was delighted to come."

"My dear Mademoiselle, we've all been delighted by your presence. Lène hadn't forgotten the encounter at Jerry."

"But you have so much choice here that a star of the Boulevard…I understand…I understand now. And then, I'm a good scout, you know…I can render homage to merit. Beside your fellows, the turntable, the tirades…like a phonograph…even with all its soul in the disk…it no longer exists..."

"You're exaggerating, Brionne," says Lène. They're intelligent…original...but men like others in a lot of places. Rienzky, the one who discovered the crowned *Noctiluca*…left his wife and children to live with a girl who's been a domestic in their house..."

"Impossible!"

"Why the devil disillusion this neophyte?" asks Denis, gently. "All the more so as that aside about Rienzky has nothing to do..."

"Nothing...?"

"I confess," says Brionne, "that I scarcely thought of what his private life might be, while he was talking, any more than the color of his braces. All I saw were his shining eyes..." She pulled a face. "So your Rienzky...a man of the same sort as the cashier at Jerry...a slut, my dear. She lived with O'Luddon, the former trainer..."

"Don't interrupt yourselves," said Denis. "I beg your pardon. Four signatures for the four o'clock post." He opens a file on his desk.

"You can tell me all that in the park, while picking some flowers that you'll take back to Paris."

"I'd like that. Can you imagine that O'Luddon had spent his last sou on her... A groom, a total gigolo...and even something else with..."

Lène and Brionne head toward the gallery. Denis follows them with his eyes. As soon as they have disappeared he gets up and goes to the bay window, waiting for the two women to go along the paths that snake before his eyes.

"I believe your man's asleep," says Brionne, coming back into the hall, her arms laden with flowers and perceiving Denis half tipped back in his armchair, his eyes closed.

"That happens quite often in the afternoon. A slight torpidity after the meal."

"It appears that it's not healthy. Doctors recommend exercise. It's true...he has a little difficult in moving?"

"A little...a lot, the poor dear."

Brionne sighs politely. "I thought I saw him at the window a little while ago...just at the moment when..."

"Would you care to shut up? Why didn't you tell me?"

"I wasn't sure."

"Oh! What if he saw us…!"

Slightly discomfited, Lène arranges the flowers that Brionne has laid out on a divan.

"What, my chatelaine? A little sisterly kiss in the corner of the eye."

"A sister like that..."

Brionne lights a cigarette. She looks around, and goes to sit down on a divan some distance away from the table, in the least illuminated corner of the room.

"So," she said, "all this art here, these frescos, the park, the flowers I've never seen before, your electric trickery, the guests…this kind of life amid what you called 'eminences' at the Jerry, all that my little rat..." She hesitates slightly. "…I believe it's enough to make one the luckiest of lucky women!"

"You're coming here for the first time; it dazzles you. That's quite natural. It's natural, too, that I should be some-what accustomed to it…"

"You can't ever be bored?"

"I have a few worries…because…" A gesture toward Denis.

"Yes…there's always something in the best of happi-ness." She crosses her legs and takes a few puffs in silence.

"Well…I'll wager that from time to time, in spite of all this, you miss the theater."

"Oh, no—not at all!"

"That's frank!"

"Have I offended you?"

"Mad, my pigeon. I'm trying to do a little psychology. I'm looking at myself, in this unique frame, with a friend, who might…who could have had an accident..."

"If I regret anything, it's the great, magnificent, baroque voyages, with a companion…as no one ever... Not very com-fortable, obviously, a heap of cares, precautions..."

"Yes, yes..."

Brionne makes rings with her smoke.

"You still love him, your romantic hero?"

"Of course... Here's the flowers." Lène puts an enormous bouquet on Brionne's knees.

"Admirable! You must tell me their names...in case anyone asks me..."

"They're discoveries by people here. Research... That one..." Lène sits down beside Brionne. "...Originally, a lily. That one, the worthy cornflower..."

Brionne lifts the spray from her knees and sets it down some distance away on the divan.

"Give me your hands... Look into my eyes."

"What's the matter?"

Brionne looks at Lène point-blank, smiles, and then becomes troubled.

"It's that you're..."

"What?" demands Léne, looking away.

"Tempting..."

An instinctive movement of the hands, trying to pull away.

"What, Jeanne d'Arc? I can't tell you that you're beautiful? You know full well. People must sing it to you often. All your friends here...these superior minds...it's obvious! Whisper it to me...shh...you see, I'm speaking very softly. He's fast asleep, your husband?"

"I think so... I...are you going to let go of my hands?"

"There...very well-behaved," says Brionne, clasping her hands over her knees. "So...two such old friends... No points of suspension in the romance? A little adventure...on the margin? Is he jealous?"

"It's very difficult to explain... Jealous? No...but it comes down to the same thing."

"Cage-bars around the dove?"

"I'll tell you about it another time. My liberty is entire... But his fashion...a fashion of seeing things, of putting himself above others...which paralyzes..."

"Yes... Oh, my puss... Terrible, men like no others. All men, in fact. Listen, then... When you come to Paris, on your own, who don't you come to see me...a little? It'll amuse you,

I assure you. I too have an interesting life...people who aren't ordinary, around men... Naturally, we're not always on the summits, like you. But then...it depends where you put the summits. My entourage is more on the order of sensations. It's only because you've made yourself Jeanne d'Arc that it's necessary to talk in apologues. Try then, one day... It will change you a little. The men, in that—there are hardly any. Those that there are...in brief, one is with one's own kind. And you know...how can I put it? There...it's necessary to see me...I'm someone. Not as an actress...that's outside. Rather as...the leader of the orchestra. It's my other celebrity. That of a...in sum, a woman to...give me your ear, so I don't make you blush..."

Brionne leans over rapidly, and plants her lips on Lène's ear. She whispers something, then sinks her teeth into the lobe, and keeps it captive with a bite in which the tongue is inserted, a little wild beast of velvet and fire.

Lène recoils with a start, but cannot free herself. With a violent shudder of her entire being, her eyes close, her head tilts, her throat swells, breathless, her lips part. Brionne passes an arm around her neck, the muscles of which are taut, holds the burning head tightly against her face, and, the lips still close to the ear: "Am I doing you any harm?"

"Let me go, let me go...I beg you," says Lène, in an almost imperceptible voice. But the embrace imprisoning her head become becomes more pressing, imperative, and, quitting the ear, moves to the parted lips, circles them, takes possession of them, aspires her breath, unleashes the little devouring wild beast again... A sharp bite responds, a reply of flame and honey returning her attack...

Brionne's free hand gropes for Lène's, clamps upon it, makes sure of its passivity, and continues its route, furiously passing through the silky pleats of the dress...

The mouths come apart. The two women look at one another, a prideful merriment in the face of the actress. Lène immediately closes her eyes and lets her head fall on to Brionne's shoulder.

"My love," murmurs the latter. "My little queen…what delights! Oh, I can glimpse many possibilities…"

Lène raises her hand to close her lips, stop the speech.

"Well, what? I haven't divined? She's fearfully deprived, the lovely beauty!"

Lène shakes her head feebly. "So many…other joys," she protests, in an indistinct voice, in which there is both pride and sarcasm.

"Jokes, without that one! The great, the only true…"

For a second time, she leans toward the abandoned head, drowns her lips, her nostrils, in the golden mass of the hair, descends again to the beautiful lips—which close this time, and contract, as if for an obstinate refusal—seizes them, forces them, breathes incoherent words into them. The hands encounter one another, collide, conflict. Brionne, the stronger, sure of all her gestures, encircles the enemy wrists, crushes the rebellious belly with one of her knees, mingles her legs with her own through the waves of fabric…

Suddenly, Lène snatches herself away, straightening up unexpectedly, wildly, whipped by a slight sound that has sobered her up abruptly, turns her head, and sees Denis, his eyes wide open, looking at them.

She pushes Brionne away, gets up, puts her hand to her hair with a gesture of terror, uncovers her face, is about to cry out.

"Don't say anything…don't say anything. I was watching you. Don't disturb yourself, Brionne. You were very beautiful, both of you…"

"Are you mad, Cécelle? Put that mirror away and sit still. Why do you look as if you want to kill someone?"

"I want to kill someone because I'm looking to see if I have a smudge on my nose?"

Cécelle puts the fragment of mirror in her pocket, re-equilibrates a cardboard box full of fragments of down on her knees, and assembles the pieces she takes out into a powder-puff.

"And see to that the kid who won't stop crying. Where have I put his dummy? Look under your behind, Cécelle."

"Let him cry. It'll do him good. When the Rockefeller comes, curiosity will make him shut up," says a hoarse voice rising from a miscellaneous heap. On a mattress lying on the floor, an old man is lying, his head at the top a black chemise emerging from an assemblage of a carpet, a skirt, a jacket and trousers.

"Isn't it time our savior bought him a rocking horse to distract him?" mocks Cécelle. "Or a little kilo of fondants?"

"You can joke, you little tart. It's a cradle he needs, the little one."

"Where would you put it, the cradle?" asks the recumbent man, "since installing Cécelle's mattress already requires putting the table out on the landing? Aah!" he groans, suddenly. "Rotten leg!"

"All we need to put him in a cradle is more comfortable lodgings," says the woman with the tangled gray hair in a black cotton smock. She goes to a wooden box half full of rags, where the nursling is wailing, and holds out a finger, which the infant begins to suck avidly.

"And then what? Central heating? It's already nice that he pays for my drugs and takes the trouble to come and see how I am..."

"A billionaire? What's a hundred, or even a thousand francs, to him?" Cécelle affirms. "You'd only have to tell him..."

"If I had two sous' worth of audacity...," the woman begins.

"You're ignorant paupers. You can't see any further than yourselves. There are millions and millions of indigents. If everyone had what they needed, there wouldn't be any Rockefellers left. We ought to thank M'sieur Aury for what he does...which nothing obliges him to."

"That's true," says the woman

"He's a man who runs a benevolent society, who takes the names of unfortunates, takes the trouble to go see them...a man who has trouble walking but who comes up our stairs with all his contraptions, where Cécelle, with her twenty-year-old legs, has to be careful not to break her neck."

"Rubbish, Papa!" says Cécelle. "Poor millionaire? He's got nothing to do. Taking five minutes on our stairs...what's that compared with Maman slaving away all day doing housework, nursing Mimile and looking after you, and me, my puffs, morning and night? And when he goes home...footmen, butlers...there's the food, there's the nice bed...does Monsieur want a little more foie gras? Will Monsieur take chamomile this evening? I tell you that they can never do enough to be pardoned for their money..." She broke off. "Oh, it stinks in here. Shall I open the window?"

"No!" cried the old man. "It's necessary that it stinks, that it's stifling, that it catches the throat! Perhaps it'll make him take account of himself. That's what I want. But ask him!"

"All right," says Cécelle. "But the quicker he arrives and goes again, leaving his wallet..."

"It's you who are right, old man," says the woman. "Cécelle has neither head nor religion. That man, when there are so many bastards everywhere, me, I venerate him."

"All the same," says Cécelle, "on going home, to the Avenue du Bois or Passy...a quarter full of town houses, anyway, what must he think in recalling that two hours before, he was in a hovel in the Rue Fallempin? Me, the foie gras would stick in my throat..."

Save for a bath-house and a little music hall, where worthy Bretonnes get together on Sundays, the Rue Fallempin, a few paces from the Boulevard de Grenelle, is nothing but sordid houses. Each one composes, for its inhabitants, the most complete combination of all the conditions against which philanthropic societies of hygiene rail. It is into that street that Denis penetrates. The pavement, like a petrified tidal wave, renders walking difficult, obliging him to weigh heavily on his cane. He goes into one of the houses, goes up two flights of stairs and knocks. A scraping of furniture. The door opens.

"Excuse me, Monsieur Aury, while I bring the little one out. You know that the space is counted in centimeters. Dogs have more room in their kennels."

Denis flattens himself against the wall, let's the box pass, and goes in.

"Bonjour, Madame Carvot, bonjour Mademoiselle. How is the invalid?"

"A little better, Monsieur Aury," says Madame Carvot, coming back in and wiping her hands on her skirt, "but it's still suppurating. It'll take a long time."

"Ah, Monsieur Aury, *bien le bonjour*," says the recumbent man, as if he were waking up. "Open the window!" he shouts at Cécelle "It's as if one were breathing poison!"

Cécelle gets up.

"Don't disturb yourself, Mademoiselle, I beg you. It doesn't inconvenience me at all."

"But Monsieur Aury," Carvot protests, "It can't be tenable for someone coming from outside."

"I can assure you that it doesn't trouble me."

He sits down on the chair that the young woman holds out, which is the one where she was working. Cécelle sits down on the end of the mattress, and, head down, exaggerating her application, continues making her powder-puffs.

"You're still suffering a great deal?"

"Oh, yes...and then, it's the morale that suffers. All one's life, a good worker, bringing home enough to live without privation, and now I'm good for nothing, sponging on these two, who never stop. Oh, they're very deserving! The young one, at the age when the soul runs and dances, always bent over her shreds...of which it's necessary to make fifty puffs to make forty sous. If it wasn't for you, Monsieur Aury, and to think that it's because of the misery this leg has brought me that interests you in us so generously, I'd be happy to pass on, yes, as I say, to rid them..."

"Come on, Carvot."

"Come on, Papa."

"I regret every time," says Denis, "not being able to do more...but there are so many other difficult situations..."

"That's what I was saying not ten minutes ago. What did I tell you, eh?"

"That's quite true," says Madame Carvot, supportively.

"Of course. We understand," says Cécelle. "We're very grateful to you."

"You have your dressings?" Denis asks.

"Yes, Monsieur Aury, but it'll soon be time to change them."

"Change them in front of me. I'll be glad to see the progress..."

"It's not pretty to look at," said Madame Carvot, "and not pleasant..."

"I know what it...does," says Denis, softly. "My own apparatus sometimes inflicts wounds..."

"Poor Monsieur!" To Carvot, she says: "Give me your leg."

She moves the carpet and jackets, uncovering the man's bony and jaundiced legs, one surrounded by bandages from the ankle to the knee. She undoes the bandages.

"Good God of wood! Excuse me, Monsieur Aury...it's just that it pulls...Ow! Gently, Mother," Carvot moans.

As the bandages come away, a composite odor of iodoform and pus escapes, Denis seems unaffected. The odor becomes so noxious, however, that Cécelle takes out her handkerchief and, trying to render the gesture natural, blows her nose as slowly as possible.

The wound appears, a long pink ulcer, spotted with gray paste and oozing sulfur-colored beads.

"Well…it's much better," say Denis, cordially.

Supporting himself heavily on his cane he leans forward, as myopic individuals do, toward the wound."

"Necessary to give it air…excuse me…," says Madame Carvot. From the table she has taken compresses, bottles, and performs operations that make Carvot groan dully. Denis takes out his watch. Then, taking his wallet it of his jacket, he places two hundred-franc bills on the bed.

"That's a good dressing," said Carvot. "It's good, all the same, what you're doing."

"It's nothing. You need so many things! Larger accommodation…"

"Oh, my poor Monsieur," moans Madame Carvot. "To think that we all sleep in here…!"

"Frightful," said Denis, simply. "If I can see a means..." He stands up.

"M'sieur Aury…" The old man extends her hands toward him. "Give me your hand, M'sieur Maury…Me, I don't ask you for anything…people like you, it reconciles one with humanity… I love my wife, and Cécelle, but if I die, be sure that there will also be your image in my eyes..."

He shakes Denis' hand and looks at him with tearful tenderness.

"It's so little…," says Denis, on the landing.

"*A vous revoir*, Monsieur Airy."

"*Au revoir*, Monsieur Aury…and with all our hearts, you know!" shouts the old man.

"*Au revoir!*"

The footsteps of the benefactor clatter heavily down the stairs.

"Two hundred bullets…and he says that he'll look for a means!"

"He said that…rather vaguely," says Cécelle.

The sound of footfalls has died away. Madame Carvot stuffs the bills into an old wallet, which she takes out of and replaces in the drawer of the table, under an iron box.

Cécelle get up abruptly. "No more glue. Zut! I'll run to the color-merchant."

"You don't have enough with what's left in the bottom?" asked Madame Carvot, a suspicion in her voice.

"Still all that to stick this evening…there'll never be enough. And if I wait till seven o'clock, Bavin will be shut and I'll be stuffed..."

"If you see Monsieur Aury…wait a little…if he sees you, he might think you were already running off to spend his bills."

"If I see him, I'll look lively! He won't have time to recognize me."

With her gaze, Cécelle rapidly explores the section of the Rue de Lourmel that extends from the Rue Fallempin to the boulevard. Not seeing Denis, she gallops to the corner of the boulevard. A waiter is idling on the threshold of a café that forms the corner.

"Hey, Nénesse, have you seen a fellow pass by...a toff, lame? Legs dragging as if he were walking in glue."

"A toff?" The waiter reflects.

"I'll bet his auto was waiting for him at the corner of the Rue Fallempin. Shit! Too late.…"

"I've seen the one you mean," says Nénesse. "look—there he is over there, outside the fruiterer's. Not a dandy, the fellow!"

Cécelle presses her pace until she is within a short distance of Denis. Then she catches up with him.

"M'sieu Aury…I beg your pardon…Marcelle Carvot. I'd like a little word with you…"

Denis stops.

"Things…no means of talking to you in front of my old folks. Oh, it's nothing bad. It's just that it's a little complicated for the good folks..."

She seems terribly embarrassed, twisting odds and ends of phrases that are burning her lips.

"Go on, just tell me what it is."

"I've never dared...and then, I'd be afraid of fatiguing you, keeping you standing…and then, if you were seen talking to me, if someone came looking..."

"Would you care to walk slowly…along the boulevard?"

Denis observes Marcelle Carvot. Thin, rather tall, not ugly, face cunning and anxious. She looks at the ground while speaking, looks up at Denis briefly at times, and then turns her gaze away, slyly rather than humbly, heavy with troubled intentions rather than embarrassment.

"It's just," she says, matching strides with Denis' stiff gait, "with regard to a young friend I have…that my parents don't know about. Oh! Say..." She stops abruptly. "Sometimes, you're something like a…kind of curé… gamekeeper…moral guardian…nothing that might perhaps stop you doing good for Papa. I swear to you that he has nothing to do with it, the poor old..."

"Go on with your secret. Your Papa will remain outside of it. I'm no moral stickler, and I know life."

They have arrived at the corner of the Rue du Commerce. A dense coming-and-going of pedestrians, newspaper-venders, vegetable barrows, the thunderous passage of an autobus, stops them on the edge of the sidewalk.

"If one can speak frankly... Say, M'sieur, here, we'll be noticed. You, a monsieur, and me, dressed as I am…not dressed, rather. There are comfortable little cafés all around..."

Denis looks at Marcelle Carvot again. She spoke the final words with a strange ease, her gaze free of all slyness, suddenly gleaming with a vulgar pleasure.

"If you wish. Lead on."

Past the zinc counter, a small, rather dark room, empty of clients, a back room where two Metro employees are playing billiards.

"Mademoiselle Cécelle," says the waiter, "What can I get you? And Monsieur?"

"He knows you?" Denis remarks, as the waiter draws away.

"I come here sometimes...when I go to the market with Mama. Oh, might as well tell you...in the evenings too, with my friend. Everyone knows you a little, when you're from the neighborhood. And then, the waiter..." She interrupts herself while the waiter serves the drinks. "He's one who has no manners."

"So?" asked Denis. "Would you care to tell me how I can be of service to you?"

"It's a dirty quarter, Grenelle. If one lets oneself listen once to a fellow...there are bands of mates...their women...one immediately has relations that drag you away..."

"To what?"

"A little of everything. Dances, excursions by auto, when one of the gang has money...."

"I see. Let's get to what you want from me."

"My friend's done something stupid. Oh, don't get looking for stories of midday at four o'clock! To cut a long story short, there's a certain sum that he needs; without that, he might be in a real pickle. And just the day before, poor thing, he'd bought me a dress with the all he had..."

"How did you explain the dress to your mother?"

"One always finds a way. She doesn't know what things cost. And then, I suppose...if it's necessary to tell you everything...that she can't stop me. Papa neither. They grumble, they don't like it, there are scenes...but one has to eat. Without me, with just Maman, there wouldn't be enough. Your two hundred francs from time to time..." She laughs. "Well, a rich man like you knows full well that two hundred francs doesn't go far. How many cigarettes like the ones you smoke does it make?"

"Would you like one?" asked Denis, tranquilly.

"Yes."

She slips the cigarette into her corsage. "I daren't smoke it in front of you. And then, the boss here doesn't like it... Don't look at me like that, M'sieur Aury. I look a fright. I came out straight after you, to catch you up. Look, I've still got my slippers on."

She raises her knee, shows Denis one of her feet, shod in felt, and mechanically lifts her skirt half way up the leg. The leg is slender, muscular, in fake black silk stockings. Denis, his head inclined over his minerva, has a fugitive flicker of the eyelids, which does not escape the young woman.

"There's all that there is of the most negligent, I know...slippers," she continues, leaning her foot negligently on one of the traverses of the table. "I'm ashamed. And I hope you haven't looked at my stockings! They're simulated. And they've surely got a ladder somewhere..."

With an abrupt gesture she imprints a kind of circular flight to her skirt, which reveals momentarily the image of one of her legs, and covers it up immediately, reveals the other, leaving the eyes with a swirl of fabric in which the double black flash of her hosiery and the pink of her young flesh have scintillated briefly. Then, raising her head, she looks at Denis, masking the acuity of her watchfulness with chatter.

"It's wretched to be poor, looking a fright. There was a painter, one day, who asked me to pose for him. There was another...he offered me anything I wanted, for me legs. No painter, him...well-to-do. It troubled him to see me going back and forth. It wasn't very difficult. To cross my legs, arrange my garters. Would you believe it! I ask you!" She goes on: "That one didn't displease me because he was...too agitated. Otherwise, perhaps with another...that would be rather amusing. It's always flattering..."

Denis listens without blinking, a slight redness in his cheeks. He says: "In sum, yes..."

250

"One can be a marvelous man, all that there is of the distinguished, superior...and in a little corner of the noggin, one has ideas...slightly unusual tastes. Oh, I know..."

"It happens," says Denis. "But I..." He dies not finish.

Cécelle precipitates her game. "However, they're nothing extraordinary, my legs," she says, pulling her skirt up a little above the knee. "The ankles, it seems...delicate enough...my dream...if I didn't live in this lousy quarter, would be a little bracelet, like some have, there...over the stocking...on the ankle..."

"For the bracelet, the dress, your friend, how much do you want? That's what you're expecting from me?"

"Oh, Monsieur Aury," says Cécelle, her eyes ablaze, "it's not just a question of money. I'd be so glad, above all, to please you, if you were to say: that's a girl, no worse than many others, once tidied up...and who's wasting her youth away in what can't even be called a hovel..."

She takes his hand gently, as if timidly, with a gesture that lets Denis' hand and her own fall quite naturally on to the leather sheath of his thigh...but she recoils slightly...

"Oh!" she says. The surprise in her voice immediately changes to compassion.

"It's my apparatus," said Denis. "I have one on each leg—and the arms too...and the neck...and around the chest...."

"Oh! Poor Monsieur!"

"It's repulsive, eh?"

"No...not when one looks at you at the same time."

"Look at me? Not every exciting. I'm old...white hair..."

"That doesn't make you old...it makes you look distinguished. And then, you have a young expression...the eyes...you can't be more than fifty."

"Not yet forty-three. Troubles..."[31]

---

[31] Previous chronological indications have suggested that Denis was born in 1889, give or take a year, so if he is now forty-two, this scene is presumably taking place in 1931 or

"Poor Monsieur Aury!"

A mechanical slide of the arm hand placed on Denis' hand has guided the fingers beyond the pad that crowns the apparatus on the thigh. They have reached the groin, remain there, and dance in tune to the young woman's words, applying a gently pressure there. Their warmth and trembling trouble Denis, concentrating a salacious irritation in that small part of him, outside the sheaths of metal and leather. He has a smile successively arrogant and indulgent, and a profound redness in his cheeks.

"It's embarrassing to get back to it...I didn't reply when you asked me how much it would be, for the dress, the...in sum, the whole lot. Oh, not much...for you, I mean...for me, as you can imagine, it's Peru!"

The maneuvering of the fingers is accentuated confidently; the eyes turn away, following the other hand, which is designing commas in the liquid spilled from the glasses on to the table-top.

"The best thing would be...what you decide for yourself."

"Yes."

Denis reaches for his wallet, and stops the gesture. "You see, my dear...it's necessary not to imagine...benevolence is very nice, but it's frightfully dear... The rich have annoyances, expenses...

"Oh, I don't doubt it," says Cécelle. She withdraws her hand negligently from the narrow hearth that she was simulating, folds her legs and arranges a lock of hair, which she twists between her fingers.

"Obviously...the angle isn't the same," says Denis, agitated. "A certain sum, relatively small for me, might assist you as broadly as you wish..."

---

thereabouts. That is of minor relevance in the present text, but has a slightly problematic significance for the temporal setting of *On demande un homme*....

"Oh, of course," says Cécelle. "You're so kind," she adds, abandoning the lock of hair and replacing her fingers where they were before. "So generous!"

She half-closes her eyes over a gaze full of effusion, and observes through her lashes the shudder that passes over Denis' face.

"So generous! And so quick to comprehend!"

More precise reptations of her fingers punctuate, as if mechanically, the effusion of her speech. Suddenly, Denis bites his lips, goes pale, and utters a hoarse groan. Then he takes out his wallet and extracts a large bill.

"Here, make your arrangements with that."

He raps the table brutally. The waiter appears. Denis pays, stands up.

"I...I hope that that will suffice. Excuse me. I have to do...I came with you at the expense of a meeting..."

"Thank you...thank you. M'sieu Aury," murmurs Cécelle, her voice humble, her vulgar gaze sparkling with triumph and challenge.

Vile, Denis says to himself, emerging from the café and staring to walk heavily, without any precise goal. *Vile, and idiotic. A surprise, good for a conscript. That's where it gets you, my lad, a taste for horror...*

That remark, coming from himself, cuts through him as if it were spoken by someone else.

He walks, in a complex state of disgust, scorn and cerebral effervescence: an extraordinary lucidity, blossoming from the brutal physical shock.

"Which will surely lead to trouble...a real pickle, as the young woman said," Denis whispers, in the voice of a feeble old man conscious of a host of organic prohibitions. "Beware of congestion! Go home without delay...hail a taxi, that's prudent..."

"Go home!" protests a lively Denis, running, jumping, tripping over, in God knows what fibers. "Go home! I'm in such good form, light. I feel perfectly at ease, enough to chat a little with a host of other selves…it seems that such a bizarre adventure is beginning, as if that little orgy were the crossroads at which, by themselves, all my decrescendos ought to end. A concrete bursting of my pustules, the fact that I let myself go…me…me!"

"Who, you?" another Denis suddenly groans, and then rolls thunderously, like a cavalry charge, thrusting aside all the other larval Denises who are beginning to accumulate in that mocking state of mind. "Who, you? The annunciator? The tabernacle of Joy?"

"Oh, don't furrow your brows so disapprovingly, King Denis!" ripostes a smiling Denis, full of forbearance. "It's not you that the honest little whore... You, the pacha of as many seraglios and sensualities that it pleases you to have! This affair doesn't concern you, doesn't even brush you... You, if you were there at all, were a spectator. The you that you were looking down on from the height of your throne was Denis Job, his nostrils full of the Fallempin garret, eyes gummed up with old Carvot's wound... You were watching him finish off appropriately the series of today's little images…his daily spoonful of the ignoble..."

"Pfft!" interjects an ironic and condescending Denis. "Throne…Job…a lot of fuss over one of those escapades that all men get up to on the sly!"

"Men!" laments a voice that submerges consciousness like a blade of light. "Which men? The true men are gods, made for the vast, the creative Joys!"

"Oh," mocks Denis Job, "where's that carnival coming from? Doesn't he know that the old boat is definitively sunk? For a quarter-pound of man-gods in a thousand centuries there are quintals of Hirchitzes, Mazous, Brionnes and Cécelles! And Carvots, sweating their cankers!"

"Not that! Not the infirm!" cried King Denis. "You know very well that it's you who go in search of them, in their lairs, ceding to the need to ward of your miseries in their sewers!"

"And even if it is," retorts Denis Job, "aren't you there nevertheless, King Denis, inviolable among your treasures…?"

"Joker! Still spattered with pus, and you talk to me about my treasures? Not even capable of steering clear of the attractions of filth. If they were real, wouldn't they provide you with enough sublime compensations?

"They compose them!" cries the voice of light.

"A joker nevertheless, that one…" mutters Denis, shrugging his shoulders.

Prey to that chattering advice, he has arrived in a square. In the middle of an intersection of large streets, there are two little verdant areas.

"I have what's needed to answer you, Denis the Apostle…and you too, King Denis," he mutters, crossing the square toward the little gardens. "But permit me to sit down. If I faint, at least I'll no longer be running the risk of being run over…"

A bench on which an aged workman is asleep, and a mother knitting. The woman makes the free space larger, with a glance of astonishment and pity for the invalid, too elegant for the popular refuge.

"Where was I? I called myself a joker twice over…for pretending that my higher parts aren't affected by my little filthy treats…and for affirming the force of the counterweight of lofty resources… Joker is a trifle brutal. Nevertheless, let's talk about it. First, let's postpone the reports of the king and the collector of ulcers…inasmuch as they're effects. If the king really picks up his scepter, the collector evaporates. But in order for the king to pick up his scepter…it would be necessary to prove that the lofty resources are intact and a panacea… To hell with it! You won't prove that…"

He smiles sarcastically, closes his eyes, pores over his thoughts, which appear in disorder throughout his being, rolling behind his forehead, tremulous and confused. His consciousness falls silent, as if waiting for the nebulous flow to condense into a precise form, or draw aside, opening a gap, delivering passage to a directive thought…

"To hell with it! And yet, beauty of the world, powers of humankind, haven't I sacrificed enough to you? Tree of my Eden, works of human genius, and you, passion that I read in the eyes of living creatures, my familiars...world of music, books, laboratories, diligent mechanisms...world in which nature and forms, by your enchanted offices, are nothing but fêtes, delights and temples...world of the mind, star within the stars, earth that ought to adhere to my soul as the other sticks to my feet...it was sufficient for me to be afflicted in my flesh for all your prestige to be extinguished? Your beauty, your grandeur, wasn't inside me, then, but outside? An illusion of my integral organism...since they reveal themselves to be impotent to save me, when I'm reduced solely to the life of the mind? And because I'm not yet blind enough, haven't fallen far enough, to dwell in the other world, the heavy earth where the Carvots swarm...here I am like the dark angel, precipitated out of heaven, tumbling through the spheres, through the void!"

Gripped by vertigo in following the image of his meditation where it has led him, Denis opens his eyes, clings on to the external world, gazes, without seeing, at children playing in the sand, a woman crossing the square with a bundle of washing on her shoulder.

"Let's put this paradoxical situation in the current style. There's no more place for me in the spiritual, nor in the material world. What remains of me? Where are you, Denis? No response, if I don't enclose that urgent question in cold data. Ergo: How have I been able, because of the innumerable stupidities of my infirmity, to let the spiritual life, which at least had its efficiency, escape from me? Why have I not been able, on the contrary, to take refuge there more victoriously than anyone else, since I knew it, lived it and enjoyed it with a plenitude as vast as is humanly possible?"

A switch. Images pass by, dancing, scattering. That of the dark angel reappears, is fixed, communicates to Denis, along with an atrocious sensation of falling and spinning, a kind of spasm of pride rising up his spine.

"Humanly? It was something else, something more, something that doesn't yet have a name, which doesn't correspond to anything in human history...that was veritably...in humans."

Like a shock to the heart, the blood rushes to his head, red-tinting for a moment the entire ambience; the spasm squeezes the soul, inflates it, a flood of spiritual blood springing from the depths.

"Of course! I've gone astray, I'm floundering...in that council of self-revision, I was using the regulation yardstick! Who am I? Stupid question! I could search the dictionary for a long time for the name of my misery! Philosophers, priests and physicians have no drugs for my diseases. The case is unprecedented. It's the joy that is diseased.

"Joy, what is that? Joy? I can see that of the traveling salesman, if his business is prospering...that of Tristan, when Iseult arrives...but he died immediately afterwards, poor fellow! That of Buddha? Of Benoît Labre? But the eye, the stomach and the loins were deprived of so many good things! That of jolly fellows with red cheeks...when the health goes, they say, all the rest goes. Let's not even talk about Dante, or Spinoza...watertight partitions 'Look at my teeth, my pectorals...that exists, and the hundred and ten an hour of my twenty-four sports car...or the discus thrown fifty meters...and the record of eleven ejaculations a night, with the twelfth on awakening...'

"I can see the joys of all those that the crowd envies—all the gladness that rests on a coup on the Bourse or an oil well—and what a fuss to safeguard it from hour to hour! Your joy, thinkers, scientists, artists...before which the universe is like one of those meals in the garden, where the wasps are on the lookout, only launching for when the jam-pot appears on the table...nothing interesting until then, in all the dishes. Do they even see them?

"So, your joy only surges, confronted by the inexhaustible germinations of the world, to fly to that which satisfies its greed, that which enters into a category of your concern. And so with all of them. No joy that circulates other than narrowed between a thousand blindnesses, like grass growing between paving-stones; none that is anything other than a tiny part of the whole. If you lose joy, good people, you can continue to live! Joy is in the margin, a luxury, a flower in the buttonhole, not the bones of your skeleton and the substance of your flesh! I got bogged down among your petty districts, good people...

"Spiritual word, material world? Ha ha! What I called my joy held them confounded in every one of its respirations, in the days when every one of my respirations was love! What I called my joy was a constellation of hearts, going from the ends of my hairs to my feet, every step of which was a kiss for the ground! Is it hazard that gives *organ* the same root as *organism*? Or have the forgers of words foreseen the great miracle, in that human victory of which I held the certainty? My organism was an organ. Every one of my perceptions a key, every reaction a song! The tune that became a hymn, my blood that bore to every fiber like the breath of the bellows the melodious stimulation. Not an instant that didn't weigh upon the open keyboard, not an instant when the instrument wasn't stirred and resonant!"

He closes his eyes, his dazed head inclining, heavy with the evoked intoxications.

"And that's why, in losing my body, I lost my physical hearts, and now, before my mind alone, the world is poor."

Scarcely had the sentence been framed than consciousness started.

"Ho! What have I just said? What did I mean? I've glimpsed an extraordinary verity!"

The forehead creases, and every crease in like a wave drawing closer to the pier of consciousness, a flotilla of ideas tacking in the mist. Then the chest dilates. An implacable serenity clears the forehead.

"That's it. I testify in the name of, and for the lesson of, humanity. A terrible lesson. The unsustainable violence of the repercussion. It's the height attained that makes the fall enormous. What a triumph, my spectacle, what a document, for whoever praises the weakness of the creature and the necessity of recourse to the divine! Unfortunately, having taken the turn of believing too much in this world derives me incurably of God. No supernatural platform on which to regain breath. Not the slightest scrap of paradise, none of those heavens in which theosophy moors the soul when the earth is too stormy. Fall. And pay. No recourse, for having staked everything, including the earth, on the earth.

"Here I am today, before that same life, on that same planet, which were my only organists. For me they had all the riches, bounties, thrones and dominations that are generally attributed to the tenant of the azure. The question of God didn't even arise. Every one of my minutes resolved it, contained the dazzling face and all the angels surrounding it. Its mystery, the great unknowable before which the myopic are hypnotized, shaking their heads and gnashing their teeth since Genesis, took its place among a crowd of other unknowables, just as mysterious, splendid and more immediate. The present offered me enough problems to fill in the time that others devote to the beyond, and they were as far from my hand as the constituent atoms of the back of the chair where I was sitting, or from my foot as those of the grains of sand to which I was standing, and so enigmatic for us, such passions to expend in knowing them... that the voyage toward the atoms seemed as worth as much as investigation of the infinitely large...

"Nothing has changed. The crash of my airplane couldn't put me beyond the life and the planet, the God that they composed superabundantly. A fly falling into a full cup. The few ripples produced on the surface don't overflow the cup. If they drag the fly over the surface, that doesn't make the surface God. I'm incapable, but I'm honest. My fifteen kilos of prostheses don't make me accuse the organists of playing false; it's the organ that has fractured...or rather, half the keyboard that's been smashed. That's why my musicians can no longer get single worthwhile chord from me."

He laughs. The woman knitting beside him starts, looks at him, and draws away anxiously

"Appeal. I'm not rigorously honest. Justice, so be it, but distributive. For a part of that which my organists played, it was me who held the scores. Life and the planet poured out the beauty and the joy in torrents, but I too poured out the torrents of my joy to life and the planet. Immensely important precision. That's where the truth that I glimpsed is nested."

Consciousness expands, savors, breathes its gains voluptuously over the rugged shadow in which the debate is laboring.

"From the moment when I attained joy, linked to my being, the blood of my blood, it gave me the power to transfigure the world, to incorporate and infuse its reality at every moment with my blood of joy. At each of your contacts with the real, cells, fibers, vibrations of my body, at each of your appeals, my prospectors, billions of antennae, my physical hearts, my soul and my consciousness responded and came running. It was thus that every one of you then became itself a soul and a consciousness, animate, instantly brightening with all the warmth of the one and all the light of the other..."

A new spacious palpitation of consciousness. A quiver of the ease of the pilgrim approaching the Ark.

"I've given. And now I'm asking, and I'm waiting. The paralyzed believer can receive God in his domicile. What can the earth offer, of itself to the congregation of its joy, deprived of its vehicles? What equivalent nourishment to the organic desire of joy to the human being to whom the idea and acceptance of misfortune is impossible...as impossible as it is for light to be its own darkness?

"Here I am, give me back the beauty of the world, in itself and in the noble works of humankind. Finished, the voyages, the free coming and going among the places, the works, the beings that made the world adorable to me; finished, the manipulation of engines and forces that showed me and delivered to me the innumerable terrestrial booty. What remains is the mind.

"What is the number of great books and great music, that of works, gestures and sentiments turned toward the exaltation of human being...capable of sustaining by themselves my spiritual being, abundant and magnificent enough for me to slake the totality of my hunger for joy? Well, what?

"Tell the truth—which is that the number is small, and quickly exhausted, and which can no longer recreate its substance! And facing that, that of the uglinesses of the world that illusion no longer disguises, that of actions, works and sentiments turned toward the diminution of human being, its crushing, its sacrifice, its glory, which needs God at every step, that of painters and songs celebrating its crimes, its gehennas, the coos and the sobs of its sempiternal amours, and that of the metaphysicians, full of its phantoms, its savagery or its despair..."

The forehead in which the justice-administering consciousness is held remains serene, but a rictus convulses the mouth.

"Millions of images of blood and mourning for a few images of joy. And yet, the joy that has become the texture of a human being, having understood its omnipotence, wants to live and slake itself, and has nothing but the earth..."

Like a logician pouring and condensing into a theorem the sum and sap of his research, consciousness itself throws to Denis the firm and precise phrases in which the resolved debate is fixed.

"A person attains the idea of the plenary joy permitted to human being on earth; if he is afflicted in his flesh, the earth cannot offer him by itself the rich nourishment that can save him, and the persistent idea of joy, the sublime conquest, the crown of human being liberated from its gods and its fatalities, that very idea, unslaked, will draw him, to slake his thirst, toward the inferior forms of terrestrial joy and their monsters."

The mixture, the intersection of the radiant mind unleashing a verity and the mind bitten by the poison of that verity.

"Corollary. My marvelous joy and my superlative image of human being are not, in the present state of the world, any better that the priests' vale of tears, since they leave that being in an even more wretched and naked misery."

The passing cloud comes apart, as if dissolved in the light, now the sole hostess of his consciousness.

"It's not a question of better, it's a question of verity. That of Joy will never be worse than those that contain the Juggernaut, St. Bartholomew's Eve and the Kishinev pogrom, and still build convents! If, as for me, the physical foundations of its adorers break, well, they will, like me, fall to the inferior earth...or, with what remains of their strength, they will be free to work for the future of an earth itself curative, an earth sufficiently resplendent with images of joy to give that joy as churches give God."

Scarcely is that thought complete than a kind of maelstrom takes possession of Denis.

"Wretch. The unreal gods have vivified themselves on their martyrs, and the faith of those that were tortured only rested on a faith of the soul. And I, who have embraced God, have received his reality in my bones and my blood, have deserted the temple and taken the host into prostitutes' cafés...

"O worst of apostates! You, who flatter yourself on having been truly a man, you who judged that no one had contemplated the real God in a more complete light than you, you do not have the right to consent to that fall!

"Get up! Don't release the chalice, wounded Bacchus! Do not flinch at the moment when that task becomes apt to your stature! The earth redeemed was fraternal and light to you when you bore it in the totality of your strength. In your turn, heavy as it is, bear it!

"Oh, heavy, heavy, for its reality is no longer anywhere but in my consciousness!"

The head leans heavily upon the minerva; the eyes close, the face is radiant.

"It's there, now, that the earth of joy turns. And no matter how your back bends, Atlas, you must not drop the world."

The eyes remain closed; the head straightens up; the fever runs through all the veins.

"You were looking for your scepter, King Denis. I'm returning it to you. I shall be all the more a king, all the more invincible now that I'm alone in guarding the adorable secret. Whoever approached me when I was entire, had their part of the secret. Whoever saw me saw the earth of joy and inhabited it with a serene certainty. I was its image and its proof. The image lacerated, they have returned to their old earth of a thousand eclipses. Each of them has only a single heart.

"And Lène…Lène, the radiant image of the image…Eve emerged from my visible strength and my triumphant verity… Lène, fragile trace of that triumph, as of my present wandering, fluttering in bewilderment to all the forms of joy… Lène…a moth…will not follow you in your new invisible reign. Too complicated for her, that new victory! Oh, the sharp dilemma! I have lost Lène, for having refused her pity. Doubtless, my misery would have been as great for her as was my joy…I didn't want that.

"Thank you, to that which in me did not want it, and preserved me for today! In shoring myself up with that harmonious image of my defeat, I would have accepted the misfortune, yielded to palliative forgetfulness, gradually buried the treasure now rediscovered, the sole verity of joy…greater than Lène…greater than our broken love…greater than me!"

The excitement increases, the temples throb; it is as if the body is licked by burning waves.

"Here I am alone on the new earth of Joy. I am the Robinson Crusoe of a land still bare of the works and forms with which humans will populate it under the sign of Joy…the sign of the true powers of the human organism, its assembled science and love. My extinct body will not extinguish the verity of human being that my body has given me. I will make that verity irresistibly visible before the consciousness that contains it is extinguished in its turn.

"It will not be Sénecé…it will be vaster still, more conclusive…irresistible, I say! I no longer have the time to forge human beings. Sénecé, like Lène, is only a trace. The idea needed my body, out there, and its actions. The neophytes of

263

the young religion of Joy needs its sorcerer, with his amulets and his miracles. I shan't create any more. I have better things to do. As a gram of radium is extracted from tons of opaque stone, I shall extract from works and deeds, although they have the appearance of matrix, even of darkness, even of crime, the sign of the eternal sun, the indestructible salt that I shall condense, and of which I shall make the sign of pure Joy.

"A pinch of bromide in a slender glass tube was sufficient to change the entire foundations of science. My grain of essential Joy will renew the spiritual foundations of the world! My infirm body can summon all the strength of its misery toward the old earth. I am armed with light...I no longer see anything but light behind the walls of things.

"You do not know, dark angel, in what world to interrupt your fall? What is a world to me? I shall drain suns...!"

Denis opens his eyes.

The bench is empty. Dusk is falling. The mother and the old workman have gone. He gets up, painfully. He goes forward, his head on fire, each of his steps dragging, torpid, frightfully heavy.

"Weigh, my apparatus. Attach me. Hold me well. Draw me well. I am the stronger! The more you draw me, the more the mind that I am will struggle victoriously, voluptuously: the mind that knows, the mind that sees, the mind..."

The congestion.

The claws, in the brain, of the red vulture.

"Scarcely had the invalid picked up in the Place Cambronne arrived at Necker...as soon as we had undone his clothing, my dear master, and seen that extraordinary assemblage of apparatus, we thought immediately: Only *Lugnault could have conceived that...*"

"That's very flattering for me, my dear friend, and you were absolutely right to telephone me immediately."

"The invalid appears to be a man of the world. His papers, in the name of Aury, did not tell us anything. To notify the address on the cards...in the provinces, in any case...to alarm his relatives...always very delicate. The congestion was benign, for the time being..."

"Will you please take me to him?"

The intern precedes Lugnault.

Denis is lying in a little room.

"Bonjour, my dear friend," says Lugnault, softly. "There's a fine face. I've been reassured. It will only be a matter of a few days...."

"Bonjour, my dear Lugnault," says Denis, with difficulty. "Slightly confused, before you...in being here...you made me so many recommendations."

"Your auto wasn't with you, then? Or Charras?"

"No...scold me." He turned to the intern. "How long will I be here, Monsieur?"

"Five days, at the most, if no complication sets in."

"Will you do me the favor of sending two telegrams?"

"Gladly."

"One...*Germain Margaut, chauffeur, chez Monsieur Aury, Bellevue.* Got that? *Remain at Bellevue with the auto. Will return*...fill in the date yourself, Monsieur. Signed: Aury."

"And the second?"

"*Lène Aury, Sénecé, via Crennes. Retained in Paris on business. Nothing serious. Will return*...idem. *Love, Denis.*"

"I'll send them to the post office immediately."

"So...," says Lugnault, alone with Denis. "You told me to scold you. When you're entirely recovered. In any case, I won't permit myself to ask you..."

"Yes, for I want you to keep the secret of this sojourn in the hospital. Can you imagine, my dear Lugnault, that I've started a philanthropic society, and that I was going to assist indigents in their homes..."

"Are there not in Sénecé, or in its immediate surroundings...miseries that would require less displacement?"

"It's because I'm hiding it. I don't want anyone around me to suspect. Listen, my dear Lugnault...this is almost a confession... For some time, I've acquired a taste for the poor. It corresponded…how that devil can I explain it?...at first…so far as I recall…because, since my last pauper, I've made a great voyage…at the end of which...that congestion... As I was saying, it corresponded, at first, to a certain…instinct…let's say of mimicry…and then, not easy to say…to a need…"

"Don't tire yourself out. Later…"

"It's not tiring me. A need…something very generous…very touching, Lugnault. You have a great heart…you'll understand. I'll call it…an amorous effusion. When I was, entirely, nothing but being, appearance, I emitted…I felt extending from myself...illuminated by me…and, illuminating me in their turn…ardent gazes, exalted hearts…in sum, all the being of all beings. I was beauty, confidence and joy. And as the sensation of beauty, confidence and joy, releases instantly from the soul all its base charges, and gives birth, during that instant, even in the utmost obscurity…to a florescence without stains…I only walked amid perfumes and light. I was the lord of all open souls…"

"I understand. But…what's the connection with the indigents?"

"It's in their homes that I rediscover, thanks to a few feeble donations…and hopeful words…that luminous opening of the soul, that instant of adoration…."

"I no longer understand very well. So many others than the poor...with your fortune, your intelligence…the scientists and artists that you've aided…more interesting, as well, for a man like you than aged consumptives…or detritus…and more interesting for the world. Would you like me to identify to you, in a minute, ten admirable chemists, and a dozen therapists, on the threshold of immense discoveries, who, for want of a few thousand francs…"

"I know…I know...it's not that. In any case, that too, I do. Not the same effusion. Or rather, no…take account, my dear Lugnault, of the mimesis…a kind of sadism of misery. Yes, sadism, if you like. The gratitude of your scientists, your artists, is mingled with pity, for me... To the poor devils, with a few sous, a few words, I give all life, all happiness, the cure,

266

me…the great unfortunate, the great incurable, whom neither money, nor words, nor art, nor science…nothing in the world…can bandage… Me, who has lost the earth…"

The invalid trembles; again the blood flows to his face.

"But that's very old, all that I told you there, Lugnault. It's over. I've rediscovered the earth. Better, even. I've…I don't know exactly what I found, just now…before the faint. It will come back. It's something admirable…the elixir of life. With which to go forth…in spite of your blessed marvelous apparatus…like a young eagle-hunter in the mountains… with which never to buckle, to give in to the suffering…

"A verity. It will come back…the salvation, the joy, henceforth ineradicable. A verity…all suns… Lugnault…!"

4

I

The Maire had given his administratees the pretext for his departure of the necessity of a cure for his wife. Madame Cahoche was not so very ill that a sojourn in Paris was necessary to put it right. In reality, Cahoche preferred to leave the Sénéçois to shift for themselves. Frignot had kept him punctually up to date of with the crumbling of Denis' work. The two men met in fixed dates in a small restaurant near the Gare de Lyon. Frignot gave him the latest news. Everything was collapsing.

"They're beginning to cut down the sculpted trees in Telluire wood."

"Why? To carry the trees home as souvenirs?"

"For heating."

The factory had suffered an accident to the current; no one had demanded that it be restored. The price of the current had reached too high a level. And people got far less help from the factory when it was a matter of repairing machines. A large number, following the example of Lauvin and Chaleix, had gone back to tools, and apparatus drawn by horses and oxen. The trouble was greater, the profits less, but the results were more reliable. Electroculture was suffering serious breakdowns, and the château was no longer interested.

The great profiteer of Denis' revolutions, in the final analysis, was Lampreux, the notary in Crennes, charged with selling the farms, the fields and the commercial capital of those who, having become rich enough to live at their ease anywhere, had left Sénécé, where their habits of pleasure and the facile life found less and less satisfaction. There were many new faces in the village. The paint on the houses in the main street, discolored by the sun and the rain, was not renewed, or even scraped off, by the newcomers. The

Séneçoises were gradually abandoning their extraordinary accoutrements in the face of the disapproval of the newcomers, who could not understand the causes of such a provocative esthetic. Some young women had gone to Paris to join the artists that had once lodged with them. Some young men were going blindly about the world, in search of employment for their imprecise talents.

At the château, half of the beautiful electrical systems that did everything were no longer working. Leveil, who was more often in Paris than in Sénecé, had started teaching a course near the Gare Montparnasse. Draguin made visits incessantly, trying to sell his inventions. Frignot did not know whether it was because lack of money was affecting those messieurs too...

"Good God!" Cahoche had cut in. "Money! And all the extraordinary people who surrounded Denis? There were scientists among them, inventions capable of making millions. If it were only Draguin's famous rain at will..."

"Oh, many avatars on that side too," said Frignot. "That business of rain, even in the best of weather, was never completely perfected..."

And, all things considered, the diminution of current, the supply rendered by the business, had hindered the research. And then again, Monsieur Denis no longer being the same man, everyone around him sensed that... In brief, he could not say exactly whether it was lack of money or because those messieurs no longer found pleasure at Sénecé. There was, in sum, still enough money to pay for Madame's fantasies. She was more beautiful than ever...although, with the life she led, she would age quickly!

The intimacy of the château was displayed basely between the two collaborators. Frignot had attached a chambermaid to Lène's service who was avid for tips, from whom he had not hidden the Maire's passion; she made excellent reports. Combining the words and attitudes of Denis and his friends with the treasons of young Stéphanie, he brought Cahoche a faithful account if the ravages that were taking place at the Maison Aury That Stéphanie had taken up her position—it had been necessary to hire domestics like everyone else—after the departure of the three young women with the names of jewels…their familiarity too disturbed, the hussies…their atmosphere, as they put it…not astonishing, in view of Madame's behavior…who spent the night away four nights out of seven…

"And in fact, saving your respects, the worst of prostitutes couldn't hold a candle to her."

"But in that case," Cahoche had said, with a cold laugh, "perhaps she's no longer interesting."

Frignot, turning very red, had stopped eating, the fork that he was holding aloft trembling slightly.

"What are you saying?" he had stammered. Then, pulling himself together, with a coarse laugh: "On the contrary…"

Denis, returning one day earlier than the date announced in the telegram from the hospital, had not found Lène at the château. She had not returned until the next day. She confessed that she had emerged from Méran's arms. She blamed Denis. After he had accepted the liaison with Brionne, he had allowed her to be carried away several times. Not without stupor, Lène had seen him complacent regarding the actress' artificial milieu. She accused Denis of having, under cover of the business affairs vaguely mentioned in the telegram, satisfied some unacknowledged passion. Denis talked about a dizzy spell, a short stay in Lugnault's establishment. He had not wanted to alarm his friends…

One point remained extremely obscure. Why had he not had the auto with him?" The chauffeur had reported that, having taken Monsieur to Bellevue railway station, he had seen him get into a third-class carriage.

Rather than admit his visits to the poor, Denis preferred to let Lène suspect the worst turpitudes.

Incoherences. Sometimes, he went with her to discreet parties in which opium and cocaine concurred with sensualities in which the mediocre intellectuality of the habitués was